Rukhsana Ahmad taught English literature at the University of Karachi before moving to Britain in 1973. She has freelanced as a writer, journalist, translator and playwright since 1985. Besides short fiction she has published *We Sinful Women*, Contemporary Feminist Urdu Poetry (The Women's Press, 1991) and a translation of Altaf Fatima's novel *The One Who Did Not Ask* (Heinemann, 1993). Her play *Song for a Sanctuary* toured London and the regions in spring and autumn 1991, was published by Aurora Metro in 1993 and broadcast by BBC Radio 4. She has recently finished her first novel *The Hope Chest*.

Rahila Gupta spent most of her formative years in Bombay and came to London at the age of 19 to do an M. Phil in English Drama. She has worked as a journalist and freelance writer for many years and is currently producing and editing publications for a housing charity on a part-time basis. She has contributed short stories, poems and polemical essays to a number of anthologies, the most recent being *The Virago Book of Love and Loss* (Virago, 1992) edited by Georgina Hammick. Also due to be published in 1994 is an autobiography of Kiranjit Ahluwalia which has been translated and written by Rahila Gupta.

Both editors are founder members of the Asian Women Writers' Collective. They live in London.

D0281386

FLAMING SPIRIT

Stories from the
Asian Women Writers' Collective

Edited by
Rukhsana Ahmad and
Rahila Gupta

Published by VIRAGO PRESS Limited, May 1994
42–43 Gloucester Crescent, Camden Town, London NW1 7PD

This collection copyright © Rukhsana Ahmad
and Rahila Gupta 1994

Copyright © in every contribution is held by the author

The right of Rukhsana Ahmad and Rahila Gupta
to be identified as editors of this work has
been asserted by them in accordance with the
Copyright, Designs and Patents Act 1988

*A CIP catalogue record for this title
is available from the British Library*

Typeset by M Rules
Printed in Great Britain
by Cox & Wyman Ltd, Reading, Berkshire

CONTENTS

···◆···

ACKNOWLEDGEMENTS

We gratefully acknowledge the support of Lambeth Council who have continued to fund us in this climate of cutbacks, specially in the area of black arts.

Warm and special thanks to Ravinder Randhawa, Joyoti Grech, Veena Stephenson, Preethi Manuel, Tanika Gupta for their commitment, unbegrudging time and unstinting support during their respective tenures. Thanks too, to the present Management Committee: Kamila Zahno, Preethi Manuel, Tanika Gupta, Sue Thakor, Parminder Chadha, Jocelyn Watson, Siu Won Ng.

Our thanks are also due to Margaret Busby for her time, Merle Collins and Pratibha Parmar for their support, and to Melanie Silgardo for keeping faith.

FOREWORD

The Asian Women Writers' Collective

As we celebrate our tenth anniversary, the Asian Women Writers' Collective continues to be a safe and supportive space for Asian women writers. Our greatest wish is to encourage new writers both in developing their own writing skills as well as in feeding into wider networks of, for example, performance poetry, radio and TV scriptwriting, journalism, visual arts, etc. *Flaming Spirit* is an important achievement in an ongoing process of recognition of Asian women's writing in Britain. Some of us have been commissioned to write for TV and radio, some are well-respected in national performance poetry circuits, whilst others are becoming published novelists. For many of us, however, writing is not a professional activity, and the collective is just as valuable for sharing our views, experiences and ideas. Within our network women have collaborated formally and informally on various creative projects and we have all benefited from a camaraderie and friendship which enriches our lives as well as our writing.

Currently, our group is predominantly South Asian and we are encouraging more women from other Asian cultures to be involved. We see the term Asian in the broadest sense; that is those whose ancestry, part or whole, is from West Asia, South Asia and East Asia, spanning the regions from Turkey to Japan and the diasporas. We want to explore our common identities as Asian women and as black women, but without making invisible the differences in our experiences and cultures. We respect this in a policy which opposes attitudes and writing which are racist, sexist, communalist, homophobic or oppressive on the grounds of disability or class.

We would like to thank all the women who are the Asian Women Writers' Collective and who have uplifted its spirit time and time again, showing us the many faces of Asian-ness. Over the past ten years, we have heard many inspiring, moving and wonderful stories but we know that we have just skimmed the surface of the sea of stories. We meet on a regular basis organising workshops, readings and events at the Oval House Theatre in Lambeth and welcome with open arms all women who want to explore and share their Asian identity through writing.

A very special thanks must be extended to our editors, Rahila Gupta and Rukhsana Ahmad for their untiring efforts in making this anthology a reality and for their encouragement of all the writers.

We would like to end on a poem from one of our workshops which was collectively written, produced by ten or so wicked women writers. Add a line if you want!

I am a Blackwoman

I am dangerous and real
sometimes bright and funny
yearning for an uppity brazen raunchy lover

I am a powerful enigmatic mysterious force of energy
fanciful and defiant
tactical and wanton

I have no sharam
I create my own Izzat

I am determined to be independent
seen as a terrified, misunderstood product of a xenophobic
society
my spirit is sagging under the weight of this dangerous world
I'm knackered over-worked and under-valued
hankering after decent childcare

But

all is not lost
I am zappily radiant
I am a treacherous revolutionary singing cynical love songs
who was left wanton and wild
raging in unity

I will be the first to find the pot of gold
underneath the rainbow

heavier than the world
lighter than the air
brighter than the sun
darker than the night

I am the colour of hope

Asian Women Writers' Collective November 1990

INTRODUCTION

As founder members of the group brought together initially by Ravinder Randhawa's determined efforts to set up a writing workshop for Asian women, we feel a great sense of achievement at the completion of a second anthology to mark the tenth year of our existence. In the early days the group used to meet at *A Woman's Place* on the Embankment, London – a place which, sadly and significantly, does not belong to the women of London any more.

Although some of the longer serving members are no longer regulars, hungrily exchanging new bits of writing or throwing ourselves into the lion's den to have our vulnerabilities exposed, we still hover, playing both a supportive and an annoyingly over-protective role.

Much has changed in this decade and we hope that the writing will reflect that. We are working in a harsher political and economic climate. Writing is a poorly paid profession at the best of times, and new young shoots require warmer, more welcoming climes than we have had recently. The fact that we are still going strong as a group is something to celebrate but let us catalogue the compromises.

The level of funding that we receive today has dropped to that which we received in 1984 from the GLC. We have lost our funding from the London Arts Board, formerly known as Greater London Arts Association. This means that instead of having a full time writer-in-residence who also did the group's administration, we now have someone for twenty hours a week.

We have no money to pay visiting writers to run workshops for the group or to pay members to run as many workshops as we did before in the community. Similarly, other support networks for individual writers have fallen away. Adult education has been decimated, funding for writers to work in schools and libraries has been cut and the publishing industry itself is in the doldrums. The political climate has altered so drastically that our agenda feels marginalised to the point of extinction.

Despite all of this – and thanks to the unpaid time from workers and other members – the group has grown. Our early conviction that there was great talent out there which needed nurturing is borne out by the excellence demonstrated by some of the new writers in this collection and the dramatic expansion of the group.

Our first publication, *Right of Way* (1988), proved to be a great impetus for new women to join. The sense of staleness that we complained of in the introduction to that book gave way to great new waves of energy and enthusiasm as younger women joined up; women from more diverse backgrounds, including women of mixed racial descent, who challenged our definition of Asian; and lesbian women whose presence gave a backbone to our well-meaning sentiments about our anti-heterosexist stance.

After the initial debates in which a conscious decision was made to be an Asian rather than a black women's group, not much attention was paid to the definition of the term Asian. The membership at that point was mainly drawn from the South Asian diaspora and discussions around literary values and traditions were held mainly within that framework. When challenged by an Iranian woman seeking membership, we had failed to broaden the definition in a meaningful and practical way. The problem was exacerbated by the fact that throughout the eighties the women's movement was being fractured by the atomisation of identity. The group was, in fact, swimming against the current by opening its membership outwards to women from 'East' and 'West' Asia. This was mainly in response to initiatives from women outside the group, Chinese women, in this instance. We decided to take a more proactive approach in our outreach and publicity. In redefining our identity as a group, we had to address questions, such as, why emphasise links between East, West, and South Asian women over and above our links with African and Caribbean women? What significance does this have for the way in which black communities are perceived in Britain? Women from mixed race backgrounds had particularly important perspectives to contribute to the question of identity. How do we avoid submerging specific cultural experiences under the broad banner of 'Asian', given the predominance of South Asian women in the group? How do we avoid marginalising women whose heritage is not bound by 'Asia' alone? These debates reflected our struggles to counter the rigid and reactionary nationalisms and religious identities being adopted by sections of the black community. Language and terminology inevitably became an issue, hardly surprising in a writers' group. In a context in which 'political correctness' became a term of abuse, we refused to succumb to the onslaught.

In our earlier years, the group had felt committed to working in our mother tongues as a way of reaching out to first generation, working-class women who did not know any English. One of our *Mehfils*, an annual event held around International Women's Day interspersed readings in English, Urdu, Hindi, Punjabi, Gujarati, and Bengali. It was an extremely well-attended and successful event, drawing women from a wide range of backgrounds. However, given the number of languages, the format proved to be taxing even for those of us who are bilingual. Apart from such occasional forays we were unable to do long-term, constructive work and attract women working predominantly in their mother tongues to join the group. This also had something to do with the fact that we met in central London, in the evenings without creche facilities so the type of women who attended were mainly young and without childcare responsibilities. We attempted to redress the situation by helping members to pay for childcare arrangements.

Given the wider interpretation of Asianness with its attendant rise in the number of linguistic backgrounds, and the increasing number of monolingual women in the group, English assumed a centrality in our proceedings which further militated against our attempts to work in the mother tongues. English may have been the coloniser's language and a mark of privilege and class in our home countries but here it also enabled us to break out of our regional identities and make common cause with the other black communities and, for that matter, the different cultures that inhabited the term 'Asian'.

As part of our outreach work, we went to workshops, readings and seminars up and down the country. Asian women who had been feeling isolated and alone came up to us from the audience wanting to become members. Membership criteria which stated that so many meetings must be attended were changed to accommodate a sort of postal membership whereby women could send in work and receive feedback by post. In fact, this collection includes stories by women from Sheffield, Birmingham, Manchester and Cardiff, to name but a few cities.

Despite the enthusiasm many of us felt for extending the facility of a writing workshop geographically so as to reach many more women in outer London, and beyond (we had hoped) by developing outreach posts, we failed to do so. This aim was consistently hampered by a lack of resources and the relative lack of the language skills needed for such a programme. An outreach worker was nevertheless appointed and workshops were taken into outer London boroughs during 1989–90, but permanent sister groups did not materialise outside central London as we had expected. However, this outreach work was stifled by the loss of our funding from GLAA. London-based workshops and work around this anthology have taken precedence for now, though links with members are maintained by our occasional newsletter, *Chitti*.

The development of the group's outreach programme remains on the agenda. There is a recognition that at present AWWC still functions in a manner which can only serve those creative women who are already independent and mobile and interested. This naturally excludes all those women who have not already attained a certain level of personal freedom and independence.

This single factor also accounts, at least in part, for the fact that middle-class women are overrepresented in the AWWC. In order to understand the pressures and influences on the group, we have looked at age, class, generation and language skills as discrete factors. No tidy categories are possible: class and language are not as neatly linked as we have implied. For instance, it is not merely first generation women, tied to their mother tongues, who are working class: the British educational system is also spewing out a second generation of women who, despite their fluency in English, are working class because of racism and poverty. We have to find ways of linking with women writing in their mother tongues so as to enable them to use the network in some constructive way; to ensure that their writing would be shown the same respect and given the kind of support which is available to those who are writing in English.

The perception of writing as a middle-class activity rather than an attainable career option and the lack of opportunities available to younger working-class women for developing their creative potential also draws women from a particular class background. Needless to say, more concrete efforts are needed to widen representation of disadvantaged groups.

However, during the last few years solidarity with working-class causes has grown steadily stronger. Workers appointed by the group, beside their support for feminist and anti-racist struggles, consistently circulated information about working-class causes and tried to represent the Collective at strikes and marches.

Yet another problem is that this political agenda carries its own cost and distances us from our communities, where so many of the cherished ideals and beliefs are embedded in religion and tradition in stark contrast with the politics of the group. This has been a period particularly fraught with division and strife amongst South Asians in Britain. The *Satanic Verses* affair, which affected Muslims more than other groups, polarised the black community into Muslims and non-Muslims. Within the Collective too, it created a painful schism. Those women who sympathised with the outrage and humiliation experienced by so many Muslims felt reluctant to echo the arguments of the freedom of speech lobby in a message of unconditional support for Salman Rushdie, even though there was deep sympathy for him, and a clear recognition of the political use of the book by the Iranian government. Those feminists who believe that freedom of speech cannot be without responsibility did not entirely agree. Still others felt that whilst the racism of the 'liberal' lobby had to be countered, it was still important to condemn fundamentalism which had the control of women's minds and bodies at its heart. Despite the depth of the differences a unanimous statement of support for Rushdie was issued at the time.

More recently, the Babri Masjid massacres in India have set up further divisions and hardening of religious identities in the South Asian community. The paradox for the Collective is how to provide space for women who identify with the Group's agenda, but feel it does not allow them to articulate reservations arising from their religious and cultural baggage.

The collective ethos of the Group is constantly under threat from the nature of writing itself. It is an activity so completely bound by individualism and subjectivity, in all its aspects: the processes of creation, of reading and interpretation, of assessment and evaluation. At each and every stage you must withdraw and make reference not only to what might be a difficult-to-define set of rational criteria, but also something quite impossible to quantify or account for, your gut reaction, your feelings. It is not surprising then that within a collective which had a clearly defined political agenda, where writing was read aloud and shared, almost every Thursday night for several years, in a spirit of sisterhood and support, it has still not been possible to develop a clearly articulated definition of a good piece of writing.

Writing, like solo flying, is deeply riddled with competition. Whether or not a group intends to do so, the manner in which a piece of writing is received by its members establishes, sooner or later, a hierarchy, a subtle sense of grading, a sense of the 'power' which 'the best' of us can exert over the rest. A particularly powerful piece would inspire you, stay with you until the next morning like the finale of a wonderful play, but it also set up the unspoken ratings. New writers can feel quite daunted by a superb piece of work.

It was inevitable that a culture developed over a period of time where 'support' became more important than criticism, as each evening brought *new* new writers to the group whose vulnerability could not be disregarded. Certain adjectives were eschewed, others permitted. A code of a kind has always operated as a sub-text. Literariness, in its Western sense, with its insistence on intertextuality, its determined pursuit of aesthetics was not viewed as a necessary or desirable goal, but integrity, emotional power, truth and an internal cohesion which follows the logic of the artistic work, together with an awareness of political significance, all in the context of our embattled lives in this country, were valued by the Collective and became the currency.

This, together with the 'workshop process', generated writing and ways of writing which were less conventional. Group poems were attempted. Characters were developed collectively, and everyone went away to try and write stories about them. Writing and the writing process itself were teased, drawn out and shared as much as it is possible to do.

Those of us who had been writing for longer and felt that we could not now progress in our work without being stretched by sharper criticism and more challenging tasks gradually found it harder to make time for these meetings which varied considerably from one week to another depending on who turned up. As individual writers embarked upon their own novels or plays it became impossible for them to read these aloud in an evening when everyone was now vying for time. They drifted away. Other women carried on the agenda of the Collective and took it forward.

Rather than approach publishers with a manuscript, the group decided to collect and publish its own work. *Read on* appeared in 1990, followed by *If I Say 'No'* in 1991. Public readings continued to generate enthusiasm and energy and gave many new writers the opportunity to present their work before new audiences.

The present collection began almost three years ago with a decision of the management committee to publish new work from the Collective. When *Right of Way* was published the group had been smaller. To represent everyone writing at that time had been a principal objective and everyone had participated in the editing process by voting on pieces for inclusion. There were only eight of us then. The active membership has remained well over forty in the past few years, touching fifty or more at times, and that was no longer possible. An editorial group was chosen but this too could not meet regularly so a further sub group of two women carried the editorial process forward. A decision was made to include work by all Asian women, living in Britain and not necessarily members, who would like their work to be considered for this anthology. Information about the publication was widely circulated when the collection process began.

Access and inclusion are difficult ideals to hold on to,

alongside of the ambition and desire to publish. We referred earlier to the changed climate in the publishing world. The space that Ros de Lanerolle had created for us at the Women's Press by agreeing to let us edit collectively was a luxury we had then taken for granted. In many ways, the literary climate is much less tolerant now, more hostile to progressive ideas. There is a tendency to dismiss egalitarianism of any kind, to deny the value of equal representation in any forum, a willingness to deride that which does not bear a stamp of approval – 'quality' as defined by some higher certification authority. This makes the publication of an anthology of work which would fully reflect the ethos in which the AWWC operated, almost an impossibility. That was a constraint under which we had to work as editors.

We now had power over the group which we as part of a writing community feel the publishing world has over us, justly or unjustly. It was a challenge to try and do justice to those old cherished ideals and remain supportive to writers, some of whom, inevitably, had to be excluded. This was made easier by the fact that other collections are also planned by the group. An anthology of poetry by members is being compiled and will be published before *Flaming Spirit* rolls off the presses.

Dilemmas aroused by the whole process remain: does success engender a kind of elitism? Were we merely shortlisting people in a spiral of reduction which would hurt more writers than it could benefit? Does success gnaw away insidiously at the values we once held dear? Does new writing have a more bitter struggle now because of these divisions? Are the 'professionals' beholden to the group and should they pay back in terms of time and support for the new writers? How do these inequalities chip away at the collective ethos of the group?

A measure of AWWC's own success as a network is that a large number of Asian women writers who are being published, performed and broadcast are, or have been, members of the group. We are liberally represented in high profile, national black arts forums. More black women writers are getting commissions from radio and TV, the only media which hold out for writers a possibility of making a living by their writing. Although this might point to the fact that we are established as a force, it does not mean that we are less marginal in the British literary consciousness, judging by the review pages of the respected papers and journals. When black writers win literary prizes or achieve unprecedented publishers' payments they preoccupy the literary establishment briefly, but are usually seen as exotic flowers of the mainstream and no attempt is made to contextualise them in any other tradition.

Within the group too, this can sometimes generate tensions, the most recent debate being between the 'published' and 'unpublished' writers. What is and what should be the relationship between these two groups? Some of these questions came to a head during the selection process for the anthology. The initial selection, about half the manuscript agreed by Virago, contained work mostly by women who had been published before. The final selection contains about half by each group.

We resolved some of these questions by adhering to the principle of the widest representation within a context of 'quality'. We spent a lot of time developing work by newer writers to which most editors would not have devoted such time. Admittedly, not all the unpublished writers needed that support – but we are aware that the collective principle continues to be under threat whilst the skills differential remains. There must be a continuing commitment to share skills from those women who were once regular attenders and who have achieved a measure of success within the writing profession.

We both have our own sense of the history of the Collective and the spirit in which writing was received and read, and, to a great extent, have been guided by that spirit. We were keen that the work should be a mix of the older and the newer, sometimes younger, perspectives and that the writing should demonstrate the range of styles, themes, approaches within the group. We made a decision to include more writers by limiting contributions to one per writer. If time had permitted more stories would have been ready for publication, but we had decided to publish in our tenth anniversary year and deadlines forced us to a cut-off point with some of the work. We hope, nevertheless, that those women who are connected with the group and could not be included here will be present and powerfully so in the next anthology.

Rukhsana Ahmad
Rahila Gupta
1994

IN YOUR OWN WORDS

Joyoti Grech

Dream that you are escaping from your pursuing torturer. You know his face. It is behind you. Before you. As you run down the long corridors of your grandmother's house away from him, you turn and shut each folding door behind you. Carefully. Quickly. Turn the key on your panic. Each folding door. Each folding door. You reach the final room, your place of security. A hundred locked doors your guardians. Dream that as you sink to safety, your cousin (twice removed) opens up a side entrance and through it walks the attacker. He pushes towards you with all his menacing weight. Your sinking does not stop, you pass through the bleeding floors. Nothing holds you up.

As you fall your legs jerk remotely. This will wake me up, you think from far away. My mind won't let me drop to smash on concrete. The heart can't take the shock. My mind won't push what my heart can't take. You think, they belong in the same body.

They do, but their allegiance is treacherous. The concrete rushes up to greet you. How do you *do*? Your body grins widely. Out pops the soul. How do *you* do?

I know where I'm headed. Down to Burger King for a Whopper. Faced with Burger King and MacDonalds on either side of the alleyway, which one do you choose to boycott? As a matter of principle you answer, MacDonalds. Ha! It's a trick question. Both of them are multinational monsters of capitalist exploitation. And what about the rainforests? There is a tree growing through your gut. Its rotting branches blossom with your kidney here, your liver there. It was no accident. You know who sowed its seed. You know who carried the burning stovepipe into your house while you were sleeping. Your body may be overcome by force but your soul is invincible.

You gather up your aura with determination. Step on out, your soul. Pick up your trail of incarnations. Such a lovely flower. And with the scent of cloves. Cloves and nails. Both the same word in Maltese and both also meaning, carn(ation). Meat. You are more than a piece of meat. You are not a piece of meat. Why, you're not a piece of meat at all. You are – well golly now you're not quite sure exactly what you are right this very minute but whatever it is that you are, it ain't gonna be beat. Or meat.

He's lurking, shifting down as close to the bottom of the page as he can manage. He thinks we're going to forget all about him if he can run enough words in between the beginning and the end. (Oh no you don't. We'll get back to you. Who do you think's got the finger on the pen here? This is *my* story.)

Your soul is feeling pretty good. Nice to get out for a change. You think, shopping. Down at the mall there is a special offer on instruments of vengeance. Two submachine guns, one chainsaw free. But there's something faintly Hollywood about such obvious tools, not befitting the necessary dignity of your intentions. And remembering the persistence of your torturer, you are driven to seek a more comprehensive strategy. Swooping into the garden, you hover over mimulus, petunias, lupins. Now foxglove, calla lilies, tall red canna stalks. Cosmos petals swaying in the utopian breeze. Water hyacinth spreads across the pool. Paradise has a sweeter perfume than the stinking room that the stovepipe inhabits.

The telephone burrs inside the pocket of your angelic raiment. On the mobile, your sister tells you that the structures of patriarchy have ivy corroding through the stones. 'Shall we bring them down now,' she asks?

You set off to join her. Clouds are gathering above the motorway. Heavy traffic on the M1. As the rain breaks, your ship steers south through the static cars. Your soul is a much better sailor than your body ever was. You approach the city. The air turns. Fumes spiral upward from the house of the torturer. Ghosts and evil memories stand sentry on every road that leads toward it.

Your sister calls back. Heaven's florist is sending on the blooms. You sail on in behind the delivery van. The ghosts dissipate in the brilliance of its heavenly headlights.

The Centre for Revolutionary Planning is two streets up from the torturer's house. You stop in there for refreshment. Your mother opens the door. 'Ah,' she says, 'is that you in your soul darling.' Her embrace fortifies you. Children's laughter fills the building. It is made of lasting materials, ancient and modern. Alpana welcome you, painted auspiciously on the steps. The rooms are hung with warm colours. You are supported and nourished. All the secretaries who ever had an office party hand lingering unwanted on their hip are deep in conference with the women strikers from Timex, Burnsalls and Grunwick. During the plenary meeting they swap tactics of resistance.

They declare the court in session and all the people of the entire world with one fraction of a glimmer of hope still shining in their heart gather together in the big yard. After a short period of music and mutual inspiration they flow outwards, a tidal wave of beautiful humanity. The verdict is: liberation.

On the pavement you wonder momentarily if it can be this easy. You look around for your mother. You want to ask her, 'Ma, does it go like this? What's the next line?' You can't see her. You're lying on your back in a used car sales yard. Beneath your head is a burnt-out carburettor. You thought it was a pillow. Where is your soul?

Someone is whistling. You recognise the torturer's tune. Never mind comprehensive strategies. You reach for your axe. 'The flowers, sweetness, don't forget the flowers,' says a voice at your ear – it is your mother's love. A bouquet appears in your hand. You use it to cover up the axe. Around the corner saunters the torturer. He approaches you with fruits and chocolate. 'All I want,' he says, lying through his pasty long-nose face, 'is forgiveness.' Weapons glint through the buttonholes on his coat.

That is not a human being, you tell yourself. That is a type. He transforms into the letter 'r'. The keyboard clatters. He is not alone. An army marches against you. His allies are armed to the fangs. Writs and orders drip from their mouths.

The institution surrounds you. In the white hallways people bellow, loud as a whisper: 'We Are Here To Help You.' 'Tell Us Your Name.' Bank notes rustle in their pockets.

The torturer is seated on a podium. He is writing down the story of your panic as if it were an invoice. He is digging and pulling into the deepest part of your very own words. He calls them his. The blood of your womb is on his hands and he would pass it off as an absence of evidence. 'Get out of there,' you try to shout. 'That's my personal diary. You have no invitation.'

He has his back to you. You drop the flowers from your axe. You want to slice him up and fry him like so many rashers of bacon.

There are no frying pans in paradise. The last tenants took all utensils with them when the lease ran out. The telephone shrills in the fog. It continues to ring, then falls into silence. No one picked it up. You shout at No one, 'That was my sister. She was calling with the map reference.' You struggle desperately to wake up. It's nearly over now, you tell yourself, glancing at the TV listings. The next programme starts at 10.45. It's an episode in a nature series. You missed the beginning.

Out on the marshes herons wheel above your head. 'Hang in there,' they tell you. 'It's coming up.' The voiceover drones through the commentator's beard. It surprises you with helpful suggestions and encouragement. 'The habitat of the predatory catweasel is often interrupted by a backhand reminder that the route to recovery is resistance.'

'Yeah sure,' you think, 'that's a great idea.' Cynicism overtook terror just this one minute ago. If you hurry you can still catch it at the bus stop. You are overwhelmed by exhaustion. 'When is this thing going to end,' you huff, checking your watch. 'I have a life to get on with. Maybe I could opt out temporarily and opt back in some time after the transformation of all human evil into heated public housing.'

The torturer is coming at you with a video monitor. It flickers with the images of your violation. He is leering at you. 'I don't want to do this,' he says. 'Tell me everything will be alright.' It is your voice. There's a spinach pattie from the Bir-Hakim bakery in your hand. You fling it at him in self-defence. The herons screech. They swing and aim for dinner. There is a hurricane of feathers and human limbs. My, those birds are hungry. Is that an eyeball or a piece of hard boiled egg? He's screaming for help now. He calls out to you by name. You point your pistol into the hurricane.

You pick off first one leg, then the other. To stop him from running away. Then one more bullet in the heart and several more into the area of most damage at the point where his now broken legs meet. You are wearing gardening gloves with green spots and flowers. There will be no fingerprints.

The herons clap their wide wings. They suggest a holiday. 'Thankyou for your support,' you call out. You wave at them from the open window of the train as it pulls off across the marshes. You are heading for the coast.

Wait. Wait. Wait. You meant to get his spirit. Leave him the body (minus the dangerous weapons) but that filthy spirit has to go. You fly off out the window in the direction of the scene of retribution. The herons flap towards you. One of them has a flimsy plastic bag fluttering insubstantially from its bill. 'You forgot this,' they coo. Oh, you think, is that what it looks like.

'Is there any room for re-education?' you ask them. 'Not with this one dearie,' they tut. 'Best to drop it in the ocean. We have a chapter down at Shoreham. They'll get rid of it for you.'

On the shingle beach at Shoreham you can hear a little boy tell his mother in Cantonese, 'I found a bee and I put it in the crab-shell.' You smile at her and she smiles back, patting the patch of pebbles beside her. 'Come and have an orange,' she says.

You hand the bag by the grubby handles over to the Shoreham heron chapter. As they dive to receive it, you notice several other similar scraps of plastic swinging from the herons' bills. A look of dawning comprehension spreads across your face. 'Did you think you were the only one, poor love?' the herons ask. 'We do this all the time.'

They circle and dip above the waves, then sing off, Ta Ta. Ah, what wonderful music. You stand and look out at the sea a while.

The air is salt and fresh.

STILL WATERS

Janet McDermott

As I enter the room, the bitter aroma of freshly ground coffee curls up from a neatly laid wooden trolley parked by the door.

'Come in and sit down.' A figure is seated in shadow at the sprawling mahogany desk beside the French windows. I let the door go and step forward, it slams to with a rude bang and we both start.

'Sorry,' I murmur guiltily. 'Shall I sit here?'

'By the fire will do.' The response is unsmiling. Dr Hinton rises from the desk to move slowly and heavily to an armchair by the purring gas fire. I sit opposite in a second chair, which gives dangerously in the middle with a faint sigh.

'So . . . I gather you wish to go down for a year,' a stern pause follows. 'I wonder if you could tell me where this interesting idea came from?'

My heart is thudding. For a moment the room vanishes in a mist of panic and only the brown, wintry garden is visible through tall windows, every last papery leaf and bare twig motionless with suspense, awaiting my reply.

'Well,' I begin, 'as you know, I haven't found it very easy set-tling in here – and I've been worrying about things at home . . .' I falter at this blatant half-truth.

'Go on,' clips the uncompromising reply.

'Because of the other things on my mind, I just can't

concentrate at all. I don't know if I can explain it any better . . .'

'Well, you're going to have to try, my dear, because so far you've given me nothing substantial. There are many students at this university with grave personal worries, who nevertheless find the strength to carry on. You must tell me precisely what the matter is so we can help you. You see, if I let you leave now, you may never find the nerve to return, and that would be a loss to Oxford and a tragic waste of your potential, don't you think?'

Despite the serious tone, Dr Hinton's eyes are kind and strangely disarming beneath strong eyebrows and short wiry grey hair. I feel defeated already, knowing there is no way to convey the immense, unbridgeable gulf between the dizzy success of my entrance exams last year and the bleakness I now inhabit.

Mummy cried and laughed and pressed her wet cheek against mine when the letter came, while Daddy sat proud and quiet, reading it over and over. Akib just slapped me on the back and said gruffly, 'Well done, Shazi, fancy you getting into Oxford, eh?' and I smiled, my thoughts already flying ahead to lunchtime and Fliss waiting by the chippy outside school, hands in the pockets of her old jeans, her close-cropped hair tousled and fuzzy, and her smiling grey-blue eyes, crinkled at the corners, squinting into the sun at the students pouring through the gates.

'You got in! Oh, Shazia!' she screamed when I told her, and hugged me wildly and unexpectedly, swinging me round in giddy circles till I clutched at her shoulders to steady myself. We stood back embarrassed, and through my denim jacket and thin kameez I could still feel the imprint of her hands on my waist, like a shock through my whole body. Sharing a packet of chips and drinking steaming tea in polystyrene cups, we huddled on a bench by the river in the cold blue December sunshine, knowing I would be late for afternoon classes, but not caring about the time or the place, weaving bold crazy futures together . . .

*

'It's not the work, I really enjoy doing the essays, and I do want to be here,' I try to explain.

'I'm glad to hear it,' Dr Hinton comments. The corners of her mouth move upwards in a faint smile and I wonder if she is laughing at me, in that veiled sarcastic way they have. It brings back shuddering memories of children laughing as I struggled to make sense of the treacherous barbed words, a language I thought I knew, but didn't.

'It's just that I feel really out of place,' I continue, resolutely.

'But, Miss Rashid, we are a college that prides itself on its high intake from the ethnic minorities, and from comprehensive schools. I see no reason why you shouldn't feel at home.'

'That's not what I meant,' I persist, ignoring the layers of meaning in her remark. 'Not out of place socially, it's more I feel out of "synch", you know? I don't feel like I'm really here. Everything feels unreal.'

A small involuntary sigh escapes from Dr Hinton's lips and she looks down, as if for inspiration, at her short, blunt-ended fingers folded over her tartan skirt. I look out through the windows again, searching for ways to explain where it started to go wrong.

The sweet-smelling grass down by the river was prickly and freshly mown. Fliss and I sat beside each other, staring at the trees on the other side as they tossed and surged like green waves in the warm wind.

'You can't go to London, you just can't,' I protested, my eyes stinging with tears as I spoke.

'But don't you see, once you're in Oxford I'll be much closer down in London than stuck up here?' Fliss replied, calm and implacable, and I saw it was already decided. 'Anyway, it's my life.' She lay back on the grass as if the conversation were over.

'But why now? Can't you wait? I've got all summer free when my exams are over, I thought we could go round Europe —'

'I haven't got any money. I'm unemployed, remember?'

'So? I've got enough for both of us – anyway, what does money matter?'

'It matters when you haven't got it. Look,' she sighed, from behind closed eyes, 'I need to get out of this pit of a town, all right? I can't live at home any more, it's really doing my head in, and I can't wait around till it suits you – there's more of a life for women like me in London.'

'How do you mean?'

She opened her eyes and looked at me searchingly, then looked away and said, 'If you don't understand, it doesn't matter.'

I wanted to say, 'Then explain it to me, Fliss, just give us a chance,' but I was scared and tongue-tied. I felt a million miles from her, although her bare, freckled arm was nearly touching my leg and I could hear her breathing.

'Can I come and see you in London?' I ventured.

'Of course! You daft or what?' she laughed, suddenly light-hearted, and jumped up, reaching an arm out to pull me up. 'Come on, you've got revision to do – and stop wittering about London, it'll be all right. You can come down every weekend if you like.'

'Miss Rashid, I don't mean to diminish what you're saying,' Dr Hinton enunciates carefully, 'but we all have our little existential crises at your age and I'm afraid life must go on. I assure you Oxford is very real, as are the rewards to be gained here. But only you can do it –'

'I know it's down to me,' I interrupt, shortly, 'but at the moment I just can't. I thought if I had some time out . . .'

'To do what precisely?' The crisp edge to her voice suggests I am running out of time.

'To go to London,' I reply desperately, and remember Fliss's room, the narrow bed, the heady, rose-scented summer nights, sounds of traffic and thudding party music drifting through the open window as we bury our shyness in warm tides of touching.

'London?' Dr Hinton repeats, flatly.

'Something happened there this summer, before I came here,' I mutter, grudgingly. I feel wary and sullen. If she pushes me, I shall just leave anyway; there are no words for this, no words that are mine.

'Something romantic, perhaps?' she probes, gently.

'Yes – no – well, yes it was, sort of,' I flounder, and suddenly there is a hard painful lump in my throat.

'Maybe the relationship ended?' Dr Hinton suggests.

The relationship ended. I repeat the words in my head like a mantra, but they make no more sense than the words on the phone that day.

'I think it's better if you don't come down this weekend –'

'But I didn't come last weekend either – is it work again or what?' She didn't reply. 'Fliss – are you all right?'

'Yes, I'm fine,' she assured me. Her low, breathy voice seemed tense, but it was so hard to tell on the phone. I tried to imagine her sitting on the bottom stair in the cluttered hallway of their shared house, nibbling her nails absent-mindedly as she spoke. 'I just think it's too much, all these weekends. I'm trying to get things going here, you know, and they expect me to spend some time with them in the house, it is a co-operative,' she lowered her voice as she said this.

'I'm sorry to be in the way,' I replied, sulkily, 'but I want to see you too.'

'Why?' she challenged.

'Don't be silly, you know why,' I laughed nervously.

'No, I don't. Tell me.' I was shocked by her angry tone and fell silent, my mind reeling among the memories of wordless secret moments we had shared. I had thought not naming it was one of the unspoken rules, so why was she suddenly shifting the goal posts?

'I think you're better off without me,' she announced when I said nothing. 'I'm just confusing things for you. You should make a new start in Oxford – travel light, you know. It's a bad idea trying to keep things going from the past.'

I remained silent; it felt like my only defence as I struggled with her words, trying to understand what she was really saying.

'Besides,' she paused, carefully, 'I'm a bit busy with Cath now, we're spending a lot of time together.'

I suddenly remembered a Sunday morning in their house, everyone slumped around the big pine table in the centre of the kitchen, drinking tea, reading pages of the dismembered Sunday paper, having arty London conversations about films and politics. Fliss was relaxed and expansive, arguing with Jez about a documentary they had seen earlier in the week, resting a foot lightly on the edge of Cath's chair. Karen was chopping vegetables methodically and depositing them in a large earthenware pot, pausing occasionally to sip her tea and gaze indulgently at the others. Her quiet industry allowed me to remain silent too, flicking idly through the colour supplement. Suddenly everyone burst out laughing at some comment Fliss had made.

'You're priceless, you are!' Cath laughed, giving Fliss's knee a quick affectionate squeeze. Fliss leapt up, grabbing Cath's wrist dramatically.

'Unhand me, woman!' she cried with mock fury and they both collapsed into fits of giggles. I was laughing too, until I caught Karen flashing Jez a quick meaningful glance, and felt suddenly confused and alone. I had blanked the incident out of my mind until now.

'What are you trying to say, Fliss?' I forced myself to ask.

'I'm just saying I don't think it's working any more,' Fliss replied quietly. 'And it'll be really difficult if you come down this weekend, it's really not a good idea.'

'When then?' I responded, coldly.

'I'll come and see you in Oxford when you get settled. It's only a couple of weeks now, isn't it?'

'Four,' I countered dully, staring at the calendar on the wall above the phone, and somehow I survived to the end of the conversation.

Mummy was cutting out material on the floor of the living-room, scissors slicing the slippery cloth with cool precision, so sure, so definite. All my life I have watched her cut cloth with neither measure nor pattern, her hands shaping it, understanding it, knowing it with the same sureness of instinct she applies to everything. I studied her dark, gleaming head bent over her work, her black hair threaded through with silver-grey, the knotted veins on her long brown hands. I could not speak, and when she looked up and smiled and asked me what time my train to London was, I turned and ran out of the house into the bright, clamorous street.

Pounding hot angry pavements, I ran past the school, through the park, across the lawns, down to the river. I flung myself on to the grass, Fliss's words already receding, her voice remote and passionless, her face eluding my clutching memory. A swallow flashed by and I turned on to my back to stare up into the cool green canopy . . .

'What happened?' Dr Hinton's voice breaks into my thoughts.

'She never came to see me,' I murmur absently and then stare at my tutor in shock as I realise what I have said.

She raises an eyebrow slightly and continues, unflurried. 'I take it the relationship between you has ended then?'

'I don't know, I don't really understand any of it,' I confess, stunned that she appears to be taking this in her stride. She waits patiently for me to continue, so I plough on recklessly. 'That's why I need some time out. I need to find out what it was all about, who I am. I know it sounds corny . . .'

'Not at all,' Dr Hinton interrupts firmly. 'But what makes you think you can't find that out here?'

'Oh, I don't think there's anyone who could . . . I mean, anyone like me . . .' I stumble, and wonder what I do mean.

'I think you'll find there is – and much closer than you think,' Dr Hinton says evenly, pinning me with an eloquent gaze. I look at her blankly and then slowly my eyes widen in amazement.

'You mean . . . you . . .?'

'You must draw your own conclusions, Miss Rashid,' she cautions, 'but never think you are alone. There are many in this university who can help you and anything you say to me is said in strict confidence.' She draws herself up briskly. 'Now, I have a letter to write, and I would like you to go away and think some more about your intention to leave before we make any firm decision.'

'Can I just sit here for a while? I won't make any noise,' I ask hesitantly.

'By all means,' she smiles and returns to her desk. I lean back in the chair, listening to the faint scratching of her pen and the hiss of the gas fire, and remember lying by the river . . .

A swallow sweeps by, flitting beneath rustling branches over the slow green river, its flight rising and falling in lifts and sighs, like my thoughts which rush towards the light glimpsed in half-remembered words, and falter again as the sense is lost, sinking into the meaningless riddle of flesh and bone and gently resistant earth. I feel my breath and know that I am alive, that my skin touches these trembling blades of grass. My eyes close against the net of shimmering green above. Reaching into the blue and red darkness behind my eyelids, I clutch at the memory of soft lips, but feel only the cool earth against my back, insisting its reality, this is all there is, this moment of birds and leaves and emptiness . . .

'Do you take milk in your coffee, Shazia?'

I look up to see Dr Hinton poised by the wooden trolley, pouring coffee from a tall white jug. She looks at me with friendly understanding, and I smile and nod in reply, realising I have made a decision.

SISTERS

·····◆·····

Sibani Raychaudhuri

I

When I was small, we always thought that everything would be all right once we came to England. Shirin, my older sister, had shown me the black dot on the map, which marked the city where our father lived, and had told me we would go there one day. I thought of England as a very special place that would bring an end to all our problems.

In those days we lived in a little village in Bangladesh where my father's family had lived for as long as anyone could remember. Amma did what she could to keep us clean and fed, but it was Shirin who always played with me and looked after me. Our main excitement, each week, came on those days when we saw the postman walking towards our house with his heavy shoulder bag. If there were any letters from Abba he would shout out '*Chitti!*' '*Chitti!*' and we would run into the lane to meet him. When the letters arrived, Shirin was the one who had to read them to us and Amma was always impatient. 'Is there any news?' she would ask, before Shirin had even had time to cut open the aerogramme. We knew what her question meant without her having to complete it. We had been waiting for over five years to get permits to go to England. I had seen Abba only twice in that time. He could not come more often than that: he was saving money for our fares. I hardly knew him, but I missed him a lot. I kept all his letters in a biscuit-tin, which he had brought for us on his first visit. The last time he came, he had arrived home with a huge case full of new clothes for us children, nylon saris for Amma, and a small radio: Shirin and I had fought over it until Amma had threatened to give it away unless we learned to share it.

We had good meals every day for a month, while Abba was there, and neighbours and relations crowded our house all hours of the day. He sat on the veranda with them, and they all smoked the cigarettes he had brought back from England. They talked and talked, while Amma and Shirin made endless cups of tea for them. When everyone had gone in the late evening, he told us stories: stories of his childhood and stories of England, that faraway place where, one day, we would all live.

Every month Abba sent money from London. When the money arrived, Shirin went with Amma to the post office to collect it. Each moment at the post office was a torture for her; she had to prove who she was, knowing that if anything went wrong she would not be given the money. Once when they were getting ready to go to the post office, I started to get dressed as well. Shirin was puzzled: 'Why are you putting on a clean dress at midday?'

'I am taking Amma to the post office.'

She smiled. 'Do you know what to do there?'

'I could find out. Why can't I go for once? You go with Amma every time.' Shirin loved me dearly, so she pleaded with Amma: 'Let Nazia take you this time. I'll tell her what to do.'

But Amma refused to listen: 'Nazia can stay and look after Kamal,' she said. I knew there was no point in arguing.

When Amma and Shirin came back, I sulked and ignored them. They didn't take any notice of me either. They were busy unpacking the groceries: sugar, tea, lentils, salt, spices. I sat on the edge of the veranda watching Kamal as he played on the baked red earth of the courtyard. He was making a series of small holes in the ground for a game of marbles. Suddenly I felt a hand over my eyes: 'Nazia, guess what we have got for you?'

I turned round and there was Shirin standing behind me with a length of silk ribbon. This was a great luxury in those days. I knew Amma had little money to spend on extras. The money Abba sent home was just enough for bare necessities. Whenever we asked for something, Amma would chide us: 'That poor man sweating over a hot oven day and night: what do you know of life?' All I knew was that Abba had to work very hard over there in England to keep us going in Jagganathpure. And I looked forward to the day when we would be allowed to join him.

II

Every monsoon our village became water-logged for days: the narrow path leading to our house from the road disappeared; the courtyard flooded – the water rose to the edge of the veranda. We lay awake at night, unable to sleep, listening to the storm. The wind rattled the corrugated-tin roof, and the heavy rain hissed through the leaves of the trees behind the house. I remember one year in particular. Shirin and I huddled together on the bed; while Kamal lay asleep on Amma's lap. We heard the frogs croaking outside in the darkness. Then we heard: *Splash! Splash! Splash!* Something came closer and closer, and then disappeared. We spent the rest of the night in fear. Shirin held me tight: 'Don't be frightened, Nazia. Look out of the window – see the lights in the schoolhouse.'

Amma heard our whispering: 'If it goes on like this, we may have to move to the schoolhouse ourselves.'

Next morning, we could see the damage. Our kitchen, a small clay hut in the corner of the courtyard, had lost its roof. Our pots and pans had washed out under the half-door and now floated in the courtyard along with vegetable-peel, burnt wood from the fire, and the body of a drowned cat. The cat had belonged to our neighbours. Kamal and I wept when we saw it. Our small vegetable patch was gone and the top of our coconut tree had been broken by the wind. Shirin wiped Kamal's eyes and put her arms round our shoulders. 'Don't worry,' she said, 'we won't be here next year.' And we thought how everything would be all right when we went to London. Dry floors, dry clothes, dry beds. 'Have you been to London?' asked Kamal. Shirin laughed and shook her head: 'Abba has been trying to get us over there since before you were born!' Kamal counted the years on his fingers – five, six, seven!

III

Then came the day when the postman's shout '*chitti*' brought a registered letter from England. Shirin had to sign a form to receive the letter, while Amma stood beside her anxiously. Kamal and I were very excited and asked hundreds of questions: 'Are we going then?' 'Has he sent the plane tickets?' We didn't stop until Amma told us off. 'Don't get too excited – there is still a lot to be sorted out.' She had become superstitious in those days; she thought that things would not come true if we expected them too confidently.

The letter, however, brought good news, and it seemed that we were on our way, at last. Abba had asked an old friend in the village to help with arrangements at our end. Mr Ahmed had already done this for another family. 'They are living in London now,' he told us, a few days later, when he dropped in to see Amma, 'on the seventh floor of a very nice, tall block of flats.' He searched for something in his pocket. 'They have sent me a colour photo.' But he could not find the photo. He shook his head and looked thoughtful for a moment. 'It's a lot of work. It takes time.' Even so, none of us had any idea just how much work it would take before we could board the plane. First we had to go to an office in Sylhet Town. We started our journey very early, before the sun rose. We were dressed up for the occasion. Amma and Shirin wore the nylon saris Abba had brought on his last visit. Amma was nervous. She kept on checking everything again and again. 'Have you taken the water-bottle?' she asked Shirin. 'Have you got the food safe?' she asked me. Then, when Mr Ahmed arrived, Amma checked everything once more. We crossed the river by the narrow, bamboo bridge. Then Mr Ahmed led us across the cracked earth of the dried-out fields towards the road, where we waited for the bus. It was a long and difficult journey: after the bus-ride came a ferry, then another bus-ride and another ferry. It was the first time that Kamal and I had been out of our village.

And, in the end, this first journey came to nothing. When we arrived at the office, a wooden sign was hanging on the door: 'Closed.' We sat down on the steps, saddened and exhausted. We had had to stand most of the way, and the day had been very hot. Mr Ahmed sighed. 'Just our luck! If that second bus hadn't stopped to collect sacks of rice from the market, we would have been here in time.' Shirin got to her feet and tucked the water-bottle under her arm: 'Let's go!' she said quietly. 'We don't want to spend the night here.'

After that first fruitless trip, we made numerous journeys to Sylhet, and, on one occasion, two Englishmen turned up in our village and asked our neighbours some searching questions about us. Amma had felt very tense and worried in case our neighbours made any mistakes – or left anything out. But Kamal and I lived in a state of euphoria. We often skipped going to school. Any day now we would be leaving for England, and, in the mean-time, we accompanied Amma wherever she went.

It was nearly two years before we were granted our final inter-view in Dhaka. A trip to Dhaka was even more of an adventure than a trip to Sylhet Town. We arrived in Dhaka the night before our interview. Mr Ahmed had arranged for us to stay with his sis-ter, whose husband was the manager of a cotton mill. We spent the night in their guest room, which had paintings on the walls, a brass pot with a plant on a small table in the corner of the room and a chiming clock on the bookshelf. Months later, I saw a clock like that in a shop window in London. Next day, at eight in the morning, we were waiting to go into the High Commission. About twenty women, young and old, all dressed in their best saris, were sitting on the wooden benches. Amma and Shirin joined them. Kamal and I sat on the floor with the other children. A man was standing at a desk: he called out the names one by one. It was midday before Amma's name was called. We followed her into the room.

We entered a large room and stood like convicts in front of a British officer, seated on a high-backed wooden chair. There was a huge shiny table between us and him. A Bangladeshi man was waiting by the officer to interpret for him. The officer asked Amma question after question about our family until there was nothing else she could tell him. Then he turned to Shirin and interrogated her as well: 'What was your grandfather's name?' he asked. 'His father's name? His mother's name?' Shirin had never met our great-grandparents, but she had been warned to expect such questions. The officer turned back to our mother. He seemed to be worried that Shirin did not have a birth-certificate. Amma was lost for words; she did not know what to say. She tried to explain: Shirin was born at home, and nobody had thought to have her birth recorded. It was not a custom then; everyone knew when she was born. The officer made some notes on the papers in front of him, and then took the papers away to another room. We waited in silence, in suspense. Those few minutes seemed to stretch endlessly. When at last he came back, the officer announced the decision.

'We have decided to allow you and your two younger children entrance to Britain to join your husband, but we have decided not to grant entry to Shirin Bibi. She is eighteen and is, there-fore, too old to go as your dependant.' I could not believe what I heard. Shirin wouldn't be coming with us. After all those years of waiting, Shirin was now 'too old'.

All the way back home, Amma was wiping her eyes on the end of her sari. Shirin didn't say a word, she only held Amma's hand tightly. Amma tried to reassure her: 'Once your Abba hears this, he'll do all he can to bring you to join us. He must know a lot of people there.' Shirin just nodded.

All our excitement about going to England had dried up at the office in Dhaka, but there was no time to brood, there was so much to do before we left. We had to arrange for Shirin to stay with our Khala, Amma's sister, in the next village. Our Khala came to collect her a few days before we caught the plane. Since we had got back from Dhaka, I had followed Shirin like a shadow wherever she went. We were going to be separated for the first time in our lives. I couldn't imagine what life would be like without her, and I didn't want to lose a minute of her company in those last days. On the day she left, when I helped her to pack her clothes, I could not speak to her – my voice was choked with tears. When we finished Shirin gave me a big hug, and I handed over to her our prized possession, the small radio. Shirin could no longer keep herself under control, and the tears flooded her eyes. We sat holding each other on the floor of the little room we shared. Then Khala came into the room with Amma and said, 'Come on! We must hurry or we'll miss the bus.' I went to the bus-stop with them – and I stood, watching and crying, long after the bus had disappeared over the dusty horizon.

IV

The dream had come true. We had come to England, but we had left Shirin behind us. Six families lived in the house Abba brought us to. We had one small room with two beds and a pile of blankets and pillows. We had to take turns for cooking, washing and taking baths. We had to dry our clothes in the room which smelt of damp and paraffin. There were always petty rows when people got in each other's way. Amma became nervous and frightened, and stayed in our room all the time. Abba was never there: he left for work early and came home late.

One day Kamal asked, 'Where can we play? Can we play in the street?'

Abba suddenly became anxious: 'Don't you two go out of this house on your own. I'll get you some games – you can play in the room.'

But Abba didn't buy us any games, and Kamal and I played on the stairs with the other children of the house.

Kamal and I were sent to different schools. Kamal's was a small primary school across the road, but mine was ten minutes' walk from home. It was big and confusing, a secondary school crowded with children. There were fights in the playground and fights in the corridors. There was lots of jostling and pushing whenever we changed rooms. On my first day I was terrified. At break I was waiting by the water-fountain to have a drink. I was standing at the edge of a crowd of boys and girls. Some were drinking; others were splashing water on us.

'Are you new here?' someone asked me in Sylheti. I nodded. Then she pulled me by the arm towards the fountain. 'You won't get anywhere here, if you wait quietly,' she said, 'you have to fight for everything.'

This was Rukeya, and this was the start of our friendship. As we walked back across the playground, she said: 'I'll take care of you until you get used to things.'

After that, I stayed with Rukeya. We spoke the same language, and, besides, most of the other girls didn't want to mix with us.

One day, when I was running down the corridor with Rukeya between lessons, two of them grabbed hold of us. They pulled our hair for no reason at all, and we punched them to make them let go. A small group of girls gathered to watch. They chanted in chorus: 'Fight! Fight!'

The noise brought out the headmistress and we were marched

into her room. Then Maxine and Fay told their versions of the story. Rukeya and I tried to tell ours. Ms Butler didn't seem to listen to us. She went on and on about our bad behaviour: 'This is disgraceful! Punching and scratching each other!' Rukeya and I kept our heads down, but we couldn't help noticing what Maxine was doing. Whenever Ms Butler looked in our direction and away from the other two, Maxine made a large pink bubble with the gum in her mouth. Fay, like us, was struggling not to laugh. Ms Butler suddenly shouted at her, 'You can wipe that silly grin off your face!'

Fay drew the back of her hand across her mouth, and the three of us giggled. That made Ms Butler furious. 'You are all on report,' she said. She handed a pink card to each of us and told us we had to ask our teachers to sign it at the end of each lesson.

We walked quietly out of her room, but as soon as we had turned the corner at the end of the corridor, we roared with laughter. Maxine nudged me: 'Have one.' She held out a packet of bubble-gum. I hesitated for a moment, but Rukeya said, 'Go on – take one!'

V

On Saturdays, there were stalls on the pavement by the tube-station, and a market in the open space behind the shops. Rukeya and I went round the market to do the weekly shopping for our families. We gave Kamal the job of carrying the bags. As yet Kamal didn't have any friends to go out with and he didn't protest too much. One Saturday, when Kamal couldn't come with us, we went to 'City Girls' in the High Street. The shop was darker than any other we'd ever been to, and music was playing loudly. We moved shyly between the racks, feeling the smoothness of the long silky dresses. Quite unexpectedly, I felt a touch on my shoulder. Someone whispered: 'Hi! I didn't know you shopped here.' I turned round to see who it was. It was Maxine. We were astonished and impressed! She was doing the same as us, only it was our first time at City Girls whereas she had clearly been there often before. Then she winked at us and led us down a spiral staircase to the basement. Here were the changing rooms – a series of cubicles with drop curtains. We exchanged glances: we knew exactly what we were going to do now. Rukeya and Maxine returned to the ground floor, and each took a long dress from the racks. Maxine's was black and Rukeya's was deep purple. I tried on a pair of tight leather trousers and a short jacket spotted like leopard-skin. We admired ourselves in the mirror and praised each other's choice with mischievous smiles. Rukeya and I knew that our parents would never let us dress up as 'City Girls'.

Every Sunday morning, Rukeya and I went to the community centre for our Bengali lessons. It was more of a club than a class. Besides our language lessons, we were allowed to listen to songs and to watch Bengali films on video. There was also a small library, which kept Bengali books, newspapers and magazines. We used to get news of Bangladesh from the centre. A few days before our school holiday ended, Rukeya called to see me and we went out together to the centre. When we entered the hall-way, a crowd was standing there. They were looking at the front page of a newspaper and talking anxiously. We wanted to know what was going on. They showed us the front page: there were photographs of bodies floating in water, people standing on a roof-top. There had been a terrible flood in Bangladesh!

Abba got home late as usual. He had already heard the news about the flood, and he looked very worried. He was restless; he couldn't stay in the room, he went to talk to other people in the house. Then he went out to see someone he knew who lived in the next street. Amma was shaking with fear about what might have happened to Shirin. I couldn't calm her down. When Abba came back he told us what he'd heard: the floods had washed away many villages on the coasts, and the small islands in the Bay of Bengal were under the sea. The electric and telephone lines had been damaged by the storm, and people were cut off from the outside world; only a few helicopters were dropping food and blankets into the damaged areas. Abba tried to assure us: 'Your Khala does not live on the coast. I heard that people in other places had taken shelter on higher ground.'

Amma wept and kept repeating: 'My Shirin must be cold and hungry. How can I eat if she hasn't had a grain of food?' That night, when I went to bed, I sat up and prayed that Shirin was safe.

VI

The summer holidays came to an end and we had still had no definite news of Shirin. Abba gathered from his friends that my Khala and her family were safe, but they had lost their home and nobody knew where they were staying. Friends kept on telling us 'No news is good news', but Amma was so depressed that she stayed in bed. I was too upset to go back to school; I stayed at home to look after Amma. Kamal went to school with other boys from the house. Every day after school, Rukeya came to see me. She used to say, 'Nazia, please come to school – it'll take your mind off your worries.'

One evening when I opened the door for Rukeya, Maxine was standing outside with her. 'Can we come in?' Rukeya asked.

'Yes,' I replied hesitantly. I rushed to tidy up the bed-clothes to make room for them. Amma was puzzled by this unexpected visit. Maxine sat on the bed next to Rukeya and handed me a letter from our form tutor: 'We have told Miss Richards about Shirin and your aunt. She has seen the news of the floods on television. We are raising money for flood-relief.'

Rukeya broke in: 'We'll give the money to the community centre, and they'll make sure it gets where it's needed.' Amma wanted to know what was going on, and why they were talking about Shirin and Bangladesh. Rukeya repeated everything in Sylheti. Amma gave thanks to Allah. When Maxine and

Rukeya left, they made me promise to come back to school next day.

Next morning I went back to school as promised. On my way there I felt I had lost touch with everything over the last month. I was completely blank when I arrived. The first lesson was a form-period. Miss Richards accepted my absence note and didn't ask me for any further explanation. She suggested that I should take a look at some of the work the other children had done in their project on Bangladesh. The work was displayed on the wall. There was also a box of books from the library. I picked up a Bengali book, *Our Bangladesh*, illustrated with large colour photographs. I sat down in the back of the classroom and started reading. Miss Richards was surprised to find that I could read Bengali; she was curious and asked me if I could translate to her what I had read. For the first time I felt like an expert.

She encouraged me to get involved in the project, and Rukeya and I went round our friends and neighbours to borrow things for display, things to read, things to listen to. They lent us photographs, things made from bamboo, tapes of *Amar Sonar Bangla* and songs by Nazrul. Rukeya borrowed her Amma's silk sari to hang behind our display. We also collected newspaper cuttings and picture-postcards from the community centre. We put a lot of effort into the project. Whatever I did, I felt I was doing it for Shirin.

When the project was completed, our class mounted an exhibition of our work in the foyer of the school. Miss Richards put a collection box in the corner of the exhibition. Boys and girls from other classes hung curiously round the place with interest. Rukeya and I and two other Bangladeshi girls acted as guides. One day, Miss Richards brought a large map of the world to our class. She pinned it up on the wall and asked me to come to the front of the class. 'Nazia,' she said, 'can you show on the map where you were born?'

I soon found Bangladesh and Sylhet, but I found it hard to

locate our village. I was sure it wouldn't be marked on the map, and I wished that Shirin was there to help me. As I was struggling to find the place on the map, I remembered Shirin, long ago, marking a map to show where London was, and tears came to my eyes. There were some giggles in the class and I realised that some of the boys in my class were laughing at me. I ran to my desk and put my head down, I didn't want to show my face to anyone. I heard their chants: 'Cry-baby! Cry-baby!' Miss Richards tried to quieten them down, but the noise grew and grew. I could also hear Maxine's voice: 'Please leave Nazia alone! Just shut up, you lot!'

Luckily, the bell for end of school went; for a moment the noise dropped slightly. Then Miss Richards called out: 'Make sure you put your chairs up before you leave!' The noise increased: there was a clattering of chairs on desks, whistles and shouts, and a rush towards the door.

Miss Richards turned to me: 'They are immature, don't take any notice of them. I'll have to talk to them in form-period.' Then she paused and helped me to wipe my eyes and face: 'I am sure you will hear from Shirin soon, I'm sure she's all right.' I dried my eyes and went back to my desk to collect my bag.

Rukeya and Maxine had waited for me outside. As I came out, they joined me and the three of us walked, arm in arm, across the playground.

SHAITAN AND THE CHAPPAL

Afshan Navid Malik

Yasmin said: 'Don't let the chappal fall upside down or God will get you.' I was frightened, but confused. Why did God want to get me.

'Nina, get down here,' yelled Ammi. I ran, dragging my chappals, or rather, Baji's chappals. She'll never find out I wore them while she was out.

Downstairs, Ammi was cleaning the rice. She never trusted Mai with cooking because of her *neechi zaat*. Sometimes I don't like Mai washing my clothes because I hate to think of her touching my things. Ammi wanted me to clean the rice. But what if I find a slug, eeyeuch! Then I won't be able to eat any rice. Abbu says I'm mad. He killed the lamb on Big Eid and poured the blood into the roots of the plum tree. Then we had really red plums. I couldn't eat them because I remembered the lamb. I was in trouble with Ammi-Abbu. There were so many plums they even had to give some to Mai. 'What a waste,' said Baji after she was so full she couldn't eat any more.

'Come on, Nina *haramzadi*, are you dreaming of your *khassam*? Curse of my life,' says my mother. She often talks to me like that. I feel very ashamed that I'm a girl. I've ruined my mother's life. I rush with the rice but accidentally-on-purpose drop the tray. All the rice spills on to the floor. My mother yells more hysterically. It'll take twice as long to clean now.

I know I'm a bad person. I have wicked thoughts and God will get me, although why he wants to I don't know. My mean self comes out, the Shaitan in me, and makes me do evil things like drop the rice. My mother knows it was on purpose and she hates me. But instead of being sorry, I'm more wicked. I smirk. My mother hits me with her chappal and I run out, chappals flying behind me. One lands upside down, its bottom facing God. I hope he's cross with her. I'm not going to turn it over.

I go to my room and lie down. I think wicked things. Like the time I turned my back on the Quran because Tariq dared me to. He said, 'Drop it on the floor or you're chicken.' I tried but I couldn't. My arms were shaking and I thought that God would appear there and then I couldn't even imagine how bad it would be, just so so bad.

What if God knows about what I did with Riffat and Tariq? We played Mummies, Daddies and babies. Riffat wanted the matchstick to be the baby. I'm scared to think these evil thoughts. '*Toba toba*,' I say to myself and touch my ears.

I try to think good thoughts. 'God, I really believe in you,' I think hard, really hard. Nothing happens. I give up, bored, and try to write a poem. It goes like this.

Pakistan my land
pure and clean
fine and special
proud I am to be Pakistani.

It sounds great. I feel very patriotic. In the war I wanted to fight. When the Indian planes flew over us we went down and hid in the shelter in the garden. The best thing about it was the glucose powder. I dipped my fingers in the box when no one was looking and licked them quickly. It was best if your fingers were already wet. You got more powder on them. I wished the bomb would fall on our house and then it would be destroyed.

It would be so exciting. Nothing exciting ever happened to me.

We were sitting in the shelter all huddled up close and I had my hands in the glucose powder when we heard the loudest blasts I'd ever heard. Great, I thought, now we'll have some fun. Then I fell asleep. Every one said later they couldn't believe how I could have slept through that. When I woke up we were going out and it was daylight. They'd got the houses on the next street. What a shame.

I heard on the radio that all the children had to fight for our country. I had dreams of standing at the top of our house throwing bubblegum at the Indian planes. They'd get all sticky and fall down and then I'd be a hero and everyone would say how great I was. Or I could fly my kite and it would get stuck round the plane and it would whiz down. I wouldn't kill the pilot. I'd convert him to being a muslim and then he could go back and be a spy.

We would win the war, because we were on the right side. Why did the Indians not realise that? Aren't they scared of God? I asked Masterji and he said, yes, we're on God's side. 'But what about them?' I asked. 'Aren't they scared of fighting against God?'

'They don't know what they're doing. Shaitan has blinded them to the truth.'

Poor Indians. They're going to lose the war because they're on the wrong side. 'I feel sorry for them but they're really awful people,' said Masterji. They hate us. I don't understand why they hate us. Ammi said it's because they're Kafirs.

Masterji says I've got to work hard for Pakistan. He says we mustn't drink Coke because it's American. He only ever drinks 7-up. It's green like the flag, he says. He's such a good man. He doesn't want to teach me because he says I'm bad. He's always teaching Baji. She's supposed to be so clever but she couldn't beat me at Ludo.

'But, Masterji!' I say with my wicked side, 'why isn't there any

Coke in Janat? I don't want to drink milk and I don't like honey.'

'You *beshurum* little girl,' he says, raising his stick. I put out my hands and he slaps them with the stick. Not too hard, like the Miss at school.

It's a serious problem though. I want to be good but I can't. Janat sounds so boring. Lakes of milk and honey and young maidens lying about. Whenever I say this to anyone they get very upset. Here's a big secret I want to tell you. When I read the *Quran* I didn't like God! *Toba toba*, I'll really go to hell now. But God sounded so cross and mean, just like the headmaster. If you grease up to him he'll like you. 'O maker of the universe, Greatest of the great, Lord of everything' and all that sort of creepy talk is what he likes. I'd get terribly bored if I were him. It must be so dull having millions of people praising you all the time.

Oh, no! the Shaitan's got me. I jump up and out into the courtyard and run up and down trying to shake Shaitan off my head. The angel on my left shoulder must have had a busy day today, scribbling away all my bad thoughts.

Suddenly a strong arm grips mine and a slap on the back of my head stings tears into my eyes. Uncle Mamoon is here. '*Shaitan-ki-bachi*,' he says, pulling me close to him. 'You're too big to run wild.' He drags me with him to my mother's room, who is still cleaning the rice. 'Shahnaz, I've told you to teach your daughter to behave in a more respectable way. I just found her running around like an *awara jummadarni*.'

'What can I do, Bhai Sahib?' moans my mother. 'She's evil, evil, I say. She never listens to anything I say. I've long given up on her. Sit down, Bhai, I'll bring you some tea,' she says, and with a mean look in my direction, she drags her feet out of the room.

'You bad little girl,' says Mamoon, forcing me to sit on his knees. 'What should we give you as punishment?' His hands are hard on my arms and I can smell a mixture of garlic and cigarettes on his breath. I'm frightened because I know I'm bad.

Mamoon looks strangely at me, with pink eyes, and rubs his bristly chin on my shoulder. I squirm. 'Sorry, Mamoon,' I say.

'Nina *haramzadi*, get out here and help!' screams my mother. I bolt out of the room, pleased at having escaped my usual punishment.

In the kitchen we are cooking chappatis. I try to pull mine into funny shapes until Ammi pushes me away and starts doing it herself. I can see Abbu and Mamoon outside, smoking. Then I see Yasmin who has arrived from the back. I dash out of the kitchen and go and sit with her near the plum tree. We're quite far from Abbu and Mamoon but we still whisper in case they hear us.

'I don't believe you,' says Yasmin.

'Don't then,' I try to stay cool.

'But how could you have done THAT, with a boy in the same room!' she says again.

I wish I hadn't told her for the hundredth time. It was when we were playing this truth game. She asked if I had any secrets and I said one big one. Yasmin said if I didn't tell her she would swear on my life never to talk to me again, and then she would break her sworn promise and talk to me. I was scared. If you swore not to do something on someone's life and then did it then God would take that life, that's what the *maulvi* told us. It took me a few minutes to realise that then I would be dead, because her swear would have been broken. So I had to tell her about the matchstick and Tariq and Riffat in the store-room.

I now sit here, cringing. She knows my secret. I always thought she was my best friend, but now she's got power over me.

'Swear to me it was true,' she says again.

'It was true,' I say.

'No, swear on your life.'

'I swear on my life it was true,' I say.

'I just can't believe it, you couldn't have,' she says again.

'Yasmin, you won't tell anyone, will you?' I ask in a sweet voice. 'Because you're my best friend and all that.'

'I won't tell anyone, but God will know, he can see everything you do.'

'But he might have been busy that day, with other things.' I cringe at the thought of God watching what we did.

'He sees everything, and anyway, even if he missed it he'll have heard you telling me,' Yasmin laughs. She's being horrible. I hate her. But if I say so, she'll probably tell everyone my secret. I sit and stare at the smoke rising from the hookah at the other end of the courtyard. Yasmin tugs at my arm.

'I won't tell any one,' she says.

'Promise?' I ask.

'Promise,' she says.

'Swear on your life.'

'I swear on my life,' she says.

Phew, I'm so relieved I jump up and start running around, with Yasmin running around behind me. We're both giggling hysterically. I run out of breath and fall down. She flops down beside me.

'What did it feel like?' she whispers in my ear.

'What?' I pretend not to understand.

'The matchstick,' she says. We both start giggling hysterically again. I look up and see Baji Neelum frowning at us.

'Ammi says come and eat,' she says. 'And you,' she points at Yasmin, 'how come your mother lets you out in the evening, you *awara* girl?'

'I am not *awara*,' Yasmin protests.

'Well, go home and stop roaming the streets then.' Neelum smirks as she says this. She is only jealous because she doesn't have any friends who live as close as Yasmin. We both wink at each other and Yasmin leaves.

We eat in the kitchen after the men have eaten. I am just about to place a huge mouthful on my tongue when I get jerked.

'Impure child,' shouts Ammi, 'eating with your dirty hand.'

'Sorry, Ammi,' I say. I always try but I never can remember. Left hand for wiping my bottom, right hand for food. Left hand for dirty evil things, right hand for clean pure things. I just can't remember. At school, Miss tied my left hand behind my back to make me write with my right hand, but it still didn't work. I use my left hand whenever I can. Even now, when Ammi turns her head, I quickly stuff lots of chappati and *salan* in my mouth using my left hand.

I go to bed worrying about how bad I am. Tomorrow we are going out. I'm going to try and be really good. Ammi and Abbu will realise what a good girl I am. I plan that I'll wear my white dupatta and white salwar to the picnic, then I'll look *sharif*. I will not run around and scream loudly.

I close my eyes. I'm not going to let Shaitan worry me tonight. I say the *Kalma* and I say to God, 'Please please give me a sign. I know you're there, please, please, show yourself to me.' I concentrate my mind and think hard. After a while I suddenly realise that it is morning. I must have fallen asleep. I jump out of bed. Today is going to be exciting, so I don't need to stay in bed for as long as possible.

We (the whole family) are going on a picnic. Chacha and Chachi have arrived with their little sons who they treat so delicately. They carry them everywhere, and worse, whenever they come to see us, we have to carry them too. I wouldn't mind but they're so fat. I bet they can eat as much kulfi as they like. Not like me. Abbu says girls have to learn self-restraint and sacrifice. Chachi rushes into the kitchen, where we are still cooking and packing the food. She embraces us one by one. First Ammi, then Baji, then me. She leaves Mai out. She kisses me on both my cheeks and then holds me there, staring at my face.

'Shahnaz, what's happened to Nina's colour?' she asks. I try and move away but am held firmly in place.

Ammi looks at me closely.

'I can't see anything,' she says after a pause.

'But she's gone so dark. She had such pretty skin before, so fair.'

I feel very embarrassed. They've discovered my secret. Every afternoon when we're all supposed to be asleep I sneak out and play in the courtyard. Once I even went into the street and played with the boys across the other side. I feel myself flush now, as I remember the heat of the sun that I love to lie in.

'She looks all right to me,' says Ammi in an annoyed tone. It's very bad to be dark if you're a girl. Ammi doesn't want people to think we're dark, because then no one will want to marry us. Or we'll have to marry horrible fat men with smelly feet. Baji Neelum tries many things to make herself light-skinned. Once she put chopped lemon and raw potato all over her face and then she lay there for nearly two hours. I thought she was dead. So, I crept into her bedroom to steal the pink dupatta, the one she never even lets me touch. I was just going to borrow it for a while and wear it in secret. I suddenly heard this scream. She'd jumped up and the stuff was running down her face and I laughed so hard it made tears come out of my eyes. I still laugh when I remember. Chachi looks at me oddly when she sees me smile.

'It's nothing to be proud of, you know. You'll be sorry you ruined your colour when you grow up.' She lets go of me.

'Your mother will tell you what it's like. Her parents were frantic when she became darker with age . . .'

Ammi looks cross. 'Now it wasn't quite like that, *behen*,' she says in a tone nicer than the way she looks.

'But me, of course, I had so many offers from the time I was sixteen. They just kept on coming. I've even forgotten some of them.'

Chachi seems to have got lost in a dream world. Me and Baji Neelum look at each other and try to suppress our giggles. Chachi carries on talking.

'There was this zamindar, he was so rich they had twelve

servants, and three horses just to ride. His land spread round their *haveli* for miles and he controlled eight kissans, but he drank, so my parents said no. Oh, and a doctor, except he had a bad leg, but wealthy family all the same. They'd heard you see, about my skin and my fair beauty,' she said spitting out the paan she had been chewing into the sink.

Ammi, Baji Neelum and I make sick faces at each other.

'What did the zamindar drink, Chachi?' asks Neelum, with a glint in her eye.

'You know, my bachi, *sharab*, and other *haram* things that I'm sure you've never even imagined. Oh, yes, he was a wicked man,' she laughs.

'So how come you married Chacha, Chachi?' I ask trying to look serious.

'It was written. My kismet was written with that man,' says Chachi with a sigh.

'Wasn't it because they caught you with him, Chachi?' I say. Both Ammi and Chachi gasp. Chachi's face puffs up until I think it's going to explode. Her breath starts coming faster and faster.

'Who told you that damned lie?' she demands.

'It was Chacha himself,' I reply.

Both Ammi and Chachi look relieved. They start to smile.

'He is such a romantic, your Chacha. He likes to think we had some, you know, romance. Like the filmy stuff, you know. The girl looks at the boy and the boy looks at the girl and they forget the whole world except for each other. But of course these things are never like the men think, my dears, as you too will learn one day.'

Chachi sighs heavily and sits down on the ground. Her fat tummy seems to wobble about and she tries to lower herself slowly, until the last minute when she just flops. She sits about, gathering her breath while we rush around packing. Baji Neelum has nearly finished cooking the stuffed parathas. Poor thing, she must have cooked fifty by now. I laugh inwardly at my latest successful avoidance of cookery. It's easy. I just do everything so badly that Ammi and Baji just can't take it. They have to rush in and take over so they can show me how to do it. I just hover about and force myself to forget everything they are saying by concentrating on trying to grab mouthfuls of food without them catching me. I'm about to steal another *shami* kebab which Ammi has just fried when I see Yasmin waving at me from the back of the kitchen, so I sneak out, on tip toe.

'What's happening?' she asks.

'We're going on a picnic.'

'You lucky thing, we never go anywhere exciting.'

'Why don't you come too?' I ask. It'll be boring with just grown-ups and Baji Neelum; I really want Yasmin to come. I try and have an imaginary conversation with Abbu, trying to persuade him that Yasmin should come.

'I can't come,' Yasmin is saying, 'I have to go to Uncle Rashid's, his wife's ill.'

'What, again?' I ask.

'Yeah,' she says miserably. This woman must spend her life being sick. Poor Yasmin has to go and look after the children and wash and clean, and it's so boring when she's not here.

We sit down by the plum tree.

'You know what you said last night,' whispers Yasmin.

'What?' I pretend not to know but inwardly I think: *Oh, no, not again.*

'About Tariq and Riffat, across the road.'

'Oh, that. What about it?' I say, pretending not to be bothered.

'Was it really true?' she asks.

'Oh, Yasmin, I've sworn on my life. How else can I convince you?'

'I just can't imagine it,' she says. 'I watched him today.'

'Who?' I ask, wishing she would go. I want to get ready for the picnic.

'Tariq, I watched him from the roof. He was playing on his bike.'

'So?' I say impatiently.

'So, I saw something else as well. I saw Baji Neelum. She was looking out of the window and smiling at Arshad Bhaijan.'

'Really!' Is Baji Neelum starting to do *Ishq*? I've heard about this business from lots of sources but I never could have believed it would happen to someone I know. It's like dying, I just can't imagine it, or getting chicken-pox. It probably hits you bad at first and then you get over it. Maybe Baji will recover by the time we get back from the picnic.

I say goodbye to Yasmin and rush to the front where everyone is loading food. Mamoon has brought a whole bucket full of ripe mangoes, soaking in iced water. Mmmm. There are huge containers of food, shami kebabs, tandoori chicken, samosas, chutnees, and a huge Thermos full of steaming hot lamb pilau. Mai's husband, the *chokidar* and a young boy will carry the food. We all pile into the *tongas* and trot along. I watch the horses' bottoms closely. Yasmin said if you keep staring at the bottom you can sometimes see the *chichi* pop out. It sounds so horrible but I can't help wishing it would happen while I was staring. The horses bounce about and sometimes even raise the hair on their bottoms, but it doesn't happen.

Chacha is talking at everyone. 'The thing is,' he says, settling back into his seat, 'that we, as Mussalmaans, have to learn to give. We have to be good, like the prophet, peace-be-with-him. Look at our young people today. Look at the girls.'

Everyone's eyes fall on me and Baji. She's covering her head with a dupatta but I'm sitting waving my legs and chewing gum. She looks down, I stare back.

'Women of today know no *sharam*,' he continues, somewhat perturbed by my returned gaze, 'and that is what is wrong with the world today. They've forgotten their eastern virtues, to be good not selfish, to sacrifice their lives for the good of the country, to live for others not – eh . . .' He stops in mid flow. I have shaken my legs so hard that one of my chappals flew off my foot and landed in the road, almost hitting a passer-by on the head. My chappal is rescued, and after more recriminations, we set off.

We arrive at the picnic spot in good moods. Ammi tells me and Baji Neelum to wrap our dupattas around us, but it's so hot mine is sticking to me. I want to throw it off and run around but I know it would not be allowed. Mamoon and Chacha have stopped lecturing and are busy talking politics. An old beggar-man has started following our party. Chacha is talking about the poor, and how Islam teaches us all to be kind and generous. The beggar, pricking up his ears, starts grovelling.

'Sahib-ji, I beg you, give me some food. My children are starving. God will have mercy on you,' he says. Baji Neelum and I giggle at the stranger, amused by his weird accent. Ammi glares at us, and we all start walking faster.

'Please, Sahib-ji, I beg you, in the name of Allah.' Suddenly my uncle stops and faces the beggar head on.

'Now look here,' he shouts, 'just clear off, you Shaitan! This country is going to the dogs because of disgusting layabouts like you.' He shoves the old man aside with the box he's carrying.

The old man falls down. We carry on walking, everyone silenced by the unpleasantness.

'He was just a miserable old scoundrel,' says Mamoon, 'who's never done any honest work in his life. He's probably wealthier than the rest of us.'

The *chokidar* suddenly trips, although we are walking on a flat surface. The Thermos flask in his box falls out and the lid comes off. Hot pilau all over the dusty road.

It would all be all right if I hadn't turned around, but I did. As we walked away, I tripped on my chappal, as usual, since I wasn't watching what I was walking on. While bending down, I saw the old man, down on all fours, scraping up the dusty pilau and shovelling it into his mouth as if his life depended on it. Of course, he was a greedy old scoundrel and, probably, richer than the rest of us. But somehow I feel the Shaitan pulled my chappal to make me look.

CASSANDRA AND
THE VIADUCT

Rukhsana Ahmad

One could say that it all began when we used to live in Derby. One day Mama came back with this book about the best walks in the Peak District, which Millie had given her, hoping that we would all begin to explore the area. On the cover was a splendid picture of the viaduct. It took me a little while to recognise it. I suppose pictures have a way of distancing themselves from reality ever so subtly, which makes it hard to identify them instantly with the real thing.

Next time we were passing through the area I asked Dad if we could stop, just to take in the scene. He had a grumble but he agreed. The three of us stood silently for a few minutes in the dusky twilight, worshipping the spectacle. The book described it as an important spot in the area, offering a view of 'extraordinary natural beauty'. I remember wondering fleetingly how we fitted into the picture. A mild-looking, grey, bespectacled Asian man, his slightly overweight, short, matronly wife dressed in navy crimplene slacks and a nondescript jumper and me, their chubby fifteen-year-old daughter, in faded 501s and a baggy, drop-shoulder top – all dressed to blend in as far as possible with the locals. Fortunately, there was hardly anyone about to notice. Only one car passed in the twenty minutes or so that we were there. I wonder why an experience like that, on the whole restful, should have led to the nightmare I now associate with the

— 42 —

image. The first time I had the nightmare can't have been too long after that wonderful evening. I have really hated the picture *and the Real Thing* ever since. But the viaduct has sunk its pylons right into the depths of my consciousness weighing me down, down, down . . .

I see it with great clarity each time, I can see the moss on the dull red brickwork, feel the strength of the row of determined arches sturdily pressing shoulders together, the deep valley lying snugly green below. I see myself, as if through a telescope, running across the viaduct, running with all my might. My muscles strain, my lungs heave, my heart beats madly, I struggle to run faster, faster, as fast as I can. I know that someone is chasing me. I keep running in the hope that I will reach the other end and be safe there. But the other end stretches further and further away from me. Finally, breathless, heart pumping madly, just as I reach the far end, I see to my horror that the bridge does not quite meet the bank. It hangs, open-mouthed and ugly over a dark, awesome chasm. The valley below has disappeared; I see reddish-brown crags and sharp granite ridges instead. Suddenly, I turn round. The person I was running away from has caught up with me. He grabs my arm, brutishly pulling it behind me, dragging the blouse off my left shoulder, snapping off the top two buttons. I turn around, horribly certain that the man means to rape me, and when I look at his face in that gasping moment of terror, I am even more horrified – the shock wakes me up each time. It's my Dad.

The first time it happened I woke up trying to shake off the dream, feeling the bedclothes with my sweaty fingers, touching my side-table and even the fringe on my lamp to drive away the horror of it. I got up, drank some water, stayed in the kitchen listening to the hum of the neon light and the fridge, trying to connect myself to the *real* reality. I watched some Superbowl on Night-Time TV, found something to nibble at and then read a book until nearly five before I could drop off to sleep again. But the next morning, when I finally woke up, the dream stuck in my chest like a bilious solid making me almost physically ill.

As I watched Dad folding the newspaper and pouring himself a cup of tea, I felt a sense of outrage building up in my head at the way he seemed unaffected by what had happened. I resented that, deeply.

'Er, sorry, I didn't hear you,' I said, noticing he had addressed something to me.

'Are you going in late today?' he repeated. 'You're not ready; it's ten to eight, you know.'

'Yes, yes, I am. I mean, I feel ill, maybe I shouldn't go in at all. I've got a double free, anyway.'

Suddenly I was utterly confused, ashamed and embarrassed at my thoughts. *I am going crazy*, I told myself. *That was a dream, that was a dream*, I repeated frantically to myself. *This is my Dad, real, kind, gentle. He loves me, like he's always loved me, one of the kindest, gentlest dads you could imagine. What's happening to me? I must not let a silly old dream confuse me.*

The nightmare did not return for a long time after that. I would think about it at odd times, sometimes when we were alone, Dad and I, and I would steal a look at him, wondering about it. Sometimes other things reminded me, strange little details, like a missing shirt button, or the hair on the backs of his fingers, or moss. But most of all I began to hate arches, and tunnels . . . and bridges . . . and towers . . . and stairs . . . without quite knowing why. Actually, after all these years, they still make me nervous and uneasy, as if there were an evil spirit rippling secretly through the brickwork, waiting to rupture the graceful symmetry with an ugly gash at any moment.

My 'mocks' took over my life for a few weeks after that and then the annual exams. Shortly afterwards we moved to London and, to tell you the truth, I was relieved never to have to see the viaduct again. Mama missed her walks, her little part-time job as a dinner lady and her quiet friendship with some of the neighbours, especially Millie, but I mention that just by the by. Basically, when Dad said we had to move, we knew we would have to, whether we liked it or not. We were that kind of family. In any case Mama always said that's how she likes things to be, and if anyone did notice or comment on how Dad always had his way, she got kind of defensive.

So, we came to live in London. I found myself a sixth-form college and Mama found the cheapest place to buy Basmati rice and *dhania* and tried cheerfully to persuade herself that Richmond Park was almost as good as the Peak District for walking. Every afternoon she would take a bus down to the park 'to stretch her legs'. You see, she comes from a family of Pehelwaans, who are, in a manner of speaking, Lahore's answer to Sumo wrestlers, so she believes strongly in plenty of exercise and lavish eating. Weight is not bad, she argues, provided you also have the energy and the muscles to carry it round gracefully.

My Dad's very different, even though they're cousins. I suppose he was raised quite differently since his parents came to live in Bradford when he was tiny. They'd wanted him to be an engineer – with a degree, the kind who are the bosses, right at the top – but he ended up instead in the local Poly with the kind of course that leads to a middle-ranking job. By the time they all realised what had happened it was too late to change anything, except that Dad really wanted more and more money so desperately that he kept moving round, changing jobs, biding his time till he had enough money to set up a specialist business, making his own solitary way to success if it wasn't going to be handed to him on a platter.

He felt utterly proud the day he took us round to see his high-street shop, smallish with a tiny office at the back, just beyond the best end of Wandsworth. On the front were bold green letters surrounded by pink neon tubing, proudly announcing the name, Unique Lighting and Electrics. 'At last I am my own boss,' he said, with great satisfaction. It took him a long while to realise that the customer was the boss, he was still the underdog. He always spoke with great pride of his 'team'. Mama had offered to work for him, but he was quite blunt with his refusal.

'It's got to look professional, Tara. If the place is full of Pakis it won't impress the customers. They'll think of us as a load of crooks, out to fleece them, without spending anything on over-heads. I want a white girl to do the shopfront. Looks less tacky, you know what I mean.'

'Well, I can learn typing and shorthand, but I don't know how to change the colour of my skin,' she said. And then more wistfully, 'I miss my little job in Derby. I used to have a bit of money to spend on little, little things, for the house, for myself and Qaiser, you know.' She was right, of course, I had noticed the difference myself: one just had to wait longer for things one needed.

'Yes, and to send more things home.' Dad never had even an ounce of graciousness.

'Sometimes, yes. One has to. I grew up in a world where you always exchanged presents and gifts, people enjoyed spending on others. No one just keeps what you give them you know, gifts do come back, one way or the other. *Hoonh*! What would you have known of all this in Bradford?'

'But I'm telling you, I don't want you doing a dinner-lady job again. If you must work, find something better to do, something that fits your position in life now.'

She looked at him without saying anything. I never could make out what that inscrutable look was, a secret 'fuck off', or 'you bastard', or 'well, this is my lot, and I shall endure it', or 'you're impossible, but I love you all the same!' For she never really looked cross or bitter in that mood, expressed in an impossible circular nod of the head, which was a 'yes' and a 'no' rolled into one. She merely looked, ever so slightly, ruffled.

The house in London was bigger. But at the bottom the

garden fell into a steep bank which rolled down to a disused railway line. We never had trains using the line, but very rarely some spare carriages would be moved round on those tracks, an activity which drove the dogs in the neighbourhood to despair. Trains frightened me a little too. Someone at school once brought in a penny that had been flattened by a train into a monstrously large, thin, misshapen coin. That was scary – just gave you an idea of what a train can do to someone's limbs, or ribs, or skull.

One particular weekend they kept moving engines and bogeys round on those tracks and that night my nightmare, the one with the viaduct, returned. This time I could hear the sound of a train rushing up behind me as this person chased me, and I felt even more breathless as I got to the end of the viaduct. And then again, the awful finale, the chasm, the rough, greedy grasp on my arm and my Dad's face waking me up. Then, all over again, the routine of not settling down for the rest of the night.

The next morning I really did feel too ill to go to college. I thought it best to stay in bed and croak in my weakest, most pathetic whine something about nausea if either of them came in to see why I wasn't up. Not going to college was not a big issue any more. Mama was sympathetic, clucked over me for a bit, felt my forehead, said I should take the pillow away, and threatened to make me her famous cinnamon and mint tea. That was a 'secret' family remedy she took great pride in promoting. But then Dad poked his head round. My stomach lurched for a second at the sight of him. Somehow the nightmare felt more real than his person. He grunted his sympathy and waved in a familiar gesture pushing away some of the fuzziness of the dream that still clung round his muscled arms and hairy fingers. His voice and the gesture made me feel, at least briefly, a trifle better.

That afternoon I considered talking to Mama about the nightmare. I worried, though, about what she might make of me for having such a bizarre dream.

'Amma,' I began, 'what do you think of nightmares?'

'They're fears, most of the time, they're your own fears, really.'

'You mean, they've nothing to do with real life – like, you know, when people have warnings, er, like premonitions, I mean?'

'I don't know, maybe they are that too sometimes. Millie said she saw her brother's coffin two weeks before he died. And she swears she recognised the pattern on its side from her dream and that's why she fainted at the funeral. Ammaji worried about nightmares, she used to throw meat to the crows to ward off any evil or bad luck, but we all laughed at her. Abbajan would say, "You get nightmares either because you're thirsty and hot, or you need to go to the toilet or, or, because you've eaten a really heavy meal at bedtime, like your mother always does, so we have to end up feeding meat even to the crows in Lahore!" She would get so annoyed at that.'

I wondered what to make of that mixed bag. My Mum had a way of doing that to you – giving you a load of common sense and then all the room for any follies you might wish to follow through.

'I can see them having that conversation, the two of them,' I said laughing, for I was fond of my grandparents and loved her little snippets about them.

I was still considering what I should say next, when she asked, 'So why are you asking? Are you having nightmares?'

'Don't you ever get any?' I turned the question round on her, I thought with some skill.

'Hmm. Sometimes,' she answered with what sounded like a careful casualness.

'What kind?'

'Any kind really, all kinds, just like everyone else, I suppose.'

'What was your last one then? Tell me,' I asked.

'Thieves, I think. I . . . I see in my dream I have forgotten to lock the kitchen door and they get in. They're all white men, and they are wearing uniforms so I think in my dream that they work for the council. They just get in and take over my bedroom and I can't open the door to get into my own room any more. I bang and shout and scream but no one hears me, and your father is not there in the house either. That was last night; then I woke up and saw that he was still not back and I realised I must have been worried at the back of my mind about being alone.'

'I see.'

'So tell me what was your nightmare? Is that what made you ill?'

'Oh, no. It wasn't that bad! Must have been the chips we had on the way back yesterday. Marilyn was ill too this morning, I spoke to her.' I was improvising freely but I knew she was still waiting for my answer. We never had secrets from each other, me and Mama, at least not officially, until then, me being the only, and, therefore, rather special child. So, reluctantly, I began.

'Mine was about a thief too. I dreamt he's trying to catch me, and I am running across this bridge, actually it looked like the viaduct in Derby. But when I get to the end I find that the bridge leads nowhere, and, and then he catches me . . .'

'And then?'

'And then I woke up. Like you said, it was the indigestion, I suppose. Did you make the cinnamon and mint tea or not?'

'I thought you didn't want it. I'm sorry. It will only take me two minutes now. Shall I make you some soft rice too?'

'Just the tea, please, Mama, I'm fine. You worry too much.' Like always, it worked; she got so distracted by her guilt at not having anticipated my need for the tea that she stopped probing my nightmare and didn't notice my confusion.

Marilyn and I had indeed stopped for chips on the way back, but I don't think too many bacteria survive at those temperatures. In fact, she'd had a lively day at the college, she'd reported on the phone. I couldn't really imagine a day at college that wasn't lively for her. She created her own amusements and titillation and adventures wherever she went.

We were an unlikely pair; our only common interest was tennis, but what really drew us close was that we were both new to London and had joined a bit later in the year than the others: the hordes of girls and boys from local schools who came to the place in little clumps and went round in little groups identifiable from a distance, the Putney Posse, Fulham Fools, Roehampton Rudes, and the Kingston Clowns – we'd nicknamed the ones we liked the least.

There were other reasons why we didn't quite fit in, which bound us to each other, I suppose. I think I was known as the rather podgy Paki with a regional accent and 'plain Jane' Marilyn, everyone had kind of hinted to me early on, had a weird background. Her mother, Jean, was an actress who insisted on calling herself an actor, besides being a lone parent who had never disclosed to anyone, including Marilyn, who her father was. Marilyn, who suspected that this was because even she herself didn't know, never liked to talk about her somewhat Bohemian family life and avoided close friendships for that reason. Before I visited her house for the first time, however, she chose to tell me all this. It was the only time I ever saw her as someone vulnerable and capable of sentimentality. For she was always full of bravado and energy, as if she were fuelled by a tireless self-charging dynamo.

Then she told me about Jez, her 'official stepfather'. His real name was Chezlov and he had paid quite a neat little sum to marry Jean in order to obtain citizenship. She had found him through an ad in *Time Out* and met him at a pub to discuss the terms of their little arrangement. She had driven a good bargain, Marilyn reckoned. Times were hard, interest rates high, not many jobs around, it was a necessary evil. Mother and daughter had talked about it and weighed up the inconvenience against the money before she committed herself. To convince the home office they had to live at the same address for a year, so he contributed towards the flat and had a room to himself.

And that was how Chezlov became Jez. It was a transmutation easy for me to understand. Many years ago I had surrendered my unusual Pakistani name, Qaiser, with its impossible glottal fricative at the beginning, to the more user-friendly Cass or Cassie. (If people assumed it was Cassandra I never argued.)

Marilyn and her mother were six months into this glorious subsidy towards the rent when I first met Jez. He worked as a carpenter, an incredible fourteen hours a day, and so managed to stay out of their way during the week. Weekends were different. He only visited his girlfriend in Southend once in four weeks because he was saving like mad. The other three weekends he spent in the flat, watching TV, reading his Polish newspaper twice over, smoking Camels and drinking countless cans of whichever beer was on special offer that week at Tesco, causing Jean much irritation and anxiety.

But Marilyn had found in him a constant and desirable target for practising her technique and testing her charms. He was well-built and attractive, despite a certain been-around-for-a-bit look about his eyes and mouth and slightly flaring nostrils. She swore that he looked a treat at the weekends, dressed only in his baggy Bermuda shorts and a silver crucifix. I gave her a little lecture about the transience of purely physical attraction and the disastrous mistakes it led people into, specially young women like herself. This made her laugh like mad.

'Hang on,' she chirped, 'I'm not gonna marry a bloody carpenter, it's just a bit of fun I'm having here. He's got a Polish girlfriend as it happens, whom he sees pretty regularly, in Southend, so don't worry, Cassie, my dear.'

To my inexperienced eyes he seemed fairly distant and impervious to the technique, which she swore had been working really well the weekend before. 'It's a potent cocktail of the coquette and the *ingénue*,' she confided.

'Great use of French lessons!'

'You can say that again,' she grinned.

When I remarked on his apparent indifference to her 'technique' she explained that that was only put on for my benefit. Though, she admitted, it had been uphill for her all the way, because he was working himself to the bone, using up all his drive and energy on work so that he had little enthusiasm left for the fun side of life. I opened my mouth to reason with her but decided not to say anything else; she was rehearsing what she described as her 'sustained flutter of eyelids' before the mirror yet again as we lounged in her room drinking milkshakes.

'Those won't do either of you any good,' Jean flung over her shoulder, not unkindly, just before she left for her performance that Saturday evening.

Marilyn was a little taller than me, so her weight problem was not so acute as mine, but we both knew that Jean was right. But we both shrugged off her throwaway advice and talked about recipes for concocting new flavours. Marilyn who was animated, getting high on the milkshake, confided that she was cooling a bottle of wine in the freezer to drink with him that evening. I hoped for her sake that she wouldn't be hurt. He obviously treated her as a kid because of what was a visible age gap. In any case, I'm certain that his limited use of English made it difficult for him to establish profound relationships with English speakers. Marilyn had raided Jean's make-up soon after she left, and was trying on various shades of lipsticks for that evening's session as she jabbered on excitedly.

Less than half an hour into this preparation Jez knocked on the door and said, with the aid of both his hands and considerable miming skill, that he was going out for a meal with a friend from Poland. And then the harder bit to convey: Would they please not put the latch on as he might be quite late but would definitely be returning?

Marilyn, glad of those long eyelashes and the sustained flutter that hid the tears so well, made light of this let-down and offered to split the wine with me. I quibbled and hesitated but she alternately teased, supported and urged me so sweetly and insistently that I agreed in the end to try a glass. It turned out to be quite an anticlimactic experience, my first encounter with alcohol, but it did loosen my tongue enough to be able to recount the nightmare which had been so much on my mind lately. Somehow, repeating the dream in the comfortable warmth of her bedroom took away the horror and fear I had begun to associate with it. Marilyn heard it all sympathetically and gave me a garbled analysis that regurgitated Freudian wisdom, imbibed through Hollywood thrillers, in its most oversimplified form.

Somehow, in the telling, I must have conveyed my worst fears, because towards the end of the evening Marilyn offered to come round and meet my Dad to sus him out. On that traitorous note, achieved on a considerably high level of alcohol, I decided to leave, as if protected by an armed guard.

I was still in time to lay the dinner table. Over the meal I casually mentioned that Marilyn would be coming for tea next Sunday and could we please do some samosas the day before? The final suggestion was fired in the direction of my mother with the fullest confidence that the said samosas would indeed be ready on the Sunday without further effort on my own part. Mama loved a request framed like that which put her under less pressure, I think, because she then knew who to ask if she did need any help. It's just that she never liked admitting that she ever needed any. She was too independent.

Dad looked interested too. 'Is she the friend you go out with sometimes?' he asked with tremendous insight.

'Yes,' I found it difficult to meet his eyes as the guilt surfaced.

'I'll get a cake from Marks,' he offered.

'Oh, no. She loves samosas,' I assured them in vain.

In the event there were several things for tea, samosas, kebabs, the cheesecake from Marks and the boiled-egg sandwiches which Mama thought were great for nutrition. I felt gauche and self-conscious when Marilyn arrived for this rather elaborate tea.

'You're the first school friend I've had round to the house since I was nine,' I explained.

'Really, how amazing. And why?'

'Well, my last visitor said something rude about my . . . about Mama.'

'What a cow!' she exclaimed.

Dad came in to join us for tea and started pressing each dish on her with a warmth and earnestness that embarrassed me no end, but Marilyn was chatting comfortably with him, even enjoying the attention, I thought. 'Great, this is easier than I thought it would be,' I said to myself, and relaxed.

Mama, who was self-conscious about her English with new visitors, had withdrawn hastily to the kitchen. I felt guilty at the way she had been slaving and decided to do the dishes for her as that was the only way of preventing *her* from doing them just then.

'She enjoyed those,' Mama was well pleased with her day's work.

'Oh, of course she enjoyed them. They were absolutely scrumptious! Thank you, you're brilliant, Amma.'

'Tut! Thanking your own mother for food. You've really become *angrezi!*' she complained cheerfully.

'You lap it up, don't you?'

'Go now, go. I can do this. Go sit with your friend.'

'I won't let you slave away alone. You can dry if you want to. Dad's talking to her, she's all right.'

There was a subtle change in the tones of their conversation, I thought, when I returned to the front room. Marilyn seemed to have moved, ever so slightly, closer to Dad and he was speaking more loudly and gruffly, in the voice he reserved for his friends. They were talking about his work. Before she left, Dad had promised her he would send Freddie down to sort out the faulty light in their bathroom.

'I think he's perfectly kind and gentle,' she whispered to me at the gate and I was relieved that she had not forgotten the reason for her visit.

Next Sunday Marilyn dropped by unexpectedly. 'I just wanted to say thank you to your Dad; Freddie came to sort out the bathroom light for us,' she said, which I thought was really sweet of her.

'I loved those kebabs and samosas,' she cooed to Mama, who was immediately galvanised into action and went to rummage through the freezer to find any left-overs. I followed her to help make the tea and Dad entertained Marilyn once again with stories and titbits about the shop. It took us a while to organise the tea this time but Mama was steady as a rock, frying *pakoras* to make up for the absence of samosas. It all looked wonderful on our best melamine tray. Chocolate biscuits on a white plate, *pakoras* arranged on a coloured serviette in a straw basket and kebabs on a delicate beige flan dish. The tea was under an embroidered tea-cosy in true Pakistani style. I felt triumphant as I walked into the front room treading carefully, fearful of my habitual clumsiness, my eyes still on the tray, listening to the gentle hum of conversation. They both stopped talking so I couldn't make out what the subject of their conversation was. Marilyn got up, gushing profusely about how wonderful it all looked and smelt! Dad just looked on with a complacent smile.

Suddenly, unexpectedly, at that moment a train rumbled past haltingly. 'Oh, a train,' I said, turning to the window to look at it.

'Didn't know you had trains round this way.' Marilyn looked surprised.

'Not very often,' I replied. In my head I could see it rushing past into the distance over a long, graceful viaduct, and, for some reason, felt inwardly terrified that it may be headed into an abyss.

Mama's entrance shook me out of my reverie.

'Come on, take please. Why are you letting it get cold, Qaiser?

Give a plate to your friend. Tut, tut! Have you never seen a train before?'

'Marilyn has solved a problem for me. She says she'll come in to the shop to help at the weekends. I've been trying to get someone since Shelagh left and haven't been able to.'

'That's nice of you, Marilyn!' I was a little surprised at this development.

'Love to. Be a nice little income for me, from what Mr Hussain tells me. It's brilliant.'

I suddenly remembered the time when I was still at nursery school and how, one day, I had asked Joanna to come round to my place and she had taken over my Crystal Barbie, for the whole afternoon, making me feel weary and cross without quite knowing why. I was glad I could understand my emotions a bit better now. I knew that now it was just a slight fear of Marilyn learning something about 'us' that I had forgotten to mention, or maybe it was, after all, a touch of possessiveness in me, about my Dad which I had not been aware of before.

The next week at college Marilyn said how much she had enjoyed working at the shop. Dad, too, had said, casually, at dinner, 'Your friend came to try out the work today. I think she might just stick it out.' Both comments confirmed a certain dread. I worried about Dad saying something hopelessly inappropriate to Marilyn or vice versa. Neither of them, I felt, quite understood the delicate balance of two quite antithetical cultures that I constantly achieved in my day-to-day living.

Three weeks passed: no crisis occurred and I began to feel a bit more secure about the situation, if a little surprised that such a working relationship was possible. Then, one Saturday, our neighbour came in with a toaster she wanted repaired. Mama being her usual gracious self, volunteered my services.

'Qaiser will get this over to the shop for you and you'll get it back soon. Maybe even today if Samee can see to it.'

I hated walking to the shop, but I smiled at Auntie Sushma as pleasantly as I could. The best part of the afternoon was over but Mama was going on repeating her instruction over and over again, 'See if he can do it while you're there, so you can bring it back with you.'

'OK, Mama,' I grunted through my teeth, as I left, glad, finally, to be getting out of the house, at least.

The front of the shop was empty as I entered. The door to the little office was ajar. I pushed it open but there was no one in there. Surprised, I pushed the second door at the back, which was the workshop area, and stood watching aghast, for neither Dad nor Marilyn had heard me open the door.

Her blouse had slipped off her left shoulder, the top two buttons had pulled open at some point and his mouth was clasped over hers. I noticed how dark his hairy fingers looked against her fair skin.

I turned and walked out of the shop as fast as I could. I started to run as soon as I stepped outside. I ran faster and faster, as if I were being chased by a train chugging furiously behind me, roaring, thunderous, as it threatened to catch up with me and flatten me out. Then, suddenly, abruptly I stopped. I could still hear that train rushing through my head. In fact, I could see it quite clearly, running across that graceful viaduct. For a second, my heart stopped. I thought I could almost hear it scream in anguish as it reached that awful naked chasm.

CULTURES OF SILENCE

······◆······

Vayu Naidu

For Deborah Levy and Gayatri Spivak

I

At eight tonight Herbrae with the green purring eyes, a voice of crushed lavender silk, rainbow-refracting earrings, and an amorous tan from Delhi, is to meet me at Don Pasquale.

I've been in the city centre from 5.30 watching the garden market fold up, easing my nervous navigation down King's Lane, the ill-marked conference rooms, the Arts Cinema and then to the quiet golden sign: DON PASQUALE. I have a beer, and then know how hot and dry I'd been. A pizzarette finds its way down my throat, the way I ease my heavy butt into the economical passage between wicker chairs, between clothed white round table and chair. The light is creamy, it settles with thickness across the page, pin-printed with the 'Life Between the Line' conference itinerary scheduled over the next couple of days. The sub-text reads: word – context – meaning. Three lectures out of the forty-five are relevant by their titles; the rest is an adventure. Why have I come? I ask myself. For intellectual upheaval. Blow hard on blocked holes, and light from fire comes through. Maybe even air, I tell myself. The lump of pizzarette is swallowed. The snack is over. I go to a book shop. Dillons. Climb stairs, turn pages, book backs, and shelve decision on buying *Literary Theory* because of the price on the jacket. Determined to leave undiminished in mind and money, I swerve past the Lit Crit quarter, past the Drama quarter and with unanticipated reflex pick out a green, grey, yellow jacket labelled *Theatre Audiences* which is overpriced, and head to the cash counter. I'm wearing a red sari. My face is blank without make-up. A Japanese man stares, follows, catches my eye, his face a map of wrinkled tourist wonder. I consciously breeze by. In these three hours in the arterial centre of Cambridge this is my first eye-contact. How do I know he's Japanese? People in book-shops don't carry a smell, neither do the pages. Between orientals too you can tell the difference. Skin, tightly stretched over cheekbones or falling in folds, it is important to note what seeps through the pores. It is the training of the mind behind the eye, like instinctively knowing the meaning between desire, lust, love and joy, that teaches you ethnique. As an Italian geologist once said, you can't teach about granite, you will just spot it. If it is good you can build monuments in the desert.

I return to Don Pasquale and wait. Herbrae arrives the way I first described her. Only now there is breath in her mouth, sound in her voice, the colour of warmth in her eyes. The uneven punctuality of King's, John's, St Mary's, Pembroke's, and Trinity's bells chime the half-hour until it is twenty-five to nine. Herbrae listens as I reply to her concerned questions. My days, their isolation, this exile. The nineteenth-century bible-box, and the nineteenth-century mystic; icons of my security. His ideas plaited with my life in a daily continent of silence. Silence, its centre, a space that clears. To watch each shade of thought shape, let loose, trap or free my actions. To take down letters that form 'betrayal', 'humiliation', 'oppression', and 'silence'. To turn them over, and to look into the mouth and belly and smooth my hands over the fish-white underside of their slippery meaning.

Then, the ten-in-the-morning greyhound streaking around the green ground, its owner with the receding hairline ambling like a juggling pin on his small, small feet, as the dog whips another orbit, beating time thin. Yes. I know the luxury of no deadlines. Herbrae too, knows the luxury of time, for the first time. To slip into it, and not have to slot time. To take it on the tongue, roll it in or flatten it out. She is a writer, with no stable space to work. She moves between geographies. Of late a new kind of writing is appearing, she says. Work which will not earn. But it appears as a gift. You can't turn it away and ask for it back. It is the quiet miracle; the silence of conception. Suddenly, the cappuccino is cold. Its cream moustaches my mouth.

We watch a film. I feel suffocated by its words, about intellectuals discussing love in North America.

II

The next morning the sun rises, spreads. Birds dash at their reflection in the smooth, clear, wide glass. I wake up to bashing beaks. A golden child comes. Spreads his smile and arms in an arc from past to present. He is a child lined in a triptych of love, himself alone. His father travels like geography; leaving great spaces of miscommunications. His mother is a morning melody, every note is in balance and even tenor. I am now an occasional visitor who shared a moment in their autobiography.

Between giggles and pleas to play football outside he is jumping from bed to floor, supporting his cold tiny hands on my buddha-serene belly. He scrambles off. I'm seizing the amoeba limbs of my brain before they spill albumin-like out of my cranium in the consistency of vaporous thought. I'm desperately trying to programme my day to make it substantial. Meet Herbrae, pick thoughts. No embroidery. Attend lectures. Just separate and smooth different coloured threads. The door bangs open. Chopin's piano concerto tinkles its way upstairs. The child has his arms filled with treasures, which he empties on the bed. Gift-wrapped kitchen devils – cook's, vegetable and meat knives – my anniversary present.

Long, long ago, my cornea had ripped in one of those exchanges after marriage. My eyes are dark, so the blood was black. You couldn't see and I wouldn't tell. For many days my eyes wept white rain. I couldn't cry. After a long time a man came by my window. Beautiful in the silver light of his hair. Stairs of sunrise dancing on his face while the gulmohur leaves shivered in the breeze as the smell of the first monsoon hung in the air. You know, the smell of first rainfall on parched earth. His eyes were clear as sky and wide as space, very dark. Sometimes even blue. He moved without touching, and touched without sense, yet kept what was his and his place. I thought then that I was alive. I cried. My eye healed, and salt tears turned blood-red with healthy glow. Only later I grew to look for the blade-edge difference between hurt, pain, grief, sorrow, loss, even the presence of absence. He gently pressed these seven silent scars in the deep, which now have grown purple teeth. The child presents me the knives and is not aware his father travelled far last night. To another hemisphere.

The child listens to my quacking, and cooing and clucking and quailing as I resonate the difference between duck and goose and peacock and chicken. 'Don't be daft!' he says. I hear his mother downstairs. I dance to several rhythms of brush, shower, pluck, pumice, scrub, wipe, dab, flush. The child, its mother and I talk, switching between precis of ontology, East-West psychology, post-modern discourse and Vedic philosophy, the child's simulations of tooting locomotive, and a lion I have drawn in his notebook which is silently screaming off the page in purple crayon.

The melody of memory is now cacaphonic and the present is soldered to a past that must remain silent.

III

The choir at King's can be heard across the cloister. Human voices dart, glisten, gleam, a goldfish rhythm as the rare and infrequent sun dances with their notes across the stained glass.

I ferret from cloister to doorway, to stair to landing, to fire-exit to the ill-marked seminar-room. The first speaker illustrates a playwright's religious sub-texts. The dead playwright had fed on a daily tonic of Christian mythology from boyhood, in Ireland, and saw early the unseen meaning – that this god, even an un-Christian one, cannot be seen or known. And for the rest of us, in not having, our condition remains as one of waiting. For him 'absence' was supreme good. With all these Zen paradoxes of a positive void, and finding prayer in poetry, he was crucified quickly by his culture's mythologists as an atheist, and lived within that freedom for the rest of his life.

There were questions that ran into answers, and comments, and observations. Then, and only then, could I pick unsteadily, as I do even now, the rice-fine rationale of Zen paradoxes: if there are no words in this culture for thoughts that exist elsewhere, then those silences and the cultures they come from *do not* exist. They have no neon-lit signposted frontiers. Therefore they cannot exist, because this culture's language has the boundaries that will always keep them out.

Not economy, nor the crown can colonise. It's simply: language. Embarrassing, all this stuff about being 'colonised', that too when you *choose* to study, live, and love, in the source of the colony. Embarrassing, when you walk the soft green thighs of the Yorkshire dales and run your hands over the dinosaur's backbone – the limestone walls that form the quilted patchwork of a landscape that undulates as it comforts. Embarrassing, when you enjoy the ritual of many teas, the radio and its intricate web of world coverage, and listen to accessible writers on their desert islands.

'Thank you' exists in other tongues; but here it must be engraved. The unseen danger is that the word sets you in the trap of an obligation called gratitude . . . Embarrassing all this. Like complaining about the scales on your teeth after several helpings of strawberry cake and ice-cream, followed by chocolate gateau.

You've read about these symptoms in sociology, economic history, Third World psyche, political economy, anthropological sociology, and the whole of theatre which gives word to the ontic space.

That warm afternoon, enclosed in a concrete rectangular space with other minds, it came to me. With the whirring of the pedestal fan, thoughts circulated. Its blades cut the thick air, which had hung like a colony of silence against a freedom of words that could shape a void.

It then struck me that, at the root of the tooth's twitching nerve, the choice of an immigrant's destination is often predetermined by the currency of language.

IV

That afternoon, my mouth is full. Pitta, Greek olives, cottage cheese. Succulent, aromatic. Not just hunger appeased, but the taste of openness – tender garlic in a summer breeze. Herbrae watches me eat. Sitting cross-legged on the floor, my neck and chin scale Trinity's gateway from the wide window.

'When were you last back?' she asks, her voice languorously stretching across the room like a sunning cat dangling from a tree's limb. I can't remember. In days and months, about two and a half years. But in tactile memory, here seems like forever. Why? she asks naturally. Here? Forever? I wonder if it is just visual reinforcements that are fortresses for comfort, for home. How do you quantify not having 'home'? By listing what isn't present from what you could remember? Couldn't be the drowsy heat. Nor the familiar faces. I believe in moving, in celebrity anonymity. What is 'back' there? Maybe the midday sun and the smell of freshly ground spices against the backdrop of sea salt humidity. What did I cease to remember? That man who travelled far told me, a long time ago, never to forget. I live now with the smell of some country's drying mouth where words gurgle up like fuel for escape. Him with the eyes so full of space has cleared my existence with language, like the forests are cleared by fire. For a long time nothing grows, just sun-squinting space and the silence of drought.

And Herbrae? Herbrae remembers crowds singing, then marching sounds, protests. A father whisked from his writing desk, his spectacles crushed under boots. His papers leaving behind a history of equality between man and man. She remembers the slamming of iron doors, the cell without memory or echo, headlines, neighbours closing gates, black ink on white paper and now . . . what words do you pick and stroke to shape and embrace Black cause and triumph when your hands are White, that too on a distant island?

This too is 'embarrassing'. Only because we've heard it so many times before and because it has become fashionable to 'listen'. There is no guilt now, just the responsibility of naming the silence. Our common language is this one which makes us know the cultures of silence. At last there is some relief. I start to see the spirits that shadow power, comfort, happiness, for which pain is a small price.

From the window, encasing the bustle of a university city's summer, with the jostle of many hues of browning bodies, and the purring of many accents of English, I felt comfort. Memory, even realisation, doesn't necessarily come in isolation.

A Seepoy was propped in his blue and white striped night-suit. Unshaven. A shrapnel blast in the right jaw. Cheek from ear to lip a gaping cave trelaced with tubes. Eyes triple-glazed with morphine, adjusting to the glare in the new ICU, and attempting to recognise the staff on duty. A school party was on a ward-visit to the war wounded. As a class, the children moved in formation from ward to ward. A latecomer little girl runs in and offers the isolated Seepoy a bunch of marigolds. No fragrance, just yellow and ochre stubs of colour. He grips them with three able fingers, two tips visibly blown off without the dressing. He looks in her face, and tears, after much resistance, roll down his shirt as he shakes, until he can't tighten his lips together to stop the flow.

Shuddering tears are the price of rescuing innocence while escaping from horror. The horror of power for complete control, or obliteration. It was a silent recognition that brought comfort, now. It was getting nearer the time, and I had to return to the afternoon session of lectures. To listen to the models of Foucault's understanding of power while studying the structure of prisons and monastic orders.

The speaker concluded with 'de-individualisation', in the case of the latter, 'is the renounced power which gives power'.

V

It's another day. The sun rises, the birds bash their beaks against the glass, the music tinkles, and I am dressed, leaning on a wooden fence looking out beyond the garden which is a husk blond following the heatwave. The golden child is playing at watering the plants with a dry, empty hose. In this way he showers me, himself and the football, and then is intent on counting the imaginary drops that fill his paddle-pool. There's a gentle breeze. Mint and rosemary waft their fragrance. I remember last evening.

The sun had cooled. Herbrae walked me through the Trinity cloister and the wooden stair where Byron had thumped his way up with the bear. Then, taking a secret iron key from her deep pocket, unlocks the small grilled-iron gate and we pad into an exclusive garden. The overpowering hedge, the rectangular lawn so assiduously trimmed, the flowers pert – details from a botanist's drawing-book. The river up ahead is swept intermittently by weeping willows like tapestry Japanese maidens teasing their lovers with rippling fingertips. The final arc of the reddened sun is disappearing. I turn to face the garden. It has the delicately pinched air of a surveying Head Butler.

I slide along the cobblestone way and all silences ring together as in a primeval ocean depth sound. It's a moment where memory is living as future. Where words fall in silence and ripple with quiet golden meaning sweeping leaves and branches to further shores. The sun drops. Its light still winks on the Tudor window panes. Now I could see the quartz from stone and the geologist's commission to build a granite war memorial in the desert. I had travelled far, slipping the noose of a colony of silence, and that man's language, from my neck. Like every child and his mother, words and their signs formed silent unbroken circles. But here it was with no treachery of compromise that the bonds of love often bring. I was free, at last, and this was not not-love.

A thud and the ball jumps high in the air. I turn. It is a forceful kick to which I must respond. A high voice trails from a window upstairs: 'Darling! You must leave her alone to breakfast!'

REBECCA AND THE NEIGHBOURS

Tanika Gupta

Savitri leant against the balcony and watched a couple far down below gesticulating wildly at each other. It was obvious they were having a fierce argument. She had studied hard for her A Levels and got her grades to get into Sussex University. It wasn't far away but it was a different world for her and she wondered how she had managed to live in such a hell-hole for so long. Every now and then she would come across old photographs of Rebecca and her eyes would fill with tears at the memory.

Savitri remembered back to when Rebecca was fifteen and restless. She had a certain mischievous glint in her eye so that you were never quite sure what she would do next. Everyone thought of Rebecca as a joker, a trickster, a teaser – someone who would do anything for a laugh. Her teachers despaired of her. If only she'd direct her intelligence to studying instead of larking around all the time! She chatted up student teachers, smoked cigarettes in the boys' loos, swore like mad and quite often was seen in local cafés during school hours. Once Rebecca was suspended for three days for trying to flush a boy's head down the toilet. She and her gang had terrorised the first-former and left him a quivering wreck. Ma was shocked.

'I must have done something terrible in my last life to merit such a child. She is such a *gunda*. Why must she fight all the time?'

'We'll never find a husband for Rebecca,' Baba sighed. 'She's far too head strong.'

But Rebecca felt different from her parents. Sometimes she found it hard to believe that she was their flesh and blood. They were so meek! Ma behaved as if she had never left their village in West Bengal; even after ten years in Petunia Mansions, she was still no closer to speaking English than she was the day she stepped off the plane at Heathrow. She worked from home as a seamstress, machining garments for some local clothes factory, and hardly ever stepped out into the world. She had no further ambition in her life than to see her two daughters do tolerably well at school and be married off to reputable families.

Baba, on the other hand, worked for London Transport as a bus conductor and he was much more worldly wise. But again, it was as if his life outside the home was a separate, almost pretend life. When they were younger, Rebecca and Savitri loved going to work with him in the holidays, sitting at the front on the top deck, pretending to drive the bus. Rebecca watched her father closely then – chatting with the passengers, calling the women 'luv' and 'dearie', joking with everyone. He looked so animated and comfortable in the outside world. And yet at home he spoke very little, just smoked his cigarettes, read the newspaper and watched the TV. He refused to speak in English at home, saying that his jaws ached from 'yakking in that foreign language all day' and he never allowed Rebecca and Savitri out after six. He said that they would 'lose their culture' by mixing with all those local 'ruffians'.

Each holiday, when Savitri went back home, Garden Estate looked more and more unwelcoming and her parents seemed to have suddenly grown old and grey. Baba had retired and spent all his time now watching TV and reading the newspapers, while Ma still worked as a seamstress and never went out.

One evening Baba switched off the television set and stared at the blank screen with a look of such sadness, Savitri knew he was thinking of Rebecca.

'Why don't you ever write to your sister?' he asked in a small voice. 'You used to love her so much. You used to follow her everywhere! Have you forgotten her?'

'What's the point of writing, Baba?' Savitri snapped. 'She never writes back. I don't even know if she thinks any more! Has she spoken yet?'

'Just because she doesn't speak, that doesn't mean she can't think. Maybe if you started writing to her again, she would remember, maybe she would wake up.'

Savitri wrote a few letters, but Rebecca never wrote back and so she gave up. It was like writing to a brick wall. Her grandmother wrote and said she was exactly the same; silent and uncommunicative. She did everything herself, bathed, ate, walked and even smiled sometimes, but she never spoke. Her cousin Sunanda wrote and told how Rebecca had grown more beautiful with time but how a terrible sadness seemed to envelop her.

Savitri remembered Rebecca's zest for life. She had wanted so much more out of life. In the evenings, in their bedroom Rebecca would share all her thoughts with Savitri. She wanted to be a film star, a pop star or a beautiful dancer . . . anything just as long as she was famous and out of Garden Estate and far away from her 'village idiot' parents.

Savitri was two years younger. She was quieter and more softly spoken, like their mother. She watched her sister closely, listened to her rantings and felt her sister's restlessness. She too wanted to break free from Garden Estate but unlike Rebecca she had her escape planned down to the minutest detail. Savitri would do it through going to university. At school, she was studious and hard-working, always coming top of the class and earning every teacher's admiration. This, of course, did not get her many friends and instead she was often shunned as the school 'swot'. But, just as they were different, the two sisters were close. Just as Savitri admired her sister's wildness and spirit, so Rebecca admired Savitri's studiousness.

'God must've forgotten to give me brains when I was born,' Rebecca joked. 'So when you popped out, he made up for it by giving you mine as well as yours.'

They'd been in Petunia Mansions for so long, they knew almost everyone in the block, some only by sight but most of the families knew each other well. The sisters had grown up in the concrete playground at the bottom of Petunia Mansions with the other children, scraping their knees and scarring their elbows for life when they fell. They had grown up with many of the children on the estate too because nearly all of them went to Garden Estate Primary and Secondary School. Miss Little, who shared their landing with them, was a large and vivacious English woman who baked them cakes on their birthdays and invited them to tea on her balcony in the summer. Rebecca was her favourite.

'I wish to God I could get out of this dreadful place,' Rebecca once confided to Miss Little. 'It's like living in a small village. Everyone knows your business and they're always sticking their noses into other people's affairs.'

'It's nothing like living in a village!' Miss Little laughed. 'You have no idea, you urban youth.'

Rebecca was put out and sulked.

'I used to live in a small house in Witney before the war. It was nice. People were friendly and helpful. We used to all meet in the local pub, men, women even youngsters. It was a lovely community.'

'So how come you left Witney and ended up here?' Rebecca quizzed insensitively. 'No offence, Miss Little, but the seventeenth floor of Petunia Mansions is a bit of a come-down after a nice English village.'

'It's a long story,' Miss Little sighed. 'But basically I made the mistake of following my heart and my husband to London. The stupid man went and died on me, leaving me with nothing but old age and his debts.' She laughed sadly and Savitri shot her sister a disgusted glance.

'I – I'm sorry,' Rebecca stammered.

'That's all right, sweetheart. You're right, though, this is a horrible place. But you both have three valuable things as your passport to freedom.'

'What's that?' Savitri asked.

'Education, youth and good looks. And remember, you can do anything you set your mind to. Just persevere.'

Peculiar as it seemed, Rebecca and Savitri grew almost to see Miss Little as their grandmother. Certainly they had more contact with her than they did with their own grandmother who lived in the village in West Bengal.

Soon after Rebecca's sixteenth birthday a new family moved into the flat below them. Within their first week they had proclaimed loud and clear to all those who lived in Petunia Mansions that they had no respect for anyone. At night, their music thumped up through the floorboards, during the day their arguments roared out through the labyrinthine corridors and every now and then one of the women would let out such a blood-curdling scream; it sounded as if someone were being murdered. Mr Jacobson, who shared their landing, had tried to complain politely about their noise but was rewarded with a punch in the nose for his trouble. Poor Mr Jacobson. Eventually, Rebecca could stand no more.

'They're disgusting!' she complained. 'And no one has the nerve to do anything about it! Everyone's scared of them!'

'They're nasty though,' Savitri commented. 'It's difficult to know quite how to tackle them.'

'Complain to the Council,' Rebecca said. 'I'll go.'

'No,' Baba said looking up briefly from his newspaper. 'If you complain, they'll start taking it out on us. It's just noise. We can bear it.'

'Your father's right,' Ma added. 'We must keep out of it.'

Typical, Rebecca thought. It was so typical of her parents to sit back and take it all without complaining. Petunia Mansions was filled with gutless cowards.

In the end, it was Miss Little who went and complained to the Council. They sent two housing officers to have a quiet chat with the Wright family. That very evening, there was a loud banging on Rebecca and Savitri's door. Baba wasn't back from work and the door banging sounded so insistent and menacing that Ma wouldn't allow the sisters to open the door.

'Come out, you dirty Pakis!' a man's voice boomed. 'I know it was you who complained to the Council.'

Ma looked accusingly at Rebecca, who shrugged defensively. The banging continued for a few more minutes and then ended as the man kicked the door with all his might.

'Black slags!' the man hissed through the letter-box. 'I'll be watching you.' And then he left.

Never before had Rebecca and Savitri tasted such fear. The whole episode only lasted five minutes but had felt like an eternity. The man's words, 'dirty Pakis', echoed in Rebecca's ears and for a moment she felt so alone. Alone because the man had targeted her family and there was no way of protecting themselves.

They were all still shaking when Baba returned later that evening.

The next day at school, Rebecca's friend Ruth pointed out a new boy in their class – Robbie Wright. She said she fancied him. Rebecca warned her friend about what a nasty family Robbie came from and how someone from his family had threatened them the night before. Ruth just shrugged and said that it wasn't Robbie's fault that his family were like that and, anyway, it didn't make any difference to her, she still thought he was gorgeous.

That same day, as Savitri and Rebecca walked back together from school, they were both silent and tense. Savitri kept trying to catch a glimpse of her sister's face through her long, unkempt hair, but Rebecca's face was closed, as if her thoughts were so private that not even Savitri was allowed to share them. As they passed by the local shops in Garden Square, a group of boys began to chant something. At first, the two sisters simply thought it was a noisy but harmless gathering and walked by without looking up. As they were about to turn the corner, a tennis ball hit Savitri's shoulder and bounced into the road.

'Ouch!' she laughed, and turned around to see which kids had kicked the ball at her by mistake.

'Wogs! Wogs! Wogs! Wogs!' chanted the boys in unison. Savitri stared at them in disbelief.

'Fuck off!' Rebecca screamed at them.

'Burn them out, burn them out, burn them out . . . ' the boys sang back.

Passers-by anxiously looked at the group of boys and then at Savitri and Rebecca, before scurrying off in the opposite direction. Rebecca stood her ground.

'Just leave us alone, you bastards!' she screeched.

Savitri urgently tugged on her sister's arm. 'Didi, let's go home.'

The boys started to lob more missiles at them, foraging around in the bin for ammunition. A bottle hit Rebecca's cheek and then shattered on the ground. Her face stung and burned with fury as she picked up a shard of the broken bottle and was about to hurl it back when Mr Jacobson grabbed her hand from behind.

'Now, now, Missie,' the old man clucked. 'Let's get you home before you get hurt more.' He pulled the two girls around the corner, linked arms with them and walked them briskly back towards Petunia Mansions. The boys' chants echoed around the square.

'Paki lover!'

Curled up in bed as dawn broke, Rebecca had her eyes still

wide open. She cursed the Wright family for having shattered her family's peaceful life. She decided that this time she was going to go to the Council and complain about racial harassment, regardless of what her parents said. They were always getting leaflets through their door from the Council, promising to act against racists, so why not test their promises out?

Savitri also lay awake, worrying about what her sister was planning.

It was no good, though. The Council was unwilling to do anything. 'We need proof,' the housing officer said.

'What sort of proof?' Rebecca asked baffled.

'Anything: witnesses, photos . . . anything.'

Rebecca bit her lip. She knew that no one in Petunia Mansions would come forward to be a witness – not even Miss Little or Mr Jacobson. She called in the police a couple of times when the Wrights deliberately got their dog to defecate on their doorstep, but the police did nothing either.

'This sort of thing happens all the time on housing estates,' a young policeman patronised. 'Neighbour disputes. You'll just have to learn to live in harmony.'

'But they're calling us names!' Rebecca shouted.

'Look, Miss,' the young policeman said, placing his helmet back on his head. 'We have far more important crimes to look into: murders, rapes, burglary. We can't go round chasing after dogs and noisy neighbours.'

'So, wait until we get murdered and then call you? Is that it?' Rebecca sneered.

The constant taunting and threats of violence were wearying. Savitri got bad results at school and it made Rebecca feel somehow ashamed of being different. She wished she were white. She knew it was wrong and she felt guilty at having such bad thoughts. Her usual friends at school were less friendly towards her, possibly because Rebecca was not so much fun to be with any more but more likely because the Wrights had a strange influence over the rest of the Estate. It was as if they brought out the worst in everyone. They were evil and made everyone think evil. British Nationalist Party stickers appeared on everyone's doors, leaflets were handed out after school by ugly young booted men who spat at the black children. Rebecca had never seen so much hatred in her time at Garden Estate.

Miss Little tried to keep their spirits up and became even more prolific in her production of cakes and good advice. 'You should study hard at school Rebecca like your sister,' she scolded. 'If you don't study, you'll never get out of this place.'

'How can I study when I'm always looking over my shoulder?' Rebecca snapped.

Miss Little ruffled her hair. 'It breaks my heart to see your family suffering like this.'

'It's got to end,' Rebecca said defiantly. 'You've got to help me.'

Miss Little sighed. 'I'll do what I can,' she promised.

Savitri's visits home became less and less frequent. Her parents, their lives and Garden Estate depressed her. She had found a new and exciting life at college, one which had less and less space for them. At the end of her second year, just when she had decided to spend the holidays in Brighton working as a waitress, Baba wrote to her. He wrote that Miss Little was on her death bed with cancer and that he and Ma had decided to return to India to be with Rebecca. Suddenly, the prospect of being alone filled Savitri with such fear, she hurried back to see them. For the first time in years, Ma and Baba looked young again. They were clearing out the flat, packing their belongings and behaving like a couple of over-excited children.

'It'll be so nice to be able to pick mangoes from the trees and eat them,' Ma laughed.

'What will I do?' Savitri wailed. 'Where will I go?'

'Come with us,' Baba tempted. Savitri decided to think on it.

She went down to the nursing-home to visit Miss Little. The moment she saw her, guilt rose inside her like a tidal wave. She hadn't even thought of Miss Little for over a year, even though she'd known she was ill – Miss Little who had been their adoptive grandmother for all those years. Her eyes lit up when she saw Savitri whilst Savitri's eyes dulled with pain when she looked down at Miss Little's small and frail body. It had all but withered away . . . only Miss Little's smile remained.

They chatted for a while. It was like the old days where Rebecca and Savitri would talk and Miss Little would listen attentively.

'I knew you'd do well,' Miss Little gasped. 'We're all so proud of you.' Savitri blushed.

'But I must tell you about Rebecca,' she continued.

'Rebecca?' Savitri stammered.

'I know why she went silent.'

'We all know,' Savitri soothed, thinking that Miss Little had lost her memory as well as her health. 'It was that constant harassment.'

'No,' Miss Little said definitely, 'I know the real reason.'

Savitri stared at her.

'She swore me to secrecy that night and I promised I wouldn't tell any of you . . . but I feel I must now because what good is my silence doing?'

Savitri's face felt hot. Miss Little began to speak in a high squeaky voice.

'The night that that terrible thing happened, Rebecca had been down to the Council offices for the fourteenth time to complain about racial harassment, only this time she had taken "evidence" with her. We had stayed up half the night before, putting together the "evidence" that the Council needed. She had clear photographs of Robbie Wright daubing a swastika on your door; photos taken by myself, dates, times, racist literature that your family had received through your letterbox and a tape recording of John Wright shouting abuse and banging on the door late one night.'

'I remember Rebecca recording that,' Savitri said softly. 'I thought she was mad at the time.'

Miss Little continued her story.

'The new housing officer was impressed by Rebecca and apparently assured her that something would be done to evict the Wrights. It was the middle of winter, already dark at five and it had been drizzling all day. As she left the Council office the new housing officer followed her out. He smiled and said he had to rush to pick up the kids and then he ran to his car. When he reached his car he'd shouted back to Rebecca. "Don't worry, Rebecca. I'll nab those Wrights if it's the last thing I do." Stupid man!' Miss Little commented bitterly. 'Someone must have heard him.'

'How do you know all this?' Savitri asked, perplexed that a neighbour should know so much more about her sister than her.

'She told me,' Miss Little said. 'Rebecca was wet through. She knew that your parents would be sitting, waiting and worrying about her so she rushed back. She said she was so busy congratulating herself as she got out of the rain and into the lift at Petunia Mansions that she didn't bother to look around her.

'As the lift doors were about to close, a man's foot jammed through the gap. Rebecca looked down at the foot and recognised the boot. She smashed her hand on to the button to close the lift doors again and again, but the doors were jammed. She kicked at the boot to try and dislodge it, but instead the doors simply opened. Robbie Wright stood in the doorway with a dirty big grin on his face. Behind him stood two other men, grinning grotesquely. He called her a "slag". Rebecca hurled herself at them in an effort to get away, but the three men threw her back into the lift, getting in with her and pressing the button to close the door . . .' Miss Little stopped and this time turned to look at Savitri.

Savitri gulped and nodded.

'Just before the door closed, one of them jammed it ajar with a crowbar. Rebecca kept pleading with Robbie to let her go as he pinned her up against the wall and unzipped his trousers. He kept muttering that they'd seen her with the housing officer and he knew that she was trying to get them evicted. He was going to teach her a lesson once and for all. Rebecca thrashed around as she tried to free herself from the men's grasp, but the more she fought the more it hurt. She tried to scream once, but one of the men held a knife to her throat and she knew that if she wanted to keep alive, she had to stay silent.'

Miss Little closed her eyes and paused.

'They took it in turns. They raped her again and again in total silence. Rebecca said she didn't remember how many times . . . she just remembered the pain. When they had finished, they kicked her in the stomach and Robbie urinated over her.'

Savitri drew in her breath sharply. 'She was gang raped!' Her voice trembled.

'We, Mr Jacobson and I, found her lying in a heap in the lift, bruised and stinking of piss. Those vicious, disgusting animals. We took her up to my flat and cleaned her up. The poor beautiful girl was in a terrible state. She was terrified in case your parents found out and so she made us swear we wouldn't tell a soul.'

'My God,' Savitri began to weep. It all made sense now. Her thoughts raced back to Rebecca. All these years, all these years she had sat silently, unable to tell anyone what had happened, unable to speak. She hadn't even been able to tell her, her own sister . . .

'She kept saying it was her fault that she'd been raped,' continued Miss Little, 'that she hadn't done as she was told. She should have listened to everyone and not caused trouble. Those bastards, they broke her wonderful spirit.' Miss Little's eyes filled with water and she lay back on her pillow exhausted with the effort. Savitri sat numb, staring stupidly at her hands in her lap.

'I wish you'd told me before,' she said bitterly.

'I know, sweetheart. I should have. I honestly thought that India would be good for her.'

'Rebecca did it though,' Savitri smiled bravely. 'She got rid of them. They were evicted.'

'But at what cost?' Miss Little murmured.

Savitri sat in deep shock for hours in Garden Square. She watched all the people go by who in turn watched her curiously. She wept and chattered to herself like a mad woman, trying to work everything out in her head. Then slowly, she walked back to Petunia Mansions, stopping and shuddering as she passed by the lifts and for the very last time, walked up seventeen flights of stairs to number 95.

She wrote a long, long letter to Rebecca. She told her everything that had happened to her in the past five years, including her talk with Miss Little on her deathbed. She begged her sister's forgiveness. She told her that she missed Rebecca, that she wanted to talk, to joke, to giggle together like they used to. She told her she was saving money for a ticket so that she could go and visit her in the winter. She wanted to see her so badly.

Rebecca didn't write back. Savitri heard no word and then one day, after four months she got her first words from her. She wrote:

> 'My dearest Savitri,
> I want to see you too. I have longed to see you.
> Please come.
> With love,
> Rebecca.'

THE MAHARANI'S HOUSE

Ravinder Randhawa

To Chitra Viswanadha (1948–92)

*The 'might have been', 'could be really', 'you never know' Maharani
had bought the mini-mansion at the bottom of the street. A mini folly
constructed by the contractor who'd built the look-alike clone-alike terraced
houses surrounding it. Was this his monument to a moment of rebellion?*

*Grandly aloof in its own garden, four square walls standing strong and
solid, deep wide windows curving in every one of them, capturing the
maximum of light available. Not content with that, the Maharani had to
add her own addition and ordered an extravagant skylight embedded into
the roof. What was she about, throwing her money to the winds? Did she
miss the light she had left behind, or did she fear someone creeping up on
her?*

Mona and husband came to the terrace in the boom years of the
eighties to look, view and buy one of the clone–alikes, but the
first thing they saw was the broken, crumbling edifice on the
corner.

They were on their way up, weren't they? Ambitious ambition
was the escalator they were on and here it appeared about to
chuck them on to a dump heap. Gaping holes where the plaster
had fallen off, shattered jagged glass in windows that sagged and
bowed, a front door that hung on one hinge: a dilapidated heap
surrounded by a garden of thick prickly weeds, which the locals
obviously used as their rubbish dump. Mona wrinkled her nose

— 80 —

at the sight of mouldy mattresses, rusty fridges and broken chairs, taken aback and not quite pleased at this introduction to the street.

'One of life's little jokes,' commented Mona, moving forward to get a better look at the crumbling heap.

'More like that slimy estate agent's joke,' said Dilip, taking the papers out of his pocket. 'Supposed to be an up-and-coming area, is it? With this heap of rubbish on the corner! And we're supposed to spend our precious money here?' They'd scrimped, they'd saved, they'd done without, counting the pennies going into their deposit fund, a house being the baseline on their pyramid of goals. Smiling wryly, they moved on up the street, Mona throwing a lingering look behind her at the decayed shell; years, perhaps decades, crumbling quietly in on themselves.

The might-have-been, may-be-really-was Maharani had come with diamond earrings, fur-wrapped and chauffeur-driven; car nosing through the middle of a grey, snowy afternoon, in which edges dissolved and buildings blurred. Patting her sedan as she stepped out, she didn't bother lifting the gold-embroidered hem of her sari, and in beautiful oblivion to its increasingly soggy state she glided over the pavement, through the garden and gave the grand splendour a look-over through her heavy-lidded eyes. And accepted. Mr Blundell was rather shocked, though very pleased to have disposed of the property, not many takers for this peculiar monument to some builder's fantasy, sitting incongruously in the backwaters of London. He gave her a sharp look. What was she about, this regalised Maharani? But perhaps to her it was the English palace it wasn't.

After a good look at the house, the shops, and a wide-eyed newspaper article which expressed snobbish surprise at the area's gentrification, given the decades of immigrant buy-ups, bedsitter economy and two highly publicised riots, Mona and husband said yes, too, smugly pleased at having their own roof over their heads, and counting the friends who still lived in flats or waited for council house offers. The only thing that marred their enjoyment of this new acquisition was the thought of their friends having to be greeted by the rubbish heap mausoleum at the bottom of the street and being judged thereby. Dilip asserted he'd get a petition organised and get the local council to at least clean it up, if not demolish it altogether. Mona sounded assent, as keen as him to be seen as a success. No matter how regularly some of their friends talked left politics and social conscience, a life in which you could demonstrate your ability not only to succeed but to outstrip the indigenous population conferred a freedom and equality that no amount of political action could achieve. 'No one's going to give you anything, you have to create it with your own bare hands' was something they had both written in their diaries.

The Maharani surveyed her kingdom and was well pleased, patting the four square walls standing strong and solid, the beautifully large windows, looking out on to the garden that surrounded the house like a frill, giving the allusion of privacy, yet allowing sight of everything around it.

Years later after purchase, when Mona and husband redecorated and refurnished, they themselves didn't think twice about doing the same as the rest and gaily carted their rubbish off to dump into the Maharani's garden: chucking away the broken futon, the sponge mattresses that had served as seats and extra beds; the ugly, tiled coffee-table presented by a DIY uncle, the planks of wood and bricks that had housed their books and 'objets d'art'. Over the wall went their student days, into the Maharani's weeds went their days of frugal living, through the air sailed the tat that had cosmeticised their lives – suddenly hitting something hard, a small shattering, reverberating in the air around them. Mona and husband giggled nervously, quickly deposited the last remnants of their old lives and hurried away.

The Maharani would go up in the evening to change and prepare herself for dinner. Dinner was usually her most important task of the day, and she looked forward to it with relish. Sometimes, the best of times, it was the pursuit of pure pleasure; some (other) times, and they were the best of times too, it was the stealthy stalk through words, nuances and glances for morsels that might prove to be useful, and yet at other times, it was for eating alone and chewing slowly on all that lived in her brain.

When Mona and husband got home after their dumping spree they sat down with satisfaction, poured tea into their new and very expensive cups (mugs having been outlawed by a Mona decree), and relaxed around their new and very expensive dining-table. Their bank account had been flush, but now was empty. They could make money, they'd proved it, and now that they were so comfortably ensconced they could make more. The bell rang, and they looked at each other without a hint of a surprise. 'Steel yourself for a grilling,' he said as he went off to open the door. Mona quickly got up to clear away the new cups, such open evidence of their ambition's trivia, and then second-thinking sat down again. Well, their community-worker friend would just have to lump it.

'The Maharani's got a new interest,' the English maid told the Indian cook, who in turn told the gardener. The gardener curled his lip and, couching his words in purest Hindustani, told her to keep her nose out of other people's affairs and to mind her own business. Outside, shivering in the bitter cold, he attacked the fledgling new weeds with the fervour of a preacher digging out sin. Inside, the Maharani and friend finished their list entitled 'Gamble and Survival'. Her fingers trailed the curves and loops of words spelling spiralling consequences, apprehension threading a minute tremble through the paper. These thoughts should have come earlier or never at all. Passion for achieving more in life than that which mere self wanted had generated rhetoric, which rhetoric had in turn swung others into her orbit. Too late for second thoughts. Second thoughts too petty

to soil oneself with. She chucked the list in the fire, action determining action, got comfortable on the sofa and reminisced about childhood days.

The next day Mona's car wouldn't start. No matter how many times she turned the ignition, coaxing and wheedling, all she got were tinny tiny clicks. Then she swore her head off. That didn't work either. She wasn't going to open the bonnet and pretend to peer knowingly. She didn't know. She got out, slammed the door and fumed. How was she going to open the shop on time at this rate? Throwing a last malevolent look at the innocent car, she stomped off to catch the bus, boots thumping on the pavement.

Passing the wall of the Maharani's house something clinked at her feet, a spark of colour shot up, glinting in the light. Bending down she picked up a piece of ceramic, shiny fish-scale patterned. Stepping into the garden, she couldn't immediately see anything that it might have come from. Hardly surprising since the garden was so weed-infested you'd have to hack your way through, every inch, not to mention the heaps of rubbish dumped by those too mean to hire a skip. Including us, she couldn't help remembering guiltily. Turning, she glanced up at the house, for the first time in years really seeing it, taking in the loose broken door, the crumbling walls, the empty windows open to wind and rain; rotting lopsided stairs leading up towards half-ceilings, through whose jagged holes she could see an equally tattered roof, grey sky looming through the holes, shedding a dull, dusty light on the devastation.

Peering up at the broken roof, Mona felt a strange disturbance, as at seeing someone humiliated, stripped of their dignity. An inscription over the door caught her eye. It looked strangely like Hindi. Her own Hindi being as broken and tattered as this house, she began to attempt an interpretation, when her mind-clock suddenly reminded her of her duties. Turning resolutely away from the house, hurrying towards the bus stop, mind flinging forward working herself into anxiety about how many customers she'd missed already. Hardly any, she knew that. But she'd coached herself into always thinking that time away from the shop was time away from customers, and time away from customers was time away from business, and time away from business was time away from money.

The Maharani drew patterns on the frosted glass, and as suddenly wiped them out, leaning her head against the coolness. To each their own, to this country its numbing cold, to the other its dust, the one leaving her dulled, the other gritting between her teeth. Waiting was the hardest thing anyone could do.

No customers queuing impatiently outside 'Mona's' fashionable fashion house. A quick disappointment blipped through her, and though Mona told herself she was being ridiculous, she couldn't keep at bay the fantasy of owning a glitzy boutique ever overflowing with customers. Reminding herself she was on the way up, she rearranged the display, channelling herself into her businesswoman's mind-set. The leaflet deal with the video shop was doing only averagely well. Half-price costume jewellery for every video hired: the marketing gem behind it was that when customers came in for their half-price jewellery, they might find a need for an outfit to go with it. She would have to renegotiate or scrap the deal. As well as doing more swotting up on marketing strategies.

Sitting down at the counter, she examined the Maharani's piece of ceramic more closely, a tinkling sound replaying in her mind. They must have broken something; though why it should matter she didn't know. One more broken item in a junkyard of a house was hardly cause for concern. And who was to say a Maharani had actually lived there? And, if she had, what did it matter? Her neighbour, the street storyteller, the street's oldest inhabitant had mentioned something, and Mona had imbibed it into her mind, liking the idea of living cheek by jowl with a romantic story, an Indian one at that.

'. . . in full swing they are,' the maid grimaced to the cook, 'she likes a do with her own lot, don't she!' Upstairs, they were howling with laughter as she, the Maharani, strutted about, acting out a wicked caricature of the king. They begged her for more. She was well high on everything and readily obliged with one, of the man called Gandhi. That brought the house down.

Early evening and going back home, Mona couldn't resist peeking into the empty shell of the 'edifice' again. Broken gas fires, torn and dirty wallpaper, an old sink hanging loose from its fittings. Dirt and decay heavy in the air. Mustering her courage, she crept up the first flight of stairs, hugging the wall, testing each step before she put her weight on it. Upstairs, she peered into an old room: a torn poster half-flapping off a wall, a rusted old cooker lying on its side, shelves hanging down. The house had been nothing but a warren of bedsits. And now, whoever owned it couldn't or didn't want to renovate it. Made business sense. Who'd be foolhardy enough to spend money in the middle of England's deepest and longest recession? But thank God some did, thinking of her customers, instinctively crossing her fingers. Lingering under the inscription, she laboriously copied it down; hand working hard at a script others called her mother tongue. Perhaps the community worker friend would be able to decipher it. He was deeply into translation projects.

The party had long gone home and now it was the Maharani's bedroom scene, but not one that anyone would have recognised. Whispers, whispers and more whispers.

That night Mona's house was subdued and quiet. And it wasn't till Dilip said quietly, as though it didn't really matter, that he might be made redundant, her faint feelings of anxiety turned into full-blown dread. She looked around at their remodelled home, now seeing the carpets and sofas and everything else as a ghastly rash extravagance. But then, they had thought they were fairly safe, their lean years behind them. There is no such thing as safe.

The Maharani wished it were a sage sitting with her, someone wise and venerable, expounding timeless truths. As it was they could only trust each other, and know that it was for the ones who would come after.

Mona's car had to go into the garage; a long expensive job. She kicked it even harder today but only on the tyre. They couldn't afford to have dents. And now on her regular rush to the bus she saw the strangest sight of all. The Maharani's garden was being cleared up. Hygiene problems, explained the workmen, apparently people had been complaining. Including us, she thought, a shadowy guilt stirring somewhere.

The Maharani unclenched her hands, breathed deeply and tried to convince herself it was better this way than the other. The other would have cost far more. Better the discovery before they jumped from the survival side to the gamble side. Not that there hadn't been and wouldn't be consequences – the least of them the gutted hole in herself. It wasn't even empty; if it was, so much the easier. What she now had living inside herself was a churning rubbish-heap of memories, grand ambitions and twisted emotions. Some things could never be attempted twice. The future looked empty, except it wasn't, she would have to spend her life filling over that rubbish dump. Applying more make-up over her paleness, she went downstairs and saw the gardener come up from the cellar. Habits of old she could always use and she asked him to tell the maid to bring her some tea.

Coming and going, morning and evening, Mona watched, and it was like watching an excavation. First went skip-loads of rubbish, secondly went the old ruined wall, thirdly the jungle of weeds and plants. One day on her way back home, she stood and looked in amazement: patterns of the past at last revealed: the clearly shaped remains of flowerbeds, paths, a fountain, a pond and far from the pond on a little oval patch a single solitary fish, finless. A fish out of water! That's clear enough, thought Mona. Also clear was where her little ceramic piece had come from.

Also clear when she got home was the letter of redundancy pinned to the kitchen door. Someone was clipping their wings well and good. That night they made a list headed 'Survival' and another headed 'Gamble'. Of course the two didn't add up.

At the weekend, fired by the revelation of the Maharani's garden, she started on her own, but hadn't gone very far before her neighbour's hello aroused her attention and curiosity. Deciding to brave verbal deluge, she leaned on her garden fence and asked the neighbour about the Maharani who used to live at the bottom of the street. Flooded, as expected, with the gossip of the last fifty years, she managed to extract, fragment by fragment, a vague story that looped and twisted upon itself.

'The Maharani, flighty piece she was, all glitter and glamour, kept a car, kept a gardener, kept a string of men, my dear, as long as your arm. She herself got it put around she was a Maharani. Not that any of us fell for it. Maharanis don't come and live at the bottom of your street everyday, do they? I grant you, that house is grand enough. Used to be, that is. And this was a proper respectable street in those days, too. We had bankers, we had solicitors, we had high-up civil servants. Not that you'd know it to look at it today. She, the Maharani,' lowering her voice and looking around, 'she even stole Mr Carruthers from Mrs Carruthers. Lived at forty-nine, they did. They moved out quick when the story got around. Myself, I never believed it. I think it was something to do with Mrs Anderson, who lived right next door to them. But the Maharani was that kind of a piece, you could hang anything on to her. Parties every night, people coming and going. And then,' lowering her voice even further and looking around again, 'there was talk of treason. Yes, there was,' nodding her head sagely, 'talk was, she was plotting against us. You know,' putting her hand on Mona's arm and leaning conspiratorially towards her, 'against us, against the empire. Now what do you think of that!'

'The Maharani was a revolutionary?'

'The mutiny it was.' Mona moved her hand away; knowing the old lady knew her so well, she didn't see her for what she was any more. And did it matter, wondered Mona, who came from where? Her parents had come here, some forty years ago, to enjoy the fruits of independence? And weren't she and Dilip doing the same, given a redundancy here and there? Dilip had begun to mutter about how the Asians were seen as too uppity and always got the push first, and then he had stopped himself. He'd almost broken his golden rule: never to think and talk racism. Success was built on hard work, not on whingeing and moaning.

The 'survival' list said that she should look for a job so that they would have one stable income; the 'gamble' list said he would take on the shop and look into expansion. She already saw the spectre of bills piling up, debts accumulating, and disaster on the horizon.

She was trudging back from an interview one day, mind grilled to a cinder, when she stopped to rest, as she often did nowadays, by the Maharani's house. Leaning against the wall, she closed her eyes and willed the house to give her a picture, a tone, a voice from the past. What had the Maharani really been up to? Had she really been gambling survival and security under a tinsel façade? Did she know that someone like Mona would one day rest against her walls, weary from fighting for her own personal survival?

'They plotted and schemed in this house. To blow up parliament no less. And the story goes they were betrayed. Yes,' said a voice on the other side of the wall, 'the other story goes that she ran away from a nasty husband to be near her English lover.'

Mona sat up straight, disorientated and confused. Touching the walls to feel their solidity, wondering if the voices had come from her own mind or whether ghosts had suddenly arisen from the past to answer all the questions crowding her mind. There were still murmurings on the other side. She crept around towards the door, giving herself a severe telling-off as she did so – a mature professional woman does not indulge in such ludicrous fancies – unseeingly colliding with the two people coming out of the house. All stared at one another as though they were seeing ghosts.

The two turned out to be a reporter and photographer from the local paper. How prosaic! To cover her disappointment in them not being emissaries from the past, she invited them back for tea. Why not? She could show off her expensive almost-new dining-table. At least that had been paid for.

The stupid reporter had a horrible habit of banging his pen on the table. They didn't really know that much more than her. The Maharani went to live somewhere in West London, grew old, died. End of story. Did she really plot to blow up parliament? Who knows? They shrugged their shoulders. Old gossip lives on in old minds, and old minds are apt to get confused. One old bloke they'd interviewed had rambled endlessly about revenge murders till the photographer had nudged his partner and indicated the video shelves: a collector's collection of sex and murder, murder and sex. The old bloke knew what he liked. They were doing a story on the house because it was going to be pulled down. Safety hazard. The editor had decided it was worth an item in the local.

Throughout the evening's meal, conversation and lullaby TV, fear and apprehension coiled within her. A fear for themselves now conjoined into flying bricks and falling walls. She didn't want their old lives to go, she didn't want the old house to go.

They were fighting for their own survival; how could she turn around and start mouthing historical importance about a house that they'd always disliked? An insubstantial cobweb of gossip from the past hardly related to the present.

In the middle of the night, taking a hammer from the cellar and throwing a coat over her nightclothes, she went down to the Maharani's house, knowing that if anyone saw her, if anyone heard her, she'd be branded quite mad.

Gentle taps, did nothing. Closing her ears to the sound, and willing everyone else to stay fast in their sleep, she banged harder, gradually cracking the cement, releasing the fish. Cradling it in her arms, she hurried home.

Is this worth it? was the question. Is this what life is about? was another. Is this a gamble worth taking for its own intrinsic good? was yet another along the road of ethical exfoliation, as they spent a Saturday looking at empty shops, as they spent the evening poring over calculators and calculations. Was this the only point to which history could have brought them? Self-aggrandisement, self-interest, self-survival? Oh, damn, she thought, realising she'd been banging her pen on the table. Well, she wasn't yet at the stage where she could go to India every year, as well as a couple of weeks in the Bahamas or Africa or wherever. Life wasn't that rosy, no need for her to start feeling guilty.

The 'fish out of water' propped up her photo albums, albums that stretched back forty years into family history. Only ten years later than the story of the Maharani. Photos of the men who wended their way to England, to labour on equal terms with the English, or so they thought. Photos followed by families, by life going on. Mona sighed and shut the album. What would she have done in the Maharani's place? In the Maharani's era? Was there such a thing as a debt to the past? Or are we only the products of our own time, no duty to anything else. She called her community-worker friend and showed him the roughly copied inscription.

'It says,' he said, 'the spirit will live on. Your new new motto?' accompanying the question with a cheeky grin.

'What does it mean?' Asking though not wanting the answer, she was feeling burdened and fragile enough as it was; a butterfly with the weight of the world on its shoulders, and smiled at her own image. She didn't have room on board for someone else's legacy.

'The present is not an island on its own,' he intoned.

'Oh, stop going into your preacher-man mode.'

'The ideals of the past make our present possible,' dragging deeply on his cigarette and blowing out perfect circles.

'For God's sake go and write a book on it. And give up smoking, it leaves a foul smell in the house.'

'There's no need to shut your mind, everything can be integrated. And it doesn't mean that you're wrong; everyone's got the right to amass a pile if they can. Those who fought for independence, freedom, fought so that . . .'

'People could live as they choose.' Interrupting him, not wanting him to get any deeper into his analysis; it might get personal. 'Look, I've got an interview tomorrow, help me with it. Please.'

Well, luck was on their side. Weren't they the lucky ones! She got a job. Their lives balanced out once again. But the 'Gamble' list was still up on the board and a tick went up for a second shop. They were fast on their way to super success or great disaster.

Driving past the Maharani's house, she found her way blocked by a medley of police vans and cars, lights blitzing a signal that something had happened. One of the gents in blue told her to reverse and take the left-hand turning. She did. Parked her car and walked right back, knowing she could gamble on being ten minutes late but no more than that. They told her to keep away. She joined the gathered crowd of onlookers on the other side. Their neighbourhood cop had agreed to give regular news bulletins, part of the new friendly-friendly approach.

Talk was, they'd found a body. 'Well, not a body, actually,' corrected another, 'a skeleton.' They didn't know whether it was a murdered skeleton or not. 'Forensic will investigate for that,' added the cops-and-robbers TV addict. Her ten minutes up, she drove off, jittery and jangled.

Old gossip was one thing. Skeletons were another. Skeletons buried in the basement indicated conflicts and passions that went beyond the ordinary. She glued back the fin, but never contemplated organising a pond for it to swim in. What had been, had been, and the motes may reflect on her life or not she didn't know; but fin and skeleton merged into each other and, despite herself, cut a space for new thoughts that drew a thin thread from the past, drawing up a kind of courage that she didn't even know she'd lacked, to look through a wider lens at the ebbs and flows . . .

AN ANSWER FOR RITA

Rahila Gupta

Someone was at the door. Jagdish Lal was being dragged out of bed by a sixth sense swirling with the vibrations of another being. The silent swishing of a sari, the gentle clinking of a bangle, the impatient tapping of fingers merged into monsoon wind.

Clutching his soaking sheet to his chest, Jagdish Lal cranked the bolt back with a deafening crash. She stood there, holding the provocative pose of a Khajurao carving, sari hugging her voluptuous body, a perfectly rounded earthenware urn sitting snugly in the curve above her hip. The mouth of the urn was staring at Jagdish Lal as it disgorged its black feathery contents into the wind's lap and from there straight into his eyes.

As Jagdish Lal twisted out of reach, he caught sight of Rita's bulging eyes, staring, wide open, and froze. A fat bunched-up tongue hung out of her mouth and a ghoulish shade of blue suffused her face.

'Now, will you let me inside?' asked Rita, her voice wrapped in canvas as it struggled to get past her tongue.

'Beti, the door has always been open for you. I have done all I can. They were put into prison despite all their bribes, despite all their string-pulling . . .'

'For two months . . . does that match up to my 21 years? I have to put my ashes to rest, my ashes to rest, to rest, rest,' the canvas creaked and scraped.

So saying, Rita disappeared. Jagdish Lal stood there a minute longer, hoping that the rain would cool his fevered brain.

Next morning, even though the harsh sun allowed no dark niches, Jagdish Lal's mind remained stuck in a cesspool of unlit images. He could not concentrate on his daily ritual. The papers held no fascination for him although the airline employees' strike, which was being led by a close friend of his, was front-page news.

He did not believe in nightmares or dreams. Weren't they just a fiction created by Freud, a diversionary tactic to dilute the irresistible pull of Marxism? Besides he had never had one – that is, until now. He was too embarrassed to tell anyone about last night and yet he could not put it out of his mind.

Madhubala came shuffling in, her two youngest kids in tow, to start her day's work at Jagdish Lal's.

'You've brought those dirty kids with you again. Make them sit on the terrace. I'm not having their snot running down all my furniture.'

'Devika has gone to the village. So there was no one . . .' the weakness in Jagdish Lal's voice made Madhubala look at him.

By now Jagdish Lal would have been bustling around in the bathroom, shaving and singing tunelessly. Instead he was lying there, without his glasses, his eyes shut with effort.

'Are you looking for a boy for Devika already? How many times do I have to tell you? Send her to school, I'll pay . . .', tired words, falling parrot-fashion out of his inert mouth.

'Shall I call the doctor, sahab? Are you not well? In all my ten years, I have not seen you lying in bed when you were not asleep.'

'No. I will be all right. It is not the body that is feeling weak. It is my mind that is refusing to get up.'

'Sahab, you have been putting too much strain on yourself. Forgive me for saying so, but we are all getting old. You have to put Rita out of your mind. You must start going to your meetings again.' Madhubala hovered, wondering if Jagdish Lal would unburden himself.

'Rita's ashes . . .' Jagdish mumbled. He was reluctant to tell Madhubala the truth. He needed someone who would stand back, not someone who would happily sieve this story through her superstitious mind and come up with a hundred different fantasies. But he also desperately wanted to be believed. It would be too embarrassing to tell anyone else.

'Let me sleep,' Jagdish Lal said with a finality that banished Madhubala to the kitchen.

Rita stood with her back to him, let her sari drop, unbuttoned her blouse and let it slide to the floor. With deft little fingers, she pinched one corner of her shoulders and peeled the skin back, her body aching with the need to relive its memories. A cheap vinyl belt shredded against Rita's body, the buckle dragging as it caught on open throbbing flesh only precariously anchored by shards of skin. A slow burning heat rose up Jagdish Lal's spine, a blistering trail left by fingernails scraping and extending outwards across his shoulders before fisting inwards into knots of pain locked into every segment of his spine. His body extended and coiled, boomeranging in on itself, as the pain locked and unlocked from the central cord.

The *whack whack* of the belt looped around Jagdish Lal's brain, like an endless circular tape with no beginning and therefore no end – both sound and echo caught in a tight embrace, image and reflection merging and driving him into insane circles. The *whack whack* drawing blood in his brain and flushing the redness into his eyes.

'You cannot live my pain, nor will I let you live through it. There is no easy redemption,' mocked Rita as she drew the skin back into place, shutting up and closing down. But the entrails lay strewn across Jagdish Lal's vision and would not be safely gathered in.

Madhubala stood directly above him, wringing the floor cloth into an iron bucket from such a great height that Jagdish Lal was getting splashed by cold, muddy droplets of water. 'Have you been crying? Your eyes are red. You had better put a vest on. The midday sun has burnt your back and left a pattern of window grilles which will hurt tomorrow.'

Jagdish Lal could not move. There appeared to be nothing wrong but he could not move. 'Tuck a sheet at either end of the window,' he told her wearily.

When she had finished, Madhubala stood there and waited. Jagdish knew that she wanted a confession. He felt an overriding desire to be alone.

'Rita . . .' he began. Madhubala's eyes were impatient. Of course, she knew that but what precisely was the matter? 'She was here last night and again just now. Something about putting her ashes to rest. She looked at me accusingly as if it was my fault. Her quiet face was disturbed . . . bulging frog-like eyes, tongue hanging out –'

'That is the effect of a cotton duppatta tightening round your neck,' Madhubala interjected matter-of-factly.

'Does that also change a thin shapeless body into a voluptuous *apsara*?' asked Jagdish Lal, irritated and embarrassed that he had referred so intimately to female anatomy.

'That is the good fortune of women who have suffered upon this earth. They are blessed with all that they didn't have. Did she talk to you brazenly and harshly?'

'Yes . . . how –' Jagdish Lal's irritation evaporated into surprise.

'I know because Rita was mild and meek. Often she would come the morning after she had been thrown again and again against a wall with iron hooks in it where the clothes used to hang. And as I massaged her aching back, I would tell her about my mother-in-law and how I stood up to her. But there was not enough anger in her to make her feel brave. So I used to say, "Didi, don't worry, your afterlife will be different." There are some compensations for us.'

Jagdish Lal tried to rub the tiredness out of his eyes. He was vainly searching for a bit more cynicism, not this easy acceptance, so that his vision assumed greater reality. 'Why didn't you tell me about this when she was alive? I could have done something.'

'Tch, your head is always buried in that paper or you're off to some meeting or other. You just think I'm a silly uneducated woman. You never pay any attention to me,' Madhubala retorted tartly, pleased that she had finally found the courage to say something that had irritated her for years.

'Why didn't Rita talk to me? She used to visit quite often,' Jagdish Lal said, half to himself.

'But would your brother have taken her back? The shame of it all . . . don't want to give in to their demands for more dowry, want to walk with head held high in the village . . . anyway did any of the girls ever say more than yes or no to you?'

'I tried to talk to them. Rita could have come and lived with me. I don't know what I could have done different.'

'It's different for us,' Madhubala muttered as she disappeared to continue her housework.

That whole day Jagdish Lal did not move. As dusk crept out of dark corners and took over his flat, he switched on the TV to people his loneliness. He stared mindlessly at the screen, and realised that his vision had started clouding over. The moistness on the inside of his eyes was being soaked up by a black velvet material.

Rita stood before him, the contours of her body thrust mockingly into his face when once they would have been shrouded in a loose *salwaar kameez*.

'How will you avenge my death? Or are you too busy uniting the workers of the world?' came the harsh muffled whisper.

'You cannot talk to me like that.'

'Once, maybe. I gave up my life because good manners wouldn't let me fight to keep it. What will you do?'

'I don't know. I've done all I could. The leader of the women's wing of the Communist Party organised a demonstration outside your husband's house at my request. Three hundred women chanted slogans for five hours. After they came out of prison, their lives became unbearable. They could not sell their house because it was said to be haunted. Local people boycotted their shop, spat on them when they dared to show their faces. What more, what more can I do to appease your soul?'

'You were the head of the household after Dadaji's death. You could have stopped my wedding. It was you who reported back to Papa that the family seemed okay, that the boy was educated. Do you think you can remove the bloodstains by humiliating the butcher?'

'What have your ashes done to my eyes? Let me see, let me see.'

'When you can see a way of putting my ashes at rest. Until then this urn will sit on your mantelpiece.' And Rita was gone.

The television blared loudly in the background as Jagdish Lal sat, blinded and bewildered. His life had been devoted to the fight against the system – wasn't that what held women's equality back? It would be different when workers had more power . . . Even in his personal life, he had made a big sacrifice by forgoing marriage so that he did not exploit women. Okay, Madhubala was a bit of an anomaly but he had educated all her children, even the girls. Ungrateful child, that Rita. And she had been so likeable when she was alive. Blaming him for his brother's actions. All his certainties lay in tatters. Nothing seemed to add up any more.

Madhubala found him sitting, comatose, in front of a flickering screen next morning. As she was shaking him out of himself, she suddenly stood stock still. There was the urn with Rita's ashes. But they had thrown them in the Ganga. She herself had accompanied the mourners on the bus and seen the scattering of ashes and chanted in harmony with the prayers that were said. It couldn't be . . . the same urn.

The line between reality and nightmare was blurring. Jagdish was not sure whether he wanted the reality of his private nightmare confirmed by someone as superstitious as Madhubala.

'What does she want? My blood?' was Jagdish Lal's pathetic whine.

'Maybe you will find the answer where she was born.'

Jagdish Lal sat like that for another day and another night, with neither food nor drink. Maybe, Madhubala was right; maybe the village held an answer. The more he thought about it, the more convinced he became. He would have to make the gruelling, dusty journey – six hours chugging along in a mail train, almost blind, for a mere 100 kilometres.

'Ashok, Ashok!' the booming stentorian sounds of the eldest son of the house echoed up the winding staircase and down the open corridors into the inner courtyard. The women of the house dropped what they were doing and hastily lifted their sari *pallu* to cover their heads. An automatic pall fell over the gossip and lively chatter that relieved the monotony of peeling vegetables to feed such a large household.

The matriarch of the family emerged from the bathroom only half dressed. Hearing a man's voice, she hastily drew the sari up to cover her head, leaving her pendulous breasts exposed to the hot sun and the rest of mankind. The children's hushed tones distorted by giggles took a minute or so to register, at which point Dadiji turned around and faced the wall.

Jagdish Lal had cultivated an absent self-absorbed look to minimise the embarrassment felt by the women for these minor indiscretions. Now, of course, he was barely able to see and genuinely too absorbed to notice.

Ashok called to his second daughter, Urmila, to bring a cup of tea for Jagdish Lal. He seemed pleased that his brother had travelled from the city when there had been no special reason to attract him to the village.

Urmila appeared in a shapeless *salwaar kameez*, eyes focused on the ground, mouthing 'yes' or 'no' as appropriate. Jagdish Lal could not hear her responses, his irritation audible in his barked command, 'Speak up, girl. I cannot see.' Her hand shook, the hot tea spilt on Jagdish Lal's clothes, scorching his neck and chest.

In a completely unguarded, impulsive gesture, Ashok Lal picked up the fly-swat hanging from the wall and beat Urmila on her back. The *whack whack* looped around in Jagdish Lal's brain until the redness flushed into his eyes. He restrained Ashok's hand and taking Urmila by the shoulder, he started walking down the stairs.

'We cannot carry on like this,' shouted Jagdish over his shoulder. 'This girl will come and live with me in Delhi.'

As they walked along the dung-covered mud roads of the village, past the great pile of hay being pulled along by a camel, Jagdish realised with a great joy in his heart that many shades of brown were assailing his eyes after what seemed like a very long time.

NAUKAR

⏤◆⏤

Anya Sitaram

The sun beamed relentlessly on the streets of Calcutta as the rickshaw-wallah toiled his way down Southern Avenue, the wooden shafts of the rickshaw rubbing against his protruding shoulder-blades and scraping away at his skin, threatening to expose his bones completely through wet, pink sores. With his thin neck straining forward, his brown hands swollen by the heat, gripping the shafts of the wagon, the rickshaw-wallah quickened his sticks of legs from an unsteady trot into a gallop and he and his livelihood careered round a bend towards Lake Gardens. Every now and again he tossed his sweating tendrils to unsettle the flies that buzzed round his head like faithful satellites.

Julia Bannerjee shut her eyes as the rickshaw narrowly missed a bus, which screamed past within two inches of them. The hood of the vehicle, which had been put up to protect her from the sun, was proving to be more of a nuisance than a comfort for it was too low for her long limbs. Only if she bent double and craned her neck forward from under the hood could she see out of the jolting carriage.

If she sat upright, her vision was restricted to the rickshaw-wallah's puny waist, puny hips and thin poles of legs. She thought it was almost obscene the way his angular kneecaps, which were the widest part of his legs, jutted out.

She hated travelling by rickshaw, not only because it was

uncomfortable but also because it was painful to see a man reduced to the level of a beast as he laboured with the task of transporting another richer, fatter, more fortunate being to her destination. Rickshaw-wallahs barely lived past middle age.

But if she did not travel by rickshaw, she would be depriving a man of his income, her husband had told her.

Her husband, Nilkant Bannerjee, had been a Marxist in his college days, a fine specimen of the earnest, vociferous, *khadi*-swathed intelligentsia prolific in Calcutta. Having completed his degree, he had joined Ashok Leyland and after several years had been sent to England to get some managerial experience, before returning to India to embark on more demanding tasks, including those of being a husband; for during his stay in the Midlands he had fallen in love with a tall, willowy, freckly and very fair English rose. His marriage to a foreigner had been his last act of rebellion before he succumbed to the cosy allure of affluence.

Julia had been in India for nearly a year now but had not yet grown accustomed to her new home; everything was still remarkable. Even Nilkant seemed different in his own surroundings – more arrogant, more conventional than he'd been in England. Perhaps it was just the confidence of being at home.

Sometimes she just wanted to shut herself away in a cool room and forget, for India had sharpened her awareness, exposed her senses to a bombardment of sights, smells, sounds, which terrified, amazed and sickened her. She was always apprehensive of venturing out into the roads swarming with people, animals, cars, buses, trams: roads choked with chaos. She would return home trembling and exhausted after an outing, having spent her nerves and energy dodging the clutching, hungry hands of hawkers, beggars, street Romeos, all thinking a white woman easy prey. Going into the city and back to her house again involved the opening and shutting of her senses, like a wound that is never given a chance to heal but half-closed, half-dried, is ripped open again, by the thing that caused it in the first place.

Calcutta reeked of poverty, death and confusion. Everywhere buildings were crumbling into skeletal ghosts of the Raj. Beggars littered the streets, and those who were too weak to beg collapsed on the pavements and lay prone for days, while skinny stray dogs sniffed at them and people stepped over them as if avoiding rubbish, until they were fortunate enough to die or be scooped up by a Mother Teresa.

Even in the dark recesses of her own house away from the excreta, from the smell of urine, betel juice and *bidis* – India's peculiar perfume – confusion would come wafting in to invade her peace with another instalment of power cuts, so that hours were spent in primitive heat and darkness, being bitten by mosquitoes and longing for the electricity to return. When she wanted to ring a friend her phone would invariably be out of order, because some workmen digging an underground railway had accidentally cut through the cables. The authorities had been planning its construction for over ten years but every time a hole of substantial depth was made the surrounding earth would cave in and fill it up again.

'Why are they trying to build an underground,' she had asked Nilkant, 'if it's proving so dangerous? Besides there isn't enough power to light this bloody city let alone run a new railway!'

'But don't you know?' he had smiled enigmatically. 'They are building it in the hope that one day when half the population of Calcutta is underground, the electricity will fail, the soil will sink and, bingo – all our problems will be solved. No more overcrowding, no more power cuts.'

The city was a seething, multi-mouthed volcano, which spouted putrid, resentful lava at intervals and threatened to explode in a devastating eruption any day. Julia would never forget an incident within the first two weeks of her arrival when her husband and she had witnessed an accident. A street-urchin had rushed into the path of an oncoming car. It was clearly the child's fault, but the sight of the limp, bleeding five-year-old rendered lifeless by a more privileged being angered the crowd that gathered round. They grabbed hold of the driver and literally tore him limb from limb. Two deaths were reported in the *Calcutta Statesman* the next day. One was a child's and the other was a driver's who had been lynched by a mob. A crime had been committed, but hundreds of people were responsible for the driver's death. No, millions. In fact, all the poor in India were responsible.

Julia was disturbed by the sinister undercurrents that flowed beneath the fragile co-existence of rich and poor, and was puzzled by the fact that all the Indians she knew seemed unaffected. It was as if they could not see.

Julia and her rickshaw-wallah reached their destination, a grey three-storey house, a little less decrepit than the other similar structures in the higgledy-piggledy warren of residential streets. Breathing a sigh and easing herself from the sweat-soaked seat, she was seized with a sudden impulse to help the rickshaw-wallah, who was wiping his face with grim relief. So in her broken Bengali, she told him to wait and rushed through the gate and into the house.

In the kitchen, the cook was preparing *aloo paratas*. Feeling awkward under his suspicious gaze, she took a couple and wrapped them in silver foil, then took a mango from the fridge in the pantry and a bottle of chilled water.

The rickshaw-wallah was squatting by his vehicle. He had poured some tobacco into his cupped left hand, which he gripped with his right hand, vigorously massaging the tobacco into a fine dust with his thumb. When he saw Julia approaching, he rose from his haunches and flicked the tobacco into his mouth.

She handed him the food, smiling, feeling gratified by her own generosity, but was a little piqued to see his unenthusiastic reception of the package at which he sullenly stared. After a few moments of embarrassed silence, Julia asked in exasperation, 'Well, what's the matter?'

'Five rupees,' he replied without lifting his eyes from the silver foil. Then Julia realised her mistake. How silly of her. She groped in her pocket, muttering apologies, feeling ridiculous as the blood throbbed in her face. Indians were lucky in that their blushes were seldom perceptible. She found a twenty-rupee note and told him to keep the change. It seemed to Julia that she had never witnessed such happiness. His sullen, haggard features were transformed by a broad smile as he thanked her repeatedly. The incident was sealed in her memory as one of the sunniest moments in time, all clouds and shadows far away.

Nilkant Bannerjee usually returned home after work at six o'clock each evening. He always looked forward to seeing his wife waiting for him, recently bathed, and smelling delightfully of Blue Grass, holding a restorative gin and tonic specially poured for him at exactly one minute before six o'clock. He loved to come home and find a clean bush-shirt laid on the bed by her fastidious white hands, find the hot, sibilant shower splattering on to the white-tiled bathroom floor, on which he would stand and feel the worries of the day rinsed away. They would go out either to the Tolley Club or dinner at the Oberoi-Grand, or maybe to a lighthearted Hindi romp at an air-conditioned cinema. They usually had to go out to escape the power cuts.

Today he had a surprise for his wife as he sat down with a second drink on the batik floor cushions, which Julia had insisted on instead of a conventional sofa.

'Darling, how would you like a dog?' Nilkant knew that Julia, like all the English, worshipped dogs. He was deflated at her answer.

'But do you think it is right to have a dog in India?'

He was irritated by her persistent pangs of guilt, which dominated all her actions and soured their conversations. So he replied, 'Oh, it's all right if you give them their proper injections and keep an eye on them.' The ploy didn't work, much to his annoyance.

'You know what I mean, Nilu. Stop playing games. How can one have a dog in a country where the majority of people cannot even afford to feed themselves? How can you spend your money on an animal when it could be used to feed and clothe a sick man?'

'Very noble of you, my dear,' Nilkant said dryly, tired of always having to justify himself. 'But Suresh's labrador has had three puppies and unless we take one, it will have to be drowned. I consider that cruelty to animals.'

'I would rather a dog died than a human.'

'I thought you British would risk your lives for the salvation of your four-legged friends.' Sensing her irritation, he added in a more serious tone, 'Look, you wouldn't think twice about having a dog in England, even though you're all aware that there are people dying in the Third World.'

'That's beside the point. How can one have a pet, feed it, fawn over it, when there's a leprous beggar pushing his rotten arm through one's front gate?'

She was so persistently argumentative, Nilkant thought. But then, he remembered, he had married her more for her stimulating company than her limpid, grey eyes.

'I don't think, my sweet, that one little labrador is going to make the slightest bit of difference to the problems of the world. It's not as if we're so hard up that we'll no longer be able to give to worthier animals.' Seeing no reaction, he lost his self-control, feeling slighted that his cherished idea of several months was met with this hostile reception. He was all the more annoyed because it was her happiness that he had been considering. 'I mean, where do you draw the line? Next you'll be saying we can't have children because India's already full of famished children suffering from rickets.' This time he knew he'd won. She desperately wanted children.

'All right, Nilkant, you have your dog.'

Julia always awoke to the raucous song of crows, which heralded the start of day; they hunched up together on rooftops and windowsills, or hovered on the stench of decaying rubbish cast out carelessly into the street. Their calls together with the wistful cries of hawkers floated into the bedroom, as isolated reminders of Calcutta's teeming multitudes.

Nilkant had already left for work when Julia went downstairs and called for breakfast. The cook came shuffling in, smelling of onions and fish and complained that there had been a *goonda* sitting at the gate since the crack of dawn who was refusing to leave until the Memsahib spoke to him.

Julia peered through the half-closed shutters of the drawing-room window and saw the *goonda* squatting by the gate. She saw him vigorously rubbing something in his palm with his thumb and recognised the rickshaw-wallah.

'Well! I hope he doesn't think I'm going to give him twenty rupees.'

She marched outside, trying to look stern, with every intention of shooing him away. She could almost imagine her husband's reaction, 'These people, they are never satisfied with what they are given. Always coming back for more.'

The little man rose to his feet, adjusting his clean white dhoti, from which his skinny legs protruded, only to be swamped in an oversized pair of black shoes. His sunken chest was just perceptible through a starched kurta, and in his hand was an umbrella, black and thin like one of his own limbs. She softened at the sight of him.

'I don't want to go shopping today, thank you,' she attempted in broken Bengali, but noticed that his rickshaw was nowhere in sight.

In Hindi he replied that he had come a year ago from Patna in Bihar to Calcutta after a series of misfortunes. He had been a *doodh*-wallah but his buffalo had died, his wife who had faithfully produced a son each year for the last eight years had developed a cataract in her left eye; and so he had come to Calcutta penniless in the hope of earning enough money to go back to Bihar and set up a small farm as well as pay for an eye operation. However in one year he had barely made enough to feed himself.

It did not matter if his story was untrue; it was plain that he needed help. Julia reached into her purse and produced another twenty-rupee note in the hope that he would accept it and leave. However, he shook his head and declined the money.

It was very kind of her, he explained, but what he really wanted was a job. His father had been in service, in a rich man's house and although he had not had any experience in service himself, he felt he had observed enough to be of help in any man's house.

Nilkant was furious: 'But, Julia, you can't allow a stranger into our home. You don't know anything about him!'

'I thought we needed a bearer.'

Nilkant spluttered in his gin and tonic. Sometimes he felt there was an invisible wall between himself and his wife, in spite of all the barriers they had leapt to cement their relationship. She knew very well that the cook, an old retainer from his mother's house in Alipur, was responsible for selecting servants. How could an inexperienced girl from England be any kind of judge? Her pig-headedness baffled him.

'Sack him. I'm not having him in this house.'

'But you haven't even seen him. You'll agree with me, when you see him.' As usual, she was calmer than him and this only served to increase his anger, which swelled like a balloon inside his head pushing out all reason. He could hardly speak.

'You're mad.' For a moment his anger subsided as he remembered their conversation the previous evening. But then it rose again, triumphant, for he felt he understood her.

'Miss Benevolent has undertaken to solve the problems of the world by folding her downy wings round a rickshaw-wallah who says he's a bankrupt milkman, the son of a noble bearer. Let everyone follow her divine example. Love thy neighbour regardless of the fact that he's a worthless rogue. Then everyone in the world will be happy, except yourself, because your cherished object of charity has run off with all your worldly goods. For God's sake, Julia, have some sense!'

'I can't just ignore poverty when it is glaring me in the face. Just grant me this one happiness.'

Nilkant was faintly reminded of his own argument the evening before. The acquisition of a pet ultimately meant enhancing one's own happiness, but he had been unable to express it in front of Julia, her idea of happiness being somewhat different. And now he was tired – he hated the recent uneasiness that had descended between them like a damp mist, leaving a sad trail of confusion in their midst. She would have her rickshaw-wallah, he had his dog.

Afterwards, whenever friends came to dinner and remarked on the quaint bearer in the crisply starched dhoti and kurta and shiny black shoes, he could not resist drawing a parallel between the puppy that gnawed at the furniture and the bearer who served the drinks: the only drawback was that it was slightly more dangerous to keep a man as a pet than a dog.

Gradually Julia was becoming accustomed to her new life in Calcutta. The dreams of England she had frequently dreamed on first arriving – its green fields, vital freshness, comfort, peace and quiet – ceased to haunt her and she began to dream of Calcutta, her Indian friends. The heat, the dust, the din, the dirt, the smells, the crowds, the flies and the dying were no longer as startling. She no longer thought of the bearer as an impoverished rickshaw-wallah, but as a curio, the result of her English eccentricity (Nilkant would tell everyone). Yet even though the bearer was often clumsy, inept at serving drinks and despised by the other servants, she insisted on keeping him, for she felt that she could detect a goodness in him, like an enduring metal, which others failed to see.

On their first wedding anniversary, her mother-in-law gave her a necklace, heavy with gold, diamonds, emeralds and rubies. In England her only jewellery of any distinction had been a string of cultured pearls. She would have balked at wearing anything richer, but in India such a necklace only merged into inconspicuousness with the many gold-encrusted silks and sparkling jewels. She thought it looked gaudy on her austere, white neck, but refusing to wear it would prove to be another source of discord between her husband and herself. She would do her utmost to prevent another spell of unpleasantness, the previous episodes still lingering in the air like stale smoke.

Far from being an object of charity, the rickshaw-wallah had been elevated to a symbol of her own sound judgement. To hear him reproached was like receiving criticisms of herself.

One day he disappeared and was nowhere to be seen for several days. Julia had to contend with the cook's supercilious glare and Nilkant's inevitable exclamations of delight, 'See what I told you! The man is totally unreliable,' all of which served to crumble her self-esteem, making her sullen and irritable.

'I can't stand the way the cook behaves towards me!' she told Nilkant, but he was not sympathetic.

'It's all a figment of your imagination. He behaves like he has always done. It's only because you're feeling foolish yourself, that you think everyone is mocking you.'

She rebelled by refusing to be sociable in the evenings during those few days when the rickshaw-wallah was away. No gin and tonic was waiting for Nilkant when he returned home from work, because it had been the bearer's job and Julia pretended each evening that she had forgotten to pour it. Nilkant went to the club alone, for Julia said she was tired after running the house all day without proper assistance. So while he sat playing bridge at increasingly high stakes, she sat reading Rabindranath Tagore by the light of a paraffin lamp, sweating abundantly and being bitten by mosquitoes.

Julia was in no mood to conceal her triumph when the rickshaw-wallah returned a week later, his shadowed eye-sockets blackened further by bruises. His nose had been broken.

'You who have no faith!' she would be heard sighing, 'And the poor man was knocked off his bicycle by a truck! Just imagine while he was lying bleeding and neglected in some gutter, you were condemning him for his inconstancy and deviousness. You who have no faith!'

Her self-esteem, which had been squashed in the last week, rose to new and excessive heights. Julia continued to rebel. One night when Nilkant and herself were to dine at his parents' house and she had been expected to dress appropriately, she belligerently refused and wrenched off her necklace, when Nilkant's back was turned, leaving it glittering provocatively on the bed.

It was gone. The discovery knocked her breath away and she had to sit on the bed while the room span round her, until her breath came back in short, agitated pants. Panic welled inside her. She tore the sheets off the bed, crawled on hands and knees on the cold stone floor, searching for non-existent crevices, then feeling a heavy sickness clogging the pit of her stomach, she began to rummage through the drawers, scattering the contents all over the room, all the time muttering, 'O my God! O my God!' under her breath, until Nilkant found her with dishevelled hair and terrified, dilated eyes, peering into the night.

'He couldn't have taken it. He's sitting downstairs looking perfectly innocent. It could have been the cook, the dhobi, an intruder, but Christ, not him!' Seeing Nilkant's severe face, she started to cry. 'Don't call the police,' she pleaded between sobs, 'we can question him ourselves.' She reached for his hand but he flinched at her touch.

'He deserves to be whipped. That necklace had been in our

family for years. It's priceless. If anything has happened to it –'

'But you're saying he's guilty even before he's proved.'

'Of course he's guilty. It's obvious.' He clenched his fist. 'The man mysteriously disappears for seven days and comes back covered in bruises. He's in trouble and needs money. So at the first opportunity he steals.'

'But he'd be stupid to steal something like that.'

'He's a desperate man.'

'Well, we should help him then.' Julia realised that she was also talking as if his guilt was a proven fact.

Her remark further enraged Nilkant who blurted out, 'You're such a perverse little idiot. For what shallow reasons did you remove that necklace when you should have worn it to my parents' house?'

For a day the house was besieged by hordes of policemen, all intent on combing through the Bannerjee's belongings, sniffing under the furniture, or standing with expressions of great authority on their faces, but in fact having little to do or say.

The Chief Inspector, less unsavoury looking than his helpers, who would have been frightening to meet on a dark night, twirled his swashbuckling moustache in thought and asked questions such as: 'But if you please, Madam, where exactly on the bed did you deposit this necklace?' or: 'But please, Madam, why did you remove it before going out?'

Julia became more and more flustered.

Nilkant did not help either. It was as if he was inflicting his last triumphant revenge on her for having employed the rickshaw-wallah against his will. At intervals he came and sat beside her, listening to the questions, and when the police left, he said, 'I have told them about the man's suspicious behaviour,' as if he were doing her a favour.

As soon as the police set eyes on the rickshaw-wallah, having interrogated the indignant cook and cleaning women, who all threatened to leave because of the insult to their good names, they knew they had their man. He was taken away for questioning. For three days he refused to admit to the crime, but as the beatings became more persistent he gave in.

'You see, Julia,' Nilkant concluded, 'he was rotten through and through. Never think that these people will be grateful. They're just out to grab as much as they can get.'

Julia was not convinced. 'If only I hadn't left my necklace there, the poor man wouldn't have been tempted.'

For a while she was wracked by guilt. Because of her the rickshaw-wallah was now subjected to worse hardships than he could ever have known. She shuddered as she remembered the chilling stories of police brutality.

As the weeks passed, the episode was gradually consigned to hazy memory, no longer her dominant thought, as the reassuring routine of the present took over. One day when the incident was all but forgotten, the Chief Inspector rang. 'Madam, we've found your necklace,' he declared.

Julia could have cried with relief, 'Oh, thank Goodness! Where did he hide it?'

There was a long silence. 'It wasn't hidden, Madam.' The policeman paused again. 'We found it while arresting a notorious burglar who we've been hunting for several months. It looks as if it was he who committed the theft. The bearer has been released.'

'Are you sure . . . that it wasn't him?'

'Yes, Madam, quite certain. Apparently the real thief was disturbed while committing the burglary. All he had time to take was the first thing that he could find. That was the necklace on the bed.'

Putting the receiver back, Julia moved unsteadily to the window, taking long, deep breaths. Outside the night was inky black. The man was free – but she felt not a flicker of relief. Just numbness. From the neighbouring buildings emerged a concert of blaring televisions. A strong breeze wafted past her, hot, oppressive.

Suddenly Julia felt the beads of sweat prick her face. She had caught sight of something. An outline against the darkness – it appeared to move. At the gate she could make out a figure. Her heart beating loudly, she strained her eyes transfixed, unable to look away. And as she stared a pair of dark eyes met hers.

THE BEGGAR KING

Smita Bhide

The house was burning. Red flames and black flames crackled at
my feet, taunting me. Without warning, the fire leapt in the air,
hurled itself in clever acrobatics over my head, across the bannisters, down the stairs, into the kitchen. It bounced between the
walls, whooshing with glee.

Shrouded in smoke, I floated after the fire, from here to there,
this way and that, unable to catch its flickering form in my out-
stretched hands. It eluded me with skill. From deep and
cavernous depths I heard the howling of a dog, calling me.

I awoke from the dream with a nervous jolt. My skin was
soaked with sweat. From the boys' room came indistinct sounds
of crying. I sat up in bed and Dilip stirred beside me, wrestling
with the sheets.

'God, it's hot,' he murmured, half-asleep. 'You OK?'

'Arun's awake,' I said, rolling out from under the covers.

'Want me to go?' he yawned.

'No, I'll do it. He's calling for me.' I stroked his shoulder, but
he was snoring again. He could sleep through a bomb-blast.

As soon as I appeared at the doorway, Arun shrieked and hid
himself in the pillows. Nikhil, my older son, bounced out of his
bed.

'He thinks you're a ghost, Mum.'

Stumbling into the room I stabbed my heel on the metal wing

of a Thunderbird 2, discarded on the floor. I cursed silently, then tried to peel the pillow away from Arun's scrunched-up little face.

'Arun, darling, Mummy's here now.'

I aimed a kiss at his ear; he sobbed and threw himself into my arms.

'Mummy! I dreamed you were dead.'

'Well, I'm not. Now go back to sleep, both of you. Everything's OK.'

My reassurances sounded hollow, even to myself. My two sons looked at me, waiting for something better.

'I'll stay for a while,' I offered, weakly.

I climbed into Arun's bed and Nikhil scrambled in beside me. I lay between them, their heads like small damp boulders, heavy with sleep on each of my breasts. Arun continued to sob for a while, soft sounds, crusty with snot, then he became quiet and peaceful again.

I lay awake for a long while. Arun had thought I was a ghost. A presence that signified an absence. He was right.

My eyes focused on the lurid orange streetlight blooming through a gap in the dark curtains. Into my mind seeped the memory of an old game I used to play: who could hold a burning match the longest?

'You've seen him, the old tramp who walks down Blackstock Road? He wears robes and a veil, and tinsel round his head. You must have seen him, Bruce. He's so strange. He just walks and walks, straight ahead, never looks at anyone. Just straight ahead.'

Bruce sipped his pint and stared at me, his face cracking abruptly into a grin.

'Yeah, I've seen him. Cross between a sheikh and Christmas fairy. Mr Wizard.'

'I call him the Beggar-King,' I murmured.

'You would.'

1982 or '83. That night we were in the George Robey, Bruce

as usual bemoaning his fate, his lifetime of miserable relationships, crap guitars, bands that came together for a few dynamic gigs before splitting in a welter of drunken bad temper and broken promises. I sat next to him with dozens of blackened matchsticks pyred up before me. As I reached for the matchbox yet again, he grabbed my hand.

'Don't *do* that. Fucking childish.'

I wondered if he was seriously depressed, or just from force of habit.

'You shouldn't give up hope,' I opined experimentally.

'You're full of bollocks!' he shouted and everyone in the pub stared and sniggered.

He was fine.

After a pause and slightly drunk by now, I began again. 'I had this dream,' I said. 'All my teeth turned black and fell out. It was dreadful! I could feel the gaps and the blood in my mouth. Like it was really happening.'

'Look at this.'

He grabbed my hand and spat a small grey lump into my palm. It was a piece of rotted tooth.

'Ugh, you shithead!' In outrage, I flung the offending morsel on to the floor and scrubbed my hand clean on his trouser leg. He scoffed.

'Other people's nightmares,' he pronounced with grim satisfaction, 'are my reality.'

He retrieved the piece of tooth, rubbed it to a pulp between his fingertips. 'This is my life. I'm twenty-two and I'm losing my teeth. I am a fucking dog-end. Shat out of England's arse. That's me.'

'Oh, save it for a song, why don't you? I'm going to get myself a huge bag of dry-roasted peanuts. Crunch, crunch!'

'How can you be such a bitch?'

He seemed genuinely upset. I laughed cruelly. 'Just lucky, I guess.'

Geoff and Kevin were at the bar, exchanging tall tales about making it in the music business. Geoff had worked in a recording studio as a sound assistant and Kevin had once been a roadie for The Clash. Now they wanted to form their own band, or get in on somebody else's. Either way, they planned to do great things. They waved politely and made room for me at the bar, and while I waited to be served I looked around and smiled a little at people that I knew. There was a whole crowd of them there that night, all waiting for a gig to start. Reg was there, Bruce's drummer, and Simon the Sheep, his keyboards player. Simon was hopelessly in love with an older woman and had been inspired to write his first song.

'I heard you playing it the other night,' I said. 'I thought it was very good.'

They peered at me with some suspicion. I didn't often speak to any of them, and if ever I did, they would withdraw with expressions of mingled fear and curiosity. But this time I had volunteered a compliment that could not be ignored. Reg nodded courteously.

'You're right,' he said. 'You tell 'im he's good.'

He thumped Simon on the back so hard that he choked on his beer. Everyone laughed and ordered more drinks, and I wondered as I always did if I would ever feel that I belonged with all these people, the scruffy punks in their battered leather jackets and their hippy rags. I wondered if I wanted to belong. I should have wanted it. We were all runaways, after all, from the same sort of tight-lipped homes in places like Kent and Berkshire and Essex. Now we all floundered together in dirty ramshackle rooms in North London, on a diet of beer and fags, takeaways and drugs. We thought big. This wasn't how it would be for ever. Oh, no. One day, we'd be famous: musicians, rock-stars, writers, actors; it didn't matter what, so long as we were unique. Our greatest contempt was reserved for those poor drones who worked in offices, worked nine-to-five, got married, got mortgaged, two kids and a Ford Escort. Easy security till the grave closed over. We were far too sussed for that. Out in the cold where we chose to be, we pressed our noses against the panes and jeered. We were on the path to glory. We were free.

Gaz wandered up, on the scrounge for a drink. He saw me and tried to turn on the charm. I gritted my teeth and willed him to go away but he hung on for dear life. Disgusted, I gave in.

'Many thanks,' he said, swigging his whisky and ice. 'Must be my lucky day. Yup, things are definitely looking up for me. Did I tell you I've fallen in love? She's gorgeous, you should see her. Blonde hair down to here, beautiful eyes, body, the works. And mad about me. Anyway, she's getting me this job in the casino where she works. West End, big hotel. I can start as a croupier – my old man used to own a casino in Spain, so I know the ropes. I'll give it six months to earn a bit, then I'm moving to Paris. I'll make it there, no sweat. I got connections there. People who know my music. Not like this scum here.'

I looked down at the puncture marks in his forearm and thought what a sucker he was. We all were. We hadn't left the rest of the world behind in our surge towards destiny. The world had left us. We were the dregs that wouldn't be washed away.

Instantly I was ashamed of such thoughts. It felt like betraying the faith.

The pub became crowded with Irish families and grimy youths. A band was setting up on the small stage. Odours of roast dinners, sweat, patchouli. Loud laughs. The bitter smell of beer on breath. Behind me I heard Bruce greeting friends, accepting drinks. Through the crush, he reached out his hand and pinched my arm affectionately. I smiled. There was a rightness to all of this. I didn't need to pretend. I felt it then with such certainty. The reels began, the stamping and whistling and clapping in time. I crept into a corner to watch.

My arm was numb under Nikhil's head. Inch by sticky inch I pulled myself free, crawled out of bed. The boys snuggled back together as if I'd never been there at all. My nightshirt clung to my skin in the close muggy atmosphere and I grimaced as I wiped my face and neck. I was thirsty, suddenly desperate for water.

The house was quiet. Only the sounds of breathing and the distant sizzle of the traffic on the roads outside. I was no longer sleepy. I crept downstairs into the kitchen, poured Evian down my throat, reflexively opened the fridge for something to nibble. More or less empty, except for a chunk of old cake wrapped in cling film. I wrinkled my nose but ate it anyway. I was always hungry. Dilip would tease me.

'Comfort eating,' he would say. 'What is it that you're really craving for?'

It was never a serious question and I never had to offer an adequate response. But I wondered now, that sultry night in the kitchen, faced with cold cake and sleeplessness. I wondered.

Bruce walked with shoulders hunched, small fox's head poked forwards. His face was a grimace, half-suspicious, half-amused. On stage he was transformed. He howled into the mike, his brows pulled down over deep little eyes, his skinny body shaking with passion. He was an elf tormented in hell. People who saw him were genuinely moved. For the briefest moment, anything was possible. They could feel joy and it would be an honest feeling. They could feel rage and it would be a clean feeling. They could fall in love and it would be safe to feel that way. On stage, Bruce was a hero. He knew it.

'Oi!'

In the street I stopped without turning and let him catch up.

'Didn't you like the music?' he said accusingly, peeved at having to follow after me, dog-like.

'No, I did. I just wanted to come out. It was hot in there.

That's all. You didn't have to leave as well.'

'I want to talk to you some more. I can't to any of them.'

'Thought they were your friends.'

'Yeah, well, friends don't always understand, do they? Want a cup of tea?'

'Yeah, OK. But I want some chips first.'

In Bruce's room I curled up on the bed, happily munching cheese-on-toast and mopping up dollops of brown sauce with long streaks of chips. Bruce scribbled fervently in a diary, cursing at the three little kittens who clambered over the furniture, pounced at each other, knocked over books and empty beercans. He stopped and looked at me piercingly.

'What you thinking about?' he said.

I shrugged. 'Khan's given us another notice to quit. Third one. We've got a week to get out, then he's moving the builders in.'

'So you gonna go?'

'Dunno. Haven't got anywhere to go, really.'

'Nah, you'll just go back home to your family. Get an arranged marriage.'

'That's racist!'

'No! You've got a way out. A way back in. You should think yourself lucky. The rest of us haven't even got that.'

'Well, that depends what you want from life.' I was enraged with him for daring to suggest that I could capitulate so easily.

'Don't we all want the same thing? Ultimately.'

I didn't reply, swallowing my food in such big pieces that it hurt my throat. Bruce grinned his evil grin, knowing that he'd nettled me. He rolled himself a spliff and sucked on it, snorting with laughter.

'Have you heard the latest Gaz-hype?'

'What, the gambling dens of Madrid?'

'He's a wanker! He's going round telling everyone that Khan's keeping one of the new flats for him. Says he's got some banker friend of his to fix him up with a special deal on a mortgage. As if Gaz could ever know bankers. They'd think he was shit on their shoes, the bastards. Christ! Gaz lives on another fucking planet.'

'Course he does. He's jacking up.'

'Makes no difference, my dear. Gaz had smack in his brain long before he ever put it in his body.'

'Don't you think you've got to be a bit desperate to be using needles?'

He winced. 'Needles! Don't even talk about needles! Ugh. I hate the thought of pain.' He took another long drag and savoured its taste. 'Nah. I just smoke it. That's civilised.'

'If you say so.'

He handed me the spliff but it made me choke. He took it back, tutting over the waste.

'Fuck, what does any of it matter anyway? When you've got the need for something . . . Life is cheap. Gear is cheap. Make the most of it, eh?'

He picked up his guitar and strummed gently. 'Listen to this.'

It was unbearably hot. I opened a window and stood gulping the cooler air from outside. I thought I should go back to bed, try and find some rest. Minutes passed, and so did the thought. I remained where I was.

It was true that I'd done all the things I'd promised myself I would never do. But I'd never blamed myself for that. I'd wanted to be with Dilip, wanted to have children with him. I'd fallen in love with this tall gaunt man, with his laugh that made his voice crack like a boy's, with the way he kissed me, loudly smacking his lips as if he were tasting something delicious, with his nervous fizzing energy that would consume him in a flamboyant burst of activity before leaving him, spirits shrivelled, in a black pit of despair. I had understood him, what moved him, and I had loved him. And he wanted to make me happy. It should have been enough.

I thought: What ever did I lose, the loss of which was so huge that nothing after that could ever fulfil it?

Out of the sky jumped a flash of electricity, making my heart jerk with fright. I gave a nervous laugh. It was only lightning.

In Bruce's room a breeze stole in through the broken windowpanes and brushed past the windchimes. The air was filled with soft sweet sounds. It was icy cold. I shivered under a thin blanket. The stink of cat shit had kept me awake most of the night. The kittens lay twined together, snoring dreamily on a pillow by my head. At the foot of the bed was Gruff, Gaz's black dog who must have somehow sneaked into the house.

Bruce woke with a start, sat up, peered at me, sank back down again.

'Wondered who you were for a minute.'

'Starving, my name is *starving*. Have you got any food?'

'I have not. You've eaten me out of house and home! Greedy gutbucket.'

'I've got a healthy appetite, that's all. You're just a scrawny anorexic. Did you know that?'

'Why don't we just get some breakfast? I really want you to shut up.'

Outside the sky was purple, filtered by a fine mist. Blackstock Road lay empty, suspenseful. We spoke in whispers, afraid to disturb the stillness until we came to the Italian cafe, a nugget of brightness and warmth. We flung the door open into a blaze of steam and the rich greasy smell of fried bread.

Bruce nibbled dry toast, sucking it soft, gulping it down with tea. He eyed me with disdain as I swiftly consumed two plates of bacon, sausages, eggs and chips.

'Have you ever considered becoming a vegetarian?'

'You toothless git. You eat like an old man.'

'You eat like a pig.'

I cackled. 'One day, when you're famous, I'll see you on telly and you'll be so flash and so cool – and all I'll be able to think of is you sucking up your toast. A human fly. Revolting!'

He glared.

'I mean it, though,' I said, through a mouthful of egg. 'About you making it. I think you've got what it takes. Talent. Your song that you've just written – it's lovely. It's the best thing you've ever done.'

He grinned, exposing his blighted teeth, his dark blue eyes sparkling with embarrassed pride.

'Yeah, I thought you'd like that song. It's about Leslie. About the memory of her, that is. How I felt when things were good. Not that they were good that much.'

'She might hear it one day. On the radio.'

'Yeah. But she won't think, I shouldn't have left him. Will she?'

The sky gleamed with early light, its clouds ready to break with rain.

I pressed my flushed face against the cold window, trying to remember the song. A melody was there, had been for years: sparking in the back of my head but always eluding identification, never igniting any useful fuses. I think in the end I'd decided it was just some pop song with a half-catchy tune. Now that I remembered that it did indeed have a meaning for me, it worried me that I couldn't grasp the whole of the memory. But I was scared to go on. To reach the end, to gain the whole, what would that entail for me?

The window was steaming up with my breath. I rubbed it clear, squinted at the street outside.

'Bruce, look. It's him.'

Past the cafe marched a small man in flowing robes. His eyes were focused straight ahead, not to the right, not to the left. He marched towards a predetermined goal. He never varied the pace of his stride. He knew where he was going.

'Yeah, right. It's your King of the Beggars.'

We rushed into the street.

'He's gone.'

Racing down Blackstock Road, we caught a glimpse of him turning the corner, heading up to Stoke Newington.

'I wonder why he dresses like that?' I panted.

'Because he's *poor*,' sneered Bruce, who loathed physical exertion of any kind.

That morning the Beggar-King was swathed in a length of red velvet, cloaked across his shoulders by a scrap of sparkly gold fabric. Around his head was a cardboard headband with a gold star pinned to the front.

'He must be Greek or Turkish. I wonder what he does.'

I slowed down to walking pace so that he wouldn't notice us. 'I've never actually seen him beg. It's just a name. I mean, he looks too proud to *beg*, don't you think? I've never even seen him talk to anyone. He's just – inscrutable.'

Bruce snorted and rubbed a painful stitch in his side. 'He's just a headcase.'

We emerged into Green Lanes. The sky grew brighter, watery sunlight over a chill wind. Traffic roared. 'The Beast London awakes,' said Bruce. 'God, I hate this city.'

'Would you go home if you could?'

'This is my home now. I got nowhere to go back to. Anyway, everything is here. The band. Opportunities. It won't happen anywhere else. If it happens at all.'

The Beggar-King put on speed. Again, we had to run to keep up with him: past the park, down Church Street, into Albion Road.

'Oi,' gasped Bruce. 'Are you gonna try and talk to him, or what?'

'I don't know. I never thought about it.'

Bruce came to a brutish standstill. 'You stupid *tart*. You've dragged me out here for *nothing*.'

'He's *gone*. I don't believe it. That was your fault, distracting me with your whining . . .'

On Newington Green, people came down out of the big Victorian houses, now converted into smart flats. They climbed into small, expensive cars and drove off, smartly.

'Yuppie bastards!' spat Bruce. 'Let's go home.'

'Got him.'

The Beggar-King appeared from a side-street at the far corner of the Green, then vanished again down an alleyway.

'You're as fucking mad as he is,' said Bruce as I ran in pursuit, pulling him by the arm.

We never found the Beggar-King. We combed the backstreets of Old Shacklewell and Canonbury. We caught a glimpse of tinsel, the flutter of a red velvet cloak; the cold streets shone with the mystery of his passing but he never appeared to us again that day.

We collapsed on the pavement, our heels in the gutter.

'We'll see him again,' I vowed. 'We'll be ready for him next time. We'll catch him and make him tell us what he knows.'

'Bet he doesn't even speak English,' said Bruce nastily. 'I've had enough of your bullshit. You make my stomach churn.'

And he set up coughing convulsively, regurgitating the phlegm of years and years of concentrated bodily abuse. I gazed at him, at his white twisted face, his streaming eyes. He would go no further with me. That much I knew.

When we arrived back in Blackstock Road, the house where I lived was on fire. Geoff and Simon, blackened with smoke, stumbled out with a set of drums. Kevin and his girlfriend Monique came to help, Gaz came, and a whole crowd of people, ducking in and out of the flames, the filthy suffocating fumes, yelling and cursing as we all tried to salvage as much as we could. As I hurried down the stairs for the last time, a crest of fire burst across the bannisters and pounced on the sleeve of my coat. I stood transfixed, watching the flames chew up the length of my arm. Kevin at the foot of the stairs roared with fear, bounded up towards me, pulled off the coat, pulled me out of the house. With a horrific crash the staircase caved in behind us.

Kevin, nearly crying, yelled at me: 'You dozy slag! You could've killed us both!'

'That was my only coat,' I muttered but no one was interested. Most people were in tears as they watched the house.

'This is Khan's doing,' said Bruce. 'He wanted you lot out and he's got the insurance as well. Cunning old bastard.'

He turned and looked me up and down. No coat, burnt boots, a carrier bag stuffed with singed clothes. That was me.

'So where you gonna go?'

I couldn't reply. The enormous and terrible loss of my home had finally begun to sink in.

He looked into my face and added casually: 'You can kip over at mine for a while. If you want. It's up to you.'

I stared at the ground for a long time, munched on my lower lip. Prolonging the end would never have worked. Bruce wrinkled his brow, annoyed at my silence.

'No,' I blurted out before he could speak again. 'No, thanks. I'll find somewhere. It's OK.'

In the middle of the crowd sat Gaz, miserably hunched on the pavement. His dog had been trapped in the house. It must have followed him in; he'd heard it barking somewhere but hadn't been able to find it. Sometime later, they carried out its charred little corpse.

My nightmare in a burning house. The song. Another life lived long ago. These things had always been there, fragments that I could piece together, make shapes with, of all different sorts. There were possibilities in those days; but no more so than now.

When I was young I believed that I could have anything I

wanted in the world, for no other reason than that I desired it keenly enough. My life was empty so I infused it with significance far beyond its meagre reality. I created a potential for miracles and lived only for that: for the promise that hovered at the corner of my eye, whispered in the margins of my waking hours and glimmered most tangibly in cold mornings such as this, before sunrise, before the real day. What that promise offered could never be possessed. That was the whole pure beauty of it. And it hadn't been lost.

Silently I tiptoed back upstairs and got dressed. Dilip didn't even stir. I packed some clothes into a large carryall, paused only for a second to look at his thin sleeping face. I wondered if he would forgive me. I left him a short letter, asking him to find it in his heart to do just that.

Dizzy with excitement, I crept down the hall and peered in at the boys. Their little mouths were puffed with sleep; I wanted to kiss them but didn't dare wake them; for a moment I almost changed my mind.

I couldn't believe I was doing this, not even as I shut the front door behind me and felt the first drops of rain speckle my face, bringing a sense of utter relief from the heat. I smiled and at the same time, wept. I hadn't lost my chance after all. It hadn't passed me by. It had waited for me, all these years, until I'd finally managed to catch up with it.

'Sometimes, when I'm dreaming, sometimes, sends me reeling, when I think of you, so close to me, what could we do, what could we be . . .'

Bruce's little song warbled in my head as I set off down the road. I walked as if to some predestined goal, my eyes focused straight ahead, not to the right, not the left. I walked like the Beggar-King.

MANO SHANTHI

···◆···

Preethi Manuel

To Prabhakar annan – your inspiration lives on

The bitterness was gathering inside, like a mushrooming mould that had grown uncontrollable over the past few weeks. A mixture of anger, disappointment and frustration. Annama felt the churning in her stomach as she saw the disappearing silhouettes of the three men walking huddled together, briefcases in hand. It had been another frayed meeting. Why, why did they always have the upper hand? The powerful hand of money, grants, funding. Mano Shanthi, the counselling centre for black people, from where Annama looked out through an askew space between the advice posters on the shop window, now only revealing an endless flow of stop-and-start traffic on the busy Kilburn High Road.

Annama recalled the early days, five years ago, when the centre was set up by a small grant from the Ethnic Minorities Unit. Who could have predicted then that Mano Shanthi would become a flagship voluntary organisation for counselling black people? Whatever its present strength, it was hardly a match for the bunch of power-wielding local council bureaucrats who had recently taken to visiting it, adept at flexing their muscles, especially when it came to curbing Labour-controlled funding. There were clear signals that Mano Shanthi was likely to be jeopardised at the slightest shift in the impending local elections. A precarious position. Balancing people's minds was more tangible, reminisced Annama, than holding on to an ephemeral vision of justice and equality which was increasingly losing popularity.

She picked on the *mittai* pink embroidery on her black polyester *shalwaar*. At twenty-nine, a dark and slender bloom of a woman who had left Kerala in South India as a nine-month-old baby in her mother's arms, Annama did fleetingly imagine herself in other jobs if only to be impressing her parents now retired near Mudumalai wild-life sanctuary. 'Our daughter in London is training to be a barrister,' or 'Oh, but our daughter's teaching English to the English!' But never for long. Once she had gone 'temping' in her holidays and worked as an administrator at Albert and Arthur Constructions. There were four men in a tiny little but exorbitantly expensive office space off the Strand They had all sat there in the same space for no less than seven years each. And one of them even smoked a cigar. Suffocating, sterile and passionless? She would rather be bungee-jumping in Oxford.

As if trying to close her wandering thoughts, Annama quickly tidied up her desk which, despite several attempts, always carried paperwork four piles high. The aftermath of the meeting had left a strange almost foreboding feeling in the crammed office space. The only redeeming feature amidst the dark wood furniture, woodchip wallpaper and untidy paper management were the anglepoise lamps lending a hazy glow which, if Annama had stopped to watch, had an almost romantic feel. But she was going to sweat this one out till tomorrow. She would follow the evening rush-hour traffic, the greyness and the red and white tail lights to Swiss Cottage Sports Centre, to a swimming-pool that would drown her rising tides. At least till tomorrow.

You could say that the swim had had little effect, or whatever effect it had had not lasted long, because the next day Annama was in relentless spirit. Why had Trevor not been there? At least Sandra had an excuse: her littlest one was then recovering from having accidentally tipped the washing up liquid into his mouth.

'Were you on a date or what?' asked Annama accusingly. Trevor, the smooth talker, answered with a furrowed forehead across his Trinidadian face, a shrug, and a woman's smile. Trevor with whom she had sneaked a night of passionate embraces, and nothing more, after a bhangra do to raise money for their photocopier. 'Don't leave it all to the founder members,' she had hissed. 'We are already balancing six pots of water on our heads.' 'What water?' Trevor had asked. That is when Neelam walked in.

'Can I speak to someone?' asked this barely 13-year old Indian girl with wavy shoulder-length hair cut squarely with a straight fringe that rounded her Dravidian brown face. A dark blue skirt and blazer over a loose-fitting white shirt, fake leather duffle bag dangling over her shoulder. She stood holding the door half-open, her deeply set moist eyes settling hesitantly on Annama. If the girl had looked more closely, she would have noticed that the sign on the pane-glass door read 'Closed'. Wednesday was Mano Shanthi's staff management day – strange title for a series of heated exchanges more akin to stock-car racing than anything else. However, it was a day away from the busy schedule of client counselling. But there was something alluring about such an interruption.

Annama gave a quick glance to Trevor and then to Sandra, who was hovering around a steaming kettle in the far corner of the open-plan office. No one objected. 'Tea?' called out Sandra. 'No thanks,' came the quiet reply from Neelam. Annama accompanied her to her desk. Neelam's movements were poised and self-assured as she sat facing Annama.

'Actually my teacher asked me to come here,' she ventured. When Annama mentioned that they were not normally open for the public today, there wasn't a sign of apology. It was almost as if Neelam had found the right person to unburden her story to and was going to do it anyway.

Neelam had been feeling sick and throwing up. Twice she had

left school to come home to rest. It was frightening coming home. 'Cause my mum died there a couple of months ago,' she said in response to Annama's interruption. Neelam's eyes flicked down momentarily, her lips pursed on one side. Annama slowed down her line of questioning from then on.

As she listened to the girl, slowly, in painful detail after detail, tell of the events that led to her mother's death by cancer, Annama could not but help feel a surge of responsibility for the fate of this young teenager on whom adulthood had been thrust so prematurely. For a 13-year-old she was immeasurably self-controlled. Although her voice and gaze had wavered, she had not shed a single tear.

The rest of the story was perplexing to say the least. Her doctor had seen her and said everything was OK except that she should rest. She had no boyfriends, never smoked or drank and hardly went out on her own. Her older sister, Kavita, was studying at college and had had to leave the day before her mother's cremation to sit her exams. At first Neelam did not sleep very well but it was getting better. She missed her Mum. Her Dad was very busy and didn't have much time for her.

Neelam stopped, as if she'd come to a natural end. Her fingers, which had till now been playing with her nails, were now digging into them. Annama's mind was whizzing around like a fruit-machine gone crazy. But nothing seemed to add up. Last night's meeting with the council officers was lingering in her mind, dulling her sharpness. The only thing she held on to was her belief in this young girl's story.

'I am going to try and help you, Neelam,' reassured Annama, 'because you're not OK.' Neelam listened with her big eyes, hands relaxing. 'But first I want you checked out thoroughly. Not at your doctor's but at hospital. Just to be safe. If I write a letter, will you take it to your doctor?'

Neelam nodded.

'I'm pleased your teacher told you to come here.'

'I think she thought my problems were cultural or something,' responded Neelam. For the briefest moment, Annama caught the flicker of her smile.

'How many are you left with?' Trevor was asking her.

'Thirteen.'

'How about if I take a couple of yours?' suggested Sandra. Sandra was the oldest worker there and the only one with children. She came from a Welsh mining family, a resolute, kindly woman with a penchant for legal peccadilloes.

'Did you know it's illegal to offer alcohol to your child at home until she's five?' ventured Sandra.

Trevor chuckled.

Annama was keen to move on to the issue of funding. If she had been dragging an unwilling horse to water she would have had more luck. 'Honestly,' she huffed, 'next time the likes of Sumanth Kumar and Clive Whatsits want to discuss "options" and "viability", you attend. Just leave me out, OK? We've got fifty clients sitting waiting on us to get a chance, sometimes the last chance, to get a grip on their lives, and when their lifeline's threatened, all you do is bloody . . .' She didn't wait to finish before her exit.

As it was only the two of them, Sandra could not help feeling mischievous. 'Did you know what Mano Shanthi means?' she teased. 'Our peace.'

'Our peace!!' the two chorused, in raucous laughter.

The following week Annama was counselling an elderly Chinese woman whose son had been 'sectioned' when the internal phone buzzed. It was Sandra. Could she take an emergency call from Dr Davies? Dr Davies? Oh, yes, Neelam Pillai's doctor. 'We appear to have located the problem,' said this authoritative female voice, 'but because of its confidential nature I need to make an appointment to see the girl myself.' Annama smiled an apology to her client while alarm bells were deadening her ears.

This could only mean one thing. *No, it can't be true. I can't be betrayed by this fledgling of a woman.* Through the rounded mellow face of Chin Ling sitting opposite her, through her pale sallow skin, slightly chapped lips and eyes pleading from their shallow orbit, the image of Neelam emerged time and time again, a hunted, haunted look, tricking your senses to distraction. Annama was glad the day ended early. She pulled out a sachet of fresh coffee from her handbag and sat sipping its aroma, hoping to dilute her thoughts.

It was Trevor who'd picked up the local newspaper. Labour had lost a couple of seats but they were still in control. 'Listen to this one,' he said, leaning his five foot eight torso against a table, 'Sumanth Kumar's heading the Policy and Resources Committee.'

Sandra linked eyes with Annama. Everyone knew Sumanth Kumar to be something of a hatchet man, articulate and ruthless – formidable qualities for aspiring local council leaders.

'Three million cuts over the next two years – it'll be a piece of cake to him,' pronounced Sandra, tilting her head back and punching out the numbers for her early morning round of calls.

'Nice touch,' sneaked in Annama, 'getting a black man to cross swords with the likes of Mano Shanthi.' She paused for thought before opening the door to the queue of clients waiting in the crisp cold, faces etched with a mixture of anxiety and gratefulness.

Late into the morning, Annama felt unable to extricate her thoughts from the meeting with Neelam. For some strange reason, the thoughts seemed too real to be imagined. By chance she glanced to one side of the faded room-divider only to catch a glimpse of a familiar figure walking hesitantly past the centre. There was no mistaking it. It was Neelam. Annama ushered her in, the young girl looking visibly shaken. A surge of emotion swept through Annama, like a tide enveloping a shore. Whatever thoughts she had of being betrayed melted into one look of anguish from Neelam.

'Neelam, you've not told me the full story.'

'No, I've just been to my doctor,' she began in a wavering voice. 'And she accused me of lying about my boyfriend.' Her eyes welled up. 'I've, I swear I've never had a boyfriend.' The tears rolled down in heavy beads, words falling out mangled in emotion. 'I'm not pregnant – no one, no man had ever touched me like that.'

Annama decided at this point that some going over familiar ground would not be amiss. 'Tell me about your mother's death,' she said, 'tell me what happened.'

This had the effect of diverting Neelam's attention and she began in short choked sentences, containing her emotion. When she came to the details of the night before the cremation, there was some hesitation.

'Were you afraid to sleep because you knew her body was downstairs?' prompted Annama.

It was then that the floodgates opened. 'Everyone else, Aunt Shreela and . . . everyone had gone home. I was upstairs in my bedroom. Crying on my pillow. Then the stairs light came on. I heard him come up the stairs, slow and heavy. But he stopped just outside my bedroom.'

'Who?'

'My Dad.'

Annama clenched her insides. The wound had burst and blood was gushing out. It was everywhere. Red, thick and luminous. A young life hanging, clinging, dangling from the corner of a high ceiling, pitching, pining voice mercilessly crushed. The gentle sobs from Neelam's heaving chest echoed into a thundering howl, bellowing the room to bursting point.

Annama held her close, arm tight around her sobbing shoulder, pushing back hair, damp and tangled with tears. When Neelam finished, the screeching inside mellowed, the room subsided, followed by a gentle envelope of calm, like the aftermath of a storm.

Annama went back to her chair. She had never been in a position where she had had to suggest abortion to a 13-year-old. But nothing she had in mind could have prepared her for what was to follow.

'He never said a word the next day – just went off to his council meetings like nothing had happened. He was even in the papers 'cause he got promoted.'

'Do you want to say . . .'

But Neelam volunteered: 'Sumanth Kumar, you know . . .'

If Annama had fallen off a ship at this point, she would have allowed the weight of the water to engulf her, let her sink down to the underworld, never face the terror of knowing life again but she was on ground and she had to fight. 'You will be OK,' ventured Annama weakly, 'but it will take time, a long time maybe.'

Annama liaised with the GP, who was somewhat offbeat. 'I must confess I did not get the impression that such things happened in Asian families.'

Annama stayed with Neelam for the afternoon of the abortion. Neither school nor home knew. The ward smelt strangely of bleach and overheating. Neelam was feeling weak and propped up on pillows when a woman was doing the rounds offering free condoms. Annama went up to her. 'There will be no need for bed no. 22,' she said firmly, coming back to hold Neelam's hand. Tightly.

A few weeks later, Sumanth Kumar was at the centre. He and three of his colleagues put forward a proposal suggesting that Mano Shanthi merge with the local hospital and provide a service for referrals from GPs. The air was charged again with attacks and counter-attacks. Annama watched Sumanth – same colouring as Neelam and the faintest family resemblance in the high cheek-bones. For anyone else, a handsomely turned out

40-year-old, and rising entrepreneur. Annama gazed at his hands gesticulating with confidence when the churning feeling began again in the pit of her stomach.

At the end of the meeting, nothing had been resolved but no one could counter with equal vigour their arguments on finance. Amidst the petty talk that followed and the snapping of brief-cases, Annama felt she was not being heard when she asked Sumanth Kumar if she could have a quiet word with him. But he had heard and their eyes met. She led him towards her table and brought out Neelam's file.

'This . . . is confidential. I didn't connect because of the sur-names. But my client – your daughter Neelam – she has decided that you should read it.' She heard him say something, felt the anxiety in him rising as he half-opened the file to catch a glimpse of its contents, a darting of his eyes, a sudden change of compo-sure. Annama stood resolute and despite her pounding heart ventured, 'When you think you are ready for a meeting, we . . . we will be waiting.'

When some days later Trevor was jubilant on opening a letter from the Policy and Resources Committee saying Mano Shanthi's funding was to continue unaltered, Annama merely gave a measured smile. Casting her eyes down, they rested on the new and coded name added that morning to her client list.

RAIN

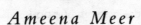

Ameena Meer

Crossing the street on a steamy grey day in September, Zerina feels as if she's walked into a memory of last summer in Delhi, the last few days before the monsoon. When the air was thick and hot, tension building in the clouds and in her forehead, where the humidity made her sinuses swell and block, so that she could barely see a few feet ahead of her.

Still the grumbling clouds hold back, occasionally letting go a thunderclap or a flash of lightning like a stinging slap across someone's cheek, a sharp insult that cuts through the skin. There is no release, just a regathering of explosive anger, like a mad woman screaming down a carpeted hallway.

The sweat gathers on the back of her neck, under her thick black hair, steaming her face, each wiry hair sticking to her fingers when she tries to brush it off.

On the subway, she has the bad luck of getting into an un-airconditioned car and the air is more suffocating than ever, the heat holding the smells of the bodies around her: sweat, deodorant, stale cigarette smoke, old hamburgers. Someone stands up as she gets in and she squeezes in between an old Chinese man, curled like a shrimp over the shopping bag he clutches in his tiny hands, and a hugely fat woman, her body overflowing into the seats beside her. No one ever rushes at rush hour.

Zerina presses her fingers into her forehead, wonders if

Gianlucca is going to call her. Wonders if she should call him. Wonders why all the men she gets involved with lately are married, or have relationships that date back more than half the length of her life.

As she squeezes herself back up to get off the train, her elbow digs into the soft breast of the fat woman and Zerina turns, as well as she can in the throngs of people, and says, 'Sorry, I'm really sorry.'

And the woman says, 'It's all right, it's all right. We're all stuck here.' Her West Indian accent is like molasses poured over the words. Zerina suffers an imaginary jab in her own breast as she walks through the turnstile.

On the sidewalk, even the feeble breeze off the ice in the Korean market is refreshing. But it's gone in four short steps across the concrete.

The humidity makes the lock stick on the door of her apartment. The key won't turn at all. She tries to force it, but her wrist aches, evidence of what a bad typist she is. Four hours on the computer and she can't unlock her door, all the veins are blue and bulging on her hand. The phone starts ringing inside. She drops her bag and all her books on the doormat and uses both hands and the force in both arms to twist and pull at the same time. She stops struggling for a minute, realising the futility of her efforts, and strains her ears to hear the muffled voice on the answering machine. 'Zerina, this is Gianlucca.' She shakes the door violently and it pops open like a vacuum lid. 'Madonna, I'm sorry you're not at home. I forgot – I told Melissa that I'd take her to a movie tonight. So we meet tomorrow, all right? Tomorrow night at seven.' Zerina stands in the doorway thinking how bloody liberated she is. The answering-machine clicks off, beeps, rewinds.

The apartment is hot, stifling with the smell of cooking – oil, garlic, cumin and onions from last night's curry. Zerina picks up her stuff and dumps it all on the floor on the other side of the door. The smell is unbearable. She runs to the windows, throwing them open with the strength she lacked earlier. One crashes against the other, a sharp crack cutting down the centre of the glass. 'Cheap glass.' She turns the fan on. She spins the taps to full blast so water ricochets off the dirty dishes and sprays greasy yellow spots all over her white T-shirt. 'Goddam it.' She gulps the water. It's still lukewarm.

Zerina spreads the newspaper out on the table and tries to read about the Middle East. Instead, she keeps seeing Prashant's face from last summer. The way he looked lying on his back, his big belly spreading and rising like a loaf of bread as she sat on top of him.

She stroked his stomach in smooth little circles, following the pale brown hairs around his nipples. Eventually, she'd slide off on to the bed and he'd roll over on his side, his stomach spilling forwards and his long hair draping his round shoulders and his beard covering his chest. With one arm under his head, the other tapping the bedcover and his chubby legs curled underneath him, he looked like a cartoon of a fat little sultan by a perverse Orientalist. She'd get up and smile at him as she threw her kurta on, in a careless, swinging movement that was unfamiliar. She suddenly felt a strange narcissistic pleasure in her own young body: pleased with her hard breasts and strong arms. She'd worked hard on her body this summer. As the hem of the kurta dropped down over her stomach, lightly tanned from mornings at the beach, she'd walk slowly across the room, each step stretching and coiling the muscles from her feet to her buttocks, like a cat.

'Mm,' he'd say, stroking his hair, 'this is perfect.'

And outside in the garden, through a crack in the window, she'd hear the sound of the sparrows and pigeons and the breeze ruffling the leaves of the trees. She could almost feel the sunlight warming the top of her head even in the curtained bedroom. She'd laugh and say, 'Of course, it is.' And she realised that she always liked a scene best if she could make it into a tableau she understood, if she could step outside and see how it looked. How she looked standing there in the doorway, the light seeping through her tissue-thin shirt: the pretty young woman and the decadent old man; wished for a minute that she was really young enough and stupid enough to believe the fantasies he'd spin out, pretty enough to make it last.

And then, faster than she can sort out – trains, planes and buses blurring into a smear of prepackaged meals and uncomfortable nights – bang, she is back in New York, the summer drawing to a hot, cloudy close. Prashant seems to have already lost interest in her, all his plans for their future obviously forgotten – she's more stupid than she guessed. He's brusque and rude on the phone. She can imagine his eyes blank and still beneath the thick eyelashes, his fingers drumming again, hard against the table, an impatient tattoo. The only thing making the painfully long days at her temp job bearable is the air-conditioning.

The sweat on her hands is making the newspaper pages stick to them. She peels the paper off her palm and takes another gulp of water. Her fingers leave inky prints on the glass. She picks up the telephone, presses two digits and puts it down. 'Not yet,' she warns herself. She rubs the fingerprints off the receiver with the edge of her T-shirt. Then she picks it up again.

Her mother's voice on the line, warm and fragrant even five thousand miles away, says, 'Hello, darling, why do you sound so unhappy?'

Zerina tries to stop herself. She says, 'Oh, it's the weather . . .'

But her mother is already off, saying, 'I just wish you would stop wasting your life and come home. Of course, you're unhappy. Living on your own like that. Why don't you get married? You know, your reputation is going to be completely spoiled.'

Zerina stares at her blank white walls. A little rivulet of sweat drips down her back, tickling her spine like the feet of an insect.

A cockroach drops off the ceiling and hits the table with a click.

Her mother is saying, 'And if you keep refusing proposals like this, people are just going to say you're too fussy. Look, there's this young economist, Ayesha's brother, he's very, very bright, from what I've been told. He's doing well, he's the top of his group, one of the rising stars in the development organisation. Don't you want to get married?'

'OK, I'll meet him,' Zerina smashes the cockroach between the pages of the newspaper.

'But are you serious? You can't just keep meeting them. You've got to take it seriously.'

'If you mean, do I want to marry him without meeting him, then, no,' she massages her forehead again. 'I can't meet someone twice or three times and be able to marry him. I just can't do it.'

'Well, how do you think arranged marriages work?' Something tickles, a cockroach is climbing through the hair on her forearm. Zerina flicks it off, shuddering. She jumps up and crushes the roach with her shoe as it tries to scurry across the floor. 'What are you doing? Aren't you listening to me?'

'All right, OK. I'll do it,' Zerina says. She has another sip of water and pulls up her T-shirt and wipes the perspiration off her upper lip. 'How are you?'

'I'm fine. We went to a dinner at the Australian Embassy last night. Everyone was asking about you. I missed you so much. Why don't you just come home? Isn't it nicer to be with us?'

'I miss you, too, Mum. And I love you.' Zerina thinks of the electricity around her mother, like the smell of her red lipstick, as she's getting dressed to go out at night and then of Gianlucca's kisses, which are hard. His teeth bite into her lips and the skin around her mouth, leaving red marks on her face and the salty taste of blood on her tongue. The receiver slides smoothly into its holder.

The loose tiles in the bathroom crack under the heels of her shoes. Zerina wipes a layer of white plaster dust off the toilet seat.

Two more days for the sink. One more day until she has a working shower. Only one more slow thick day, the sweat shining like polish on her forehead. Her shorts drop around her ankles and she steps out of them, leaving her shoes underneath. She lets her T-shirt fall beside the shorts, enjoying the cushion of soft cotton against the soles of her feet before they touch the gritty floor.

Naked in the kitchen, Zerina washes all the pots and pans. The soapy, greasy water splashes her chest and stomach. When she's finished, she scrubs herself. On full blast for twenty minutes and the water's still not cold, but with the fan blowing across her back, her skin feels almost cool, a slight shiver on the back of her neck. She pours dripping handfuls of water over herself. She wiggles her toes in the puddles they make around her feet. When she stops, the wooden floorboards are soft and swollen with water. She opens the refrigerator, the blast of cold air making goosebumps rise on her wet skin. Standing there, her back against the eggs and the butter tray, she drinks the milk straight out of the carton, in long gulps that seem to rise from her fingertips to her forehead.

Zerina lies in the middle of the living-room carpet. The fan whirs. Its head turns back and forth, sweeping air in sheets across her body. She closes her eyes.

She wakes to the sound of the phone ringing. In the darkness, she thinks it's her alarm clock. She jumps up, trying to silence it. The receiver bumps off. 'Hello? Hello?' says a tiny voice.

'Hi,' croaks Zerina, the heat making it almost impossible for her to move. Her body is slippery with sweat.

'Madonna, you were sleeping . . .'

'Mm,' Zerina rubs her eyes. Bits of dirt and hair from the carpet stick to her arms and shoulders, sprinkling her face as she moves.

'Were you dreaming about me?' The room is alternately pink and green from the flashing neon lights across the street.

'I don't remember.'

'Listen, Zerina, I want to see you.'

'Tomorrow. At seven.' She stretches and rolls on to her stomach, brushes the fuzz off her bottom. A sudden breeze blows the newspaper across the room.

'Now, baby. I want to see you now. Melissa and I – I don't know, I'm crazy.'

'Oh,' Zerina's pulse thumps in her wrist, her breath quickens. 'What happened?' She imagines her fingers digging into the muscles on his shoulders, his neck, feels his tongue in her ear. Her skin tingles. She wishes he were here already. A page of newspaper flies over her leg. She holds her breath.

'She's jealous. She's always jealous, always thinking I'm betraying her with every woman I know. Forget it, Zerina. I just want to see you.'

'She's got good reason to be.'

'She doesn't understand me like you. I'm at a pay phone, Zerina – I'll be there in twenty minutes.' A lightning bolt illuminates the room like an electric light, the crash of thunder like the switch clicking off.

'You just had a fight with your fiancée and you're coming over here?'

'We'll just talk,' pleads Gianlucca.

'Gianlucca, I'm tired and – no. I'm not dressed.'

'That's how I like you.'

'I'll see you tomorrow, all right? Don't worry, it'll work out. OK? Sleep well.' The newspapers thrash around the room. Zerina remembers the heart-shaped face of Prashant's wife smiling out of a photograph on his desk.

The phone starts ringing again, making the floorboards vibrate. Three loud blasts through the room, then a pause. The code she and Prashant made up for each other. It rings again. Zerina picks up the receiver and twists the cord around her hand. One quick snap. Tiny sparks hiss off the coloured wires.

Suddenly, the room rings with silence. The apartment feels

remote and abandoned. Prashant's fading voice echoes, bounces from the corners to the high ceilings.

Zerina takes a breath and the gulp of air washes into her, fresh and cool.

She hears the clicking on the fire escape. First, small, hesitant taps. Then the wind slows, sucking in a long deep breath, before letting go. Torrents of rain pour down like overturned buckets. The water hits the metal, hanging on the railings like strips of torn cloth, before splashing down on to the sidewalk below.

Zerina gets up and climbs out of the window.

DEATH RITES

···◆···

Maya Chowdhry

Varanee sits holding Alex's hand, he cocks his ear as if he can hear the sound of Buddhist chanting but it's inside his head. Alex gently opens his eyes, his eyelashes fluttering, and beckons for Varanee's ear.

Alex whispers, 'Let's have some monks chanting for the service, perhaps at the wake too. Better than piped orchestral.'

Varanee sits bolt upright and wonders: Maybe death brings some psychic awareness, maybe he saw the book; I thought he'd gone blind. Varanee looks at the book, *The Tibetan Book of The Dead*, puzzled.

The room is the white-wall sterile type found in most hospitals; you'd think they'd have primrose yellow, or white with a hint of blue, just to get away from that 'you'll be dead soon' feeling when you look at the walls.

Alex leans over and feels the cloth Varanee's wearing; it's rough cotton.

'Stop wearing that white sari,' Alex mumbles. 'Men wear kurta pyjama and anyway I'm not ready for white yet.'

Varanee ignores him and picks up the book.

Alex continues, 'And the nurse said, meditation or no meditation no more candles, it's a fire hazard.'

Varanee still ignores him, he's not listening, his mind seems elsewhere in memories and other places.

Varanee returns, 'Shall I read it to you?' and when Alex nods he begins: 'Your Bardo body seems much like your human body, but it has certain forms of perfection. It is born of hopes and desires and signs of what is to come.'

Desires, Varanee thinks to himself, recalling a conversation with Avani. And suddenly before he knows it he's thinking out loud.

'Avani said I was vain.'

Alex interrupts, remembering Avani in drag at the Khush Klub swanning around in a scarlet sari and gold slippers: 'What does he know?'

Varanee continues: 'He also said that he was bisexual because he'd been a woman in his last life. I said, "Well, honey, I'm a man and a woman in this life so what was I in my last life?" and he said, "Confused." '

Alex starts to laugh and then cough, his fragile flesh sagging around his ribs as he convulses. He spits out.

'Don't make me laugh, I'm not up to it.' Varanee smiles and Alex doesn't react. Varanee thinks to himself, he really can't see. Varanee's eyes drop and Alex can't see that either.

Varanee continues to read to Alex, 'Look at the bodies of your friends; they are dying, help them. See their imperfection, do not die with them.'

'That's not in the book,' Alex mumbles.

'I know, it's a thought I had,' Varanee replies.

'Read then,' Alex whispers, squeezing his hand impatiently.

But Varanee is lost in another death memory.

' "Look for your womb door," I said to Steve as he lay gasping for his last breath, and he spat out: "I'm taking the one marked Club Fuck," and I said, "No, not that kind of a door." And before I could explain he coughed and departed from this world. Into Club Fuck I suppose, to be reincarnated as a bouncer; he always said they got the best pick.'

Light cuts through the blinds from the streetlights outside. In the dark the orange shafts of lights streak the bed. At least the room's more colourful now, Varanee thinks to himself. Varanee lights an incense stick and wafts it around the room.

'Have you been farting, Alex? It pongs in here.'

Alex ignores him and turns away. Varanee tries to take his hand, Alex pulls it away.

'I didn't mean . . .' Varanee stumbles.

'It's the smell of decay,' Alex whispers, his breath hissing through his teeth.

'Don't say that.' Varanee knows he didn't think before he spoke; he knows he has to get used to what to say to the dying. They worked so hard in their relationship not to be dysfunctional, to be honest, and now it was all being thrown out the window as he tiptoed around the 'words to say to the dying'.

'The truth is another's lie. Finish the book, there's not much time,' Alex breaks through his thoughts, wondering what to say when you've not much time left to say it, wanting to say a lifetime of words when you don't know if you'll have a week, an hour, a minute, how long, and what do you say?

Varanee interrupts Alex's thoughts, 'Don't worry, you don't have to – I mean, you can – I mean, I can read it after, if necessary, after, you know . . .' and even he can't say the specific words, the ones they avoid in every conversation, the words around are easier like, 'will', 'funeral', but not that word.

'I think I'll absorb it better if I'm alive, don't you?' Alex says, trying to sound cheerful, to match the emphasis on the word 'alive'. Alive, that word's easier to say than its opposite.

Varanee continues to read, 'Approaching your womb door, you will see signs of the continent of your next birth. If you are to be born a pleasure-seeking god, you will see temples full of gold jewels. Enter there if you can.'

'And I thought I was a pleasure-seeking god in this life,' Alex croaks.

At work they found out Alex had it because he was off sick,

and finally he had to tell them. It leaked out like tear gas, filling every corner of the office. The woman across the hall picked up his drawings with marigold rubber gloves on. Then, Sorry we have to let you go, not enough work. And even if he'd had the energy to fight them because it was discrimination, what was the point?

I sat holding his hand, he was sobbing and I was reading a chapter from Louise Hay's *You Can Heal Your Life*, pausing in between paragraphs to pass him tissues. 'Let's do some affirmations,' I said. 'No,' he said, 'I'm sick of theory.' We lay on the floor kissing until the tears stopped and daylight had evaporated. We lay in the dark, the silence like death's shadow.

Varanee walks out of the hospital room. For hours it seems he's been walking down long white-walled corridors, suddenly a trolley whizzes by him; lying on it is a woman covered in blood, blood splashes on his hand as she passes. He stares at his hand thinking, 'Is it absorbing into my pores, whose blood is it?' It begins to dry. He retraces his steps around the corner.

The doctor pulls the curtain around the blood-stained woman. Varanee looks at his hand again and mutters to himself.

'This is the dried blood of a dead woman.' Varanee faces the wall whispering, 'I couldn't get any of them to take me seriously, the others, I mean. When Billy had lost his sight I would sit and read to him and he would say not that death book again. Let's have *Ecstatic Pleasures of a Swimming Pool-Attendant*. And I would say, "It's called *The Tibetan Book of the Dead*, and it's important and you should listen, it'll help." And he'd squeeze my hand and say, "If you insist," and I did. "Your suffering is due to your own bad karma, nothing more. Meditate on your guru." "You're my guru," he would say, and I replied, "Okay, if you must," and continued. "Your favourite deity, Primordial Trinity, or the Great Symbol. If you cannot, a good spirit, of your own age, will come and count out your good deeds with white pebbles. An evil spirit, also of your own age, will count out your bad deeds with black pebbles." Then I said, "Don't lie about your age when the judgment comes." "I've already had my judgment," he said, "I've accepted I'm going." "Okay," I said, "but that's this life and you'll be assessed on that to prepare for your next. I mean you don't want to be born an insect, do you?" "This society," he says, "has stepped on me and squashed and flattened and smashed my brains so much I would have got off lightly if I'd been an insect."

'Later, when Billy was lying down and his breathing was rough and scratchy, I said, "Let's practise." And I got beer-bottle tops and started counting out. "You may be frightened and lie about your evil deeds. The Lord of Death will then consult the Karma Mirror which reflects good and evil truthfully. Then the Lord of Death will tie a noose around your neck and drag you away. He will chop off your head, tear out your heart, pull out your intestines, eat your brain, drink your blood, chew your flesh, and gnaw at your bones. It will be horrible. Remember that you cannot die. Your mystic body will rematerialise."

' "I won't judge you," I said, and offered Billy the bottle tops and he counted them out. "How do I know what is good and evil?" he said, counting them out. I said, "I think if it doesn't harm someone then it's good, otherwise it's evil." He continued counting: "Is it evil even if you didn't know you were harming someone?" "I don't know," I said. He went on, "One for Jerry, one for Andy, one for Shane," and we soon ran out of bottle tops.

' "Even insects don't die like this," he said, closing his eyes. "You're not, are you?" I interrupted. "No," he said, "so undignified," he muttered.'

A nurse comes up to Varanee, watching him whisper to the wall.

'I think you're on the wrong ward,' she spits out and tries to usher him away.

He shows her his hand. 'This is the blood of a dead woman.'

'What did you do?' she starts screaming and I drag her to the curtain and part it and see the blood-drained, blood-stained woman.

And I say, 'Dead on arrival, she splashed me.'

And the nurse tuts and says, 'This is a hospital.'

And I say, 'I know and Alex knows,' and I slam my hand on the white wall and make a blood-stained hand-print and leave.

Varanee sits on the top deck of a number 47. In the rain the street looks sad. He gets off five stops early, standing in the rain on the pavement, feeling like there's no point going home, feeling like he might as well wait in the road on the bus route between the hospital and a house they both know.

Alex is asleep, he stirs and drifts off again.

Varanee is mumbling to himself. 'What it doesn't explain, this Bardo, is who else will be there. Will friends be there? It doesn't seem so. I decide that we will be alone in these forty-nine days. That is, you go for the full forty-nine days' death journey, if you don't get enlightened on the other days along the way.'

Alex opens his eyes, the irises are cloudy, his face is red and blotchy. 'Is it time? Oh, it's you, I thought it was time to choose my womb door.'

Varanee looks at him surprised, 'You've been listening then.'

It seems like neither of them are in the room, and that the room is as dark as the bottom of a well. A voice booms, 'You will experience visions of the realm of your future existence. Do not be attracted to them, do not follow them, for they lead to a long and painful Bardo.'

'It can't be more painful than this,' Alex interrupts, drifting back from the well-like darkness. 'I know I'm not enlightened, not in the least bit. That's why I'll go the whole forty-nine days for sure.'

Varanee stares at Alex straight in the eyes, he needs the honesty they have been avoiding.

Alex drifted in and out of sleep. He said the gods had all been to visit him in the last few days and that they were taking him on a boat trip. And he said, 'Yuck, I hate boats, they make me sick.' The gods said, 'Don't worry you won't be sick on this boat.' Anyhow, he said, he was taking a sick bag just in case. And I put a recyclable poly bag by his bedside.

Varanee sits by his home-made altar and continues to stare at Alex. Alex doesn't respond, maybe he can't, or maybe they don't want to face their Death Rites.

Varanee's dazed and talks out loud: 'I expect you're wondering about me, whether I'm doing this for my own benefit. That in the near future I shall be taking this very journey. The answer is NO, NO, NO, NO, and I still can't believe it.

'My karma allocation is slightly on the negative side. But then it's not all to do with the personal, there are larger things involved. Like the bad karma of whole nations. Shall we call this a die-in, shall we call it fate, or is that avoiding the political implications of this situation. Is it a seed planted from the gods or the FBI?

'Shall I be philosophical and say, "What a journey Alex has had! What a life journey!" Shall I lean over the bed and count out some black and white pebbles for him, measure his life, our love?'

Varanee throws himself on the altar screaming, 'Fuck your pebbles. Compassionate One, my guru, and the Primordial Trinity, save me from suffering.'

Varanee stuffs the objects from his altar into a poly bag. His eyes are full of tears and things he doesn't want to see. He says, 'Alex says he'd like to come back as a deer, with a sleek body, fast ears and a sense for running out of danger.

' "Deer get eaten by wolves," I said.

'And he said, "Men get eaten by hate." '

THE BAMBOO BLIND

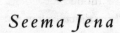

Seema Jena

It was late afternoon in October. Darkness had not crept in yet. She could still see some blue-grey patches through the window. An eeire dampness clung to the air after the shower of rain earlier on in the day as though it were complementing her state of mind. She tried hard, but eventually they came, tears. Wiping her face, Razia threw away the magazine she had been trying to read. She could not tear herself from the thoughts that had been nagging her the whole day. While anxiously awaiting Razak's return, she reproached herself for her behaviour towards her husband, but things were getting out of control and had to be dealt with decisively, she thought, defiance returning to her face.

From some corner of the house, voices could be heard sorting out the menu for the evening meal. 'One adds the *garam masala* last, you daughter of an owl!' her mother-in-law's voice boomed through the wall.

Thinking it was expected that she should offer some help, Razia tied her long disarrayed tresses into a knot and stepped out of her room, but realised that the family may feel awkward with her there. She switched on the television.

The news was relating the plight of the Kurds. Skipping through the channels to see if anything interesting was on, she realised that all the meaty bits were stacked away for the evening. Razak had once explained that such an arrangement suited people in this country as they went out to work during the day, even the women. She envied their good fortune. Unlike her, they were not confined to four walls, where one day was little different from the next, like the daily tearing off a page from her wall calendar. However, none of the other residents ever seemed to be conscious of the monotony, not even the women. Her thoughts drifted towards a different scene in a far off place, to the life behind the *chilman* (the bamboo blind), to the house where she had grown up, her father's.

Razia's father, Syed Mazhar Ali Shah, was regarded very highly among the leading citizens of the city. His family had lived in Lucknow for at least a hundred years. Now in his late sixties, Mazhar sahab had retired from the daily hassles of the tobacco business and had passed it on to the able hands of his four sons. Their house stood out from the rest of the houses in the street and apart from housing twenty-five humans of all shapes and sizes (excluding the servants of course), it was a monument to the tradition, culture and high values her ancestors represented. Razia had spent all her childhood and teens in this house. The façade had nothing to distinguish it from the other old houses of Lucknow. The front door opened on to the road, there was no compound wall, with just a few steps leading from the door to the street. What formed the most significant feature of the house was the massive inner courtyard which divided the house into two sections. There there were the anterooms, which housed the offices and provided space for the dozen employees, typists, accountants and the babus, where clients came to meet the younger Mazhars for business transactions and where they would sit talking, discussing, bargaining and hassling all day long.

Then there was the back section of the house which constituted the women's quarters. The front of this wing, opening to the courtyard, was covered by the *chilman*. Fifteen women of different ages, starting from the ten-month-old Farhana (Mazhar sahab's youngest granddaughter), to Amma (Mazhar sahab's mother), who was eighty-five, as well as all children under ten, inhabited this section of the house. The women, though hidden from the men behind this veil of thin bamboo strips held together with jute strings, scrutinised every movement that went on in the courtyard as well as kept a note of the people who visited the house. If at times, they felt that they had missed out on some juicy bits, they were extracted from the servants with great dexterity. However, the world behind the fifty-foot-long bamboo blind was very active, and each member of it was engaged in something throughout the day. Amma always had her *pan* box open, making pans for the whole house. Begum Mazhar supervised the kitchen and the daily shopping list, allocating various chores to the servants. It was quite a job to be the unofficial head of such a large family.

Razia had loathed the whole arrangement behind the bamboo blind. 'That's a woman's life; our mothers had this life and so did their mothers,' Amma explained, moving the ground betel nut in her toothless mouth. 'Don't sin in this life, so you can face Him on the day of judgment,' she had said gravely. No one complained except her. Razia had completed her matriculation and with great difficulty persuaded the family to let her enrol in the local women's college. Suddenly, one day her scholastic career was terminated. A fellow student who also happened to be the daughter of her father's best friend eloped with a Christian boy she had met during an inter-college essay competition. The entire community was shocked. 'Ya Allah!' Begum Mazhar had exclaimed, raising her right hand to her forehead, 'that too, with an infidel! *Toba toba!* What is this world coming to? Tch . . . tch . . . tch.'

After the incident Razia was told by her brothers that she had acquired all the education that she would ever need and it would be worthwhile if she learned how to prepare *biryani* and learn zardozi embroidery from her sisters-in-law. 'These talents are far more valuable than any college degrees in a marriage,' said

Rizvan, the eldest. She secretly wished that no one would ever come forward to marry her, but she knew that with her father's reputation and the dowry she would bring with her, many fathers looking for 'nice' girls had been encouraged to approach the mullah's wife, who forwarded their applications to Begum Mazhar, with exceeding promptness.

One afternoon, a few months after the scandal of the elopement had died down, Nargis *khala* had rushed into the terrace, where Razia was drying her hair and announced breathlessly, 'I have got something here.' Her hand, hidden in her dupatta, shook. 'What would you give me if I show you this?' she said, taking out the hidden treasure, a coloured photograph of someone. 'This is the boy *bhai jaan* has seen this morning.' Not again; must be some fat, ugly, stupid brat of some rich father, she thought. Her aunt went on with added gusto: 'He approves. The only thing he is worried about is that the boy lives in Vilayet and his family is there too.'

Razia pricked up her ears. 'Vilayet!'

She was no longer indifferent to the remaining bits of information pouring out of Nargis *khala*'s lips. Marrying someone living in England would be a dream come true. She glanced gingerly at the photograph left behind by her aunt. She studied the young face, the smart blue suit and the mischievous smile, the last observation making her blush. From that day on, she fasted and prayed that the alliance would come through. Her prayers were answered and a few days later the date of the wedding was fixed.

The *nikaah* was a grand affair. Half the distinguished population of Lucknow turned up for the reception. After the wedding the couple went to Simla for a weekend. These were the most memorable days in Razia's life. Razak was very kind and considerate. He told her that his family lived together in Britain, that he had a large family and that she would not miss home and added, 'In many ways it is just like Lucknow.' She tried hard to hide the smile creeping up to her lips.

Razak's house in Manchester was not as palatial as her father's, but it sheltered fifteen people under its roof. Here, each family was allotted a room. Their's was in a corner. For Razia the most attractive feature about the room was the window which over-looked the street that ran along the side of the house, although the view was not in any way spectacular. The street was lined with semi-detached houses like their own. The same people pursued the same activities day after day – children leaving and returning from school, the postman shoving mail twice a day through the flaps with his podgy fingers, people emptying their garbage into the bins. But the window was her sanctuary in a house where most of the people were still strangers.

She was ill at ease and uncomfortable with Razak's sisters, who spoke of sales, salons and the latest video releases, particu-larly the eldest one, Hasina, who always stared at Razia when they were together, minutely observing and judging her younger brother's wife.

After Razak had returned with her to Britain, he was busy with the new extension to the shop and had very little time to take her out. They had gone out only twice in all the months they had been in the country, once to visit some special relatives and family friends as was the custom for newly weds. Razak stayed the whole day at the shop and in the evenings went out for a drink with a friend. Razia tried to picture what a pub looked like. Once when they were alone, she had broached the subject. He had replied matter-of-factly, 'Oh, it's just like a café, where one orders things to eat and drink, lot of noise, smoke, nothing grand.' She wanted to ask if that was all then why go there every-day, but checked herself, recollecting her grandmother's parting advice, 'Want to keep a man in your fist, never ask too many questions.'

Razak was in many ways easy to please; she forgot all her dis-appointments with his gentleness and love. His only plea to her was that he would not tolerate any complaints against his family.

His mother was old, his sister had problems, his sister-in-law was illiterate, but she was different, she was educated, should she stoop to their level? After that, Razia stopped mentioning her daily discomforts to her husband, until yesterday. She screwed up her nose as she recollected yesterday's scene and the confrontation she had with Razak's family.

Razia looked out of her window quite frequently whenever she had nothing to do and Razak's sisters had crowded into the living-room. That her mother-in-law did not approve of her standing near the window or sitting on the sill was made clear by the arching of her eyebrows whenever she caught Razia in the act, though she had never verbally expressed her disapproval. The day before when Hasina dropped in, Razia had greeted her and got up to leave the room, mumbling some excuse.

'Do we stink?' Hasina's voice was sharp as a knife. 'Yes, tell me, do we stink? Or are we not good enough for you, that you prefer the window gazing to us?'

In her confusion Razia could only mutter, 'But *baji*, what harm is done to anybody if one looks out of a window?'

'*Chup; badtameez!* In your family do they talk back to elders?' Hasina's voice had increased its volume to such a degree that the children had left their games and gathered in the living-room to watch the game that engaged the grown-ups. Razak's mother, feigning to be deaf during this verbal exchange, suddenly shot a warning look at her daughter, silencing her. Hurt and humiliated, Razia ran out of the room with her mother-in-law in tow.

Once in Razia's room the older lady started speaking, '*Na, na, bete*, don't be upset with Hasina. She means well. What will people say if they always find you near the window?'

Razia could feel the tears trickling down her cheeks, she tried her best to suppress the sobs rising within her.

Her mother-in-law went on in the same sugary tone, 'You come from a decent family, do I have to tell you what is right and what is wrong . . .?' the old lady's voice trailed to a halt when she saw that Razia had started crying.

Her mother-in-law adopted a cajoling tone, 'Go to the shops tomorrow, one of the boys will take you, buy a sari . . . some bangles, *hain*. Now stop crying, Razak will be back soon; one shouldn't show a tearful face to a husband when he comes home, how would it make him feel? So unwelcome,' she patted Razia's back and left the room.

Razia decided to settle matters with her husband as soon as he got back. Once he was in, she banged the door and started the tirade of accusations: for always being partial to his family, her loneliness in a strange country, his lack of concern for her. She stumbled with the words, not knowing the right lines for the occasion, never having experienced the rage she felt at that moment. Razak could only stare at his wife, his mouth half-open, looking stupid and helpless. When he finally got the whole picture of the day's events he promised he would try to see a way out of her misery. She heard him trying to coax his mother, who sounded equally concerned by Hasina's behaviour. '*Allah mian! Why don't you give me death instead of all this?*' she exclaimed, the catch-phrase which put an end to all arguments in the house.

Razia's thoughts were jostled by the familiar hoot of the car horn in the porch. He was late, trying to avoid her, she thought bitterly. She switched off the television. That morning, he had left hurriedly, not wanting another tearful scene with his wife. She had spent the whole day in her room, reading and watching television. She was looking forward to the evening and to seeing how Razak fulfilled his promise. 'Let's see how much of a man he is,' she kept telling herself.

Razak came in carrying a cardboard box. 'This is the answer to all your problems,' he said, looking fondly at her.

He summoned his eldest nephew to hold a chair for him on which he stood and screwed two thick nails into the frame of the window. He removed something long and noisy from the box and hung it from the nails and inspected it with a knowledgeable frown. The object was white and shiny, with thin strips held together with strings.

'This is known as a venetian blind. See, if you pull this string the strips flatten and if you pull the other string, the strips open up and you can see everything outside, even if the window is covered, come here and see for yourself.'

Dumb with disbelief at what she was being told, Razia got up from the chair, walked up to her husband and stood beside him. 'What?'

He turned to her, beaming like a knight in shining armour. 'Happy? See, I told you, I would do something.'

Razia was speechless for a few moments. Later when she was able to speak she said, 'In Lucknow, we call it the *chilman*.' She looked at his kind and earnest face and smiled. She did not wish to seem ungrateful.

THE GUEST

Leena Dhingra

Ekadashi is the eleventh phase of the moon and a day on which many people observe a fast. My grandmother, whose name, Chand, means moon, has always fasted on that day. She started fasting when she was twenty to commemorate an event that changed her life. She told me about it that summer. That summer when Mrs Collins came to stay.

It was the year of my lower sixth. My parents were to be away in New York for five months and had arranged for my grandmother from India to come and stay with me. I'd tried arguing that I could easily manage on my own, that I was seventeen after all and that people of my age left home, held jobs, lived independently and even got married and produced children. Ravi, my elder brother, offered to come up from university every weekend. They just laughed us off, pronounced a little speech that, as a student, my responsibility was to study and theirs was to make sure I had the support to concentrate on my work! I let the matter slide. I knew from experience that what I called a discussion they would call an argument or rudeness. Like the time Mum let me go to assertiveness-training classes with Annie, and then said I was being rude whenever I tried to put into practice what I had learned. I complained to my friends Cheryl and Annie about the overprotectiveness of Indian parents and the injustice of it all.

Of course, deep down, I knew that they were right and I was really quite pleased that Chand-Nani, my grandmother, was coming. I just wasn't very good at listening to deep down in those days.

So Nani came with all her usual paraphernalia: her special milk pan, her herbal concoctions, her incense, her murthis, her Gita, her pictures, her prayer cushion, oil lamp, Ganga water and all the fragrant eccentricities that reminded me of India. The first two weeks went off fine and we settled into our routines. We shared the cooking and other chores. She went for walks, visits, said her prayers and, as usual, went regularly to the Saturday jumble sales from where she gleaned nearly new clothes to take back to India for 'the refugees'. This was a bit of a standing joke in the family. Nani herself had been a refugee and had lost everything in the partition. But even though that was years ago, she still collected clothes to distribute and would seek out the needy.

One weekend Ravi came up and, on the Sunday, Nani went to leave him at Victoria station. It was the day of her fast, when she had only one small meal of fruit in the evening. I was on my way to Annie's to revise when I realised that Nani had forgotten her keys. Obviously I couldn't go and was discussing notes on the phone when the doorbell rang. I opened it and there stood Nani with an odd-looking stranger – all mousy browns: grey-brown hair, brown felt hat, brown coat with threadbare patches, brown shoes with grey dust, and carrying a small brown case and a brown paper carrier-bag. Standing next to my grandmother in her ochre silk sari and maroon woven shawl, she could not have presented a stronger contrast.

'So sorry, darling, I forgot my key. This is Mrs Collie, we met at Victoria station and I've invited her to come and stay with us for a while. Will you put the kettle on, sweetheart, and make us all a cup of tea? I'll just light my jauth and join you in the kitchen.' With this, Nani breezed past me, slipped out of her shoes and disappeared down the hall leaving us staring at each other.

'The name is Collins, Mrs Collins,' said the stranger stepping forward and articulating every syllable as though I didn't understand English.

I didn't realise my mouth was wide open until I had to close it to reply.

'I'm sorry. My grandmother does mispronounce . . .'

Mrs Collins darted a quick and critical glance over the hall, taking in the shoe rack, the coats, the pictures, the smudges around the door handles. In the kitchen, she pushed her bag and case under a chair, barricading them in with her legs and giving me a hostile look as she sat down. I put the kettle on and dashed off to find Nani in her room, sitting there all serene, folded palms, staring into the flame of an oil lamp and counting her never-ending beads. She did this every morning and evening. I sighed loudly. When she had finished, she looked at me and just smiled through my indignant questioning.

'What's so strange? I told you. We met at Victoria station. She needed help – a place to stay – and so I invited her here.' Nani smiled, so disarmingly. Such a beautiful smile. 'It's just for two or three days, until she can find the friends she came to stay with.'

'But, Nani . . . one doesn't . . . we don't . . . we don't know her!'

'Do we really know anybody? Do we know ourselves? Think about it.' She looked at me strangely as though across a great distance. 'For the present,' she said mysteriously, 'Mrs Collie is our guest!'

Honestly! This is ridiculous I thought, but all I managed to say was: 'Her name isn't Collie. It's Collins. Collies are dogs like Lassie.'

Suddenly my grandmother whizzed out of the room apologising down the hall. When I reached the kitchen she and Mrs

Collins were having a little tête-à-tête, as the kettle steamed away around them. It was really all too absurd.

I drifted back to my books and saw the telephone was still off the hook. Annie! What was I going to tell my friends.

By dinner, Mrs Collins was looking decidedly more at ease: her bags were now in a corner of the kitchen, she'd removed her hat, coat and shoes, was wearing Nani's slippers and inspecting the spices.

'I was already in service by the time I was your age – seventeen, isn't it, dearie? Started at the bottom and worked my way to the top. I always had my standards, see. I'll give this kitchen a good scrub up after dinner.'

'Why? Is it so filthy?' I said, sitting down. Nobody seemed to notice.

'This is just a simple meal, Mrs Collins, and not too spicy.' Nani put the dishes on the table.

'Oh, don't worry about me. I can eat all sorts. Worked in the house of a man who'd been out in India. They had a native cook. They'd brought him back from India they had. He cooked all sorts – native food, English food. I ate everything. Never been fussy, I haven't.'

Suddenly, she leaped out of her chair, rummaged through her carrier and triumphantly pulled out a greasy brown paper bag. 'I nearly forgot. I've a pork pie here we can all share.'

'A pork pie!' I burst into a fit of nervous giggles, anticipating the consternation of my vegetarian grandmother – and on the day of her fast too. But Nani just took out the pie, put it in a plate, and even cut it with her own hands as though it was the most natural thing to do.

That evening when Nani requested me to be more polite, I challenged her, 'What politeness do you want? English politeness or Indian politeness?' I said. 'Do you want me to say please, thank you and sorry properly, or do you want me to curb my independent opinions?'

'What about just showing respect to another.'

'But she's . . .'

'She's our guest. And a guest is a god.'

'It's utterly unbelievable. I mean, you just wouldn't believe it,' I complained to my friends Annie and Cheryl. 'I explained to her that she could be from anywhere, that they were closing the asylums these days and that all sorts of people were wandering around in the streets. But she took no notice, just smiled.' Annie and Cheryl listened greedily. 'I mean, last night,' I continued, 'I got out of the bed in the middle of the night because I could hear her creaking and shuffling around.'

'Where was she sleeping?'

'Well, Nani offered her the couch in the living-room, she looked around the room and then said, "No, it wouldn't be proper." So we put her on a camp bed in the hall. In any case, when I got there she was out of the bed and had crept into the living-room, and guess what she was doing?'

'What?'

'Well, she was going round to all the pictures, all the statues – you know, the dancing Shiva, the Durga, the Krishna, and all – and making the sign of the cross over them!'

'How odd!' exclaimed Annie.

'She probably thinks it's all the Devil's business. I've met people like that,' intervened Cheryl. 'You know, the commandments and all. Graven images. Some people take that all quite literally!'

Before I could have my next burst of righteous indignation, Cheryl said, 'I think it's really kind of your Nan to help a stranger. Don't you agree, Annie?'

'Well, I suppose it is, if you look at it that way. But Dee is right. She could be from anywhere.'

That evening, when I came home, a makeshift clothes line had been erected by the kitchen window on which Mrs Collins's clothes were drying, the kitchen itself had been rearranged so as to provide a little cosy corner in the sun in which Mrs Collins was comfortably sitting in one of Nani's 'refugee' dressing-gowns, darning her stockings. As I slipped out of my shoes in the hall, I noticed that the kitchen floor looked as though it had been polished.

'There's fresh tea in the pot, dearie,' she called out. 'Your gran's out and said you're to study till she returns.'

I frowned, dropped my bags and came in to pour my tea. The floor had definitely been polished.

'And when you've finished you will dry the cup and put it away and not just leave it dripping on the draining-board,' she said through her teeth as she tried to break the thread with them.

In my irritation I spilt some tea on the floor.

'Wipe it with the floor cloth, will you, dearie? It's over the bucket under the sink.' She said this without looking up, pre-empting my reaching for the dishcloth. I did as I was told.

'It's good to have standards,' she announced in a firm lilt as I left the kitchen fuming with irritation.

When Nani came in, Mrs Collins melted all over her. 'Good evening, madam, let me take those bags, madam, and madam, do sit down, madam, and tea?'

Nani was all smiles and her new, strange, distant look appeared to have acquired a kind of radiance.

That night again, the floorboards creaked as Mrs Collins crept around the house when she thought we were all asleep. She inspected the paintings, the statues, the books. She opened the drawers and cupboards. I warned Nani that when Mrs Collins left on Thursday one of us should be there when she packed. Nani just nodded but did not seem unduly concerned. So I felt that it was my duty to keep an eye on things and every night I crept around after her to try and see what she was up to. Once, I had to hide in the hall cupboard and wait until she was in her bed snoring before I could get out and climb back into mine. I went to sleep during French in school and was given a detention.

When I came back from school, Nani announced that Mrs Collins would be staying on because her friends hadn't yet returned. She was out collecting some of her things from some left-luggage place. Just like that!

I wrote to Ravi and told him he must come at once as there was an emergency.

That night, Mrs Collins got up as usual, and I crept after her. The living-room door was ajar and in the mirror above the fireplace I was greeted with the most extraordinary sight: Mrs Collins wearing an apron and cap, twirling round the room in a dance and smiling every time she caught her reflection in the mirror.

Ravi didn't come, he just called. Nani had picked up the phone.

'No, baba, there's no need for you to come now, we're all fine. Also I have a friend staying with me. Yes, quite right, it is nice company. And a help too.'

I dashed across the hall to get to the phone, determined to tell Ravi the truth about the dusty grey-brown stranger. But as I passed the kitchen I realised that Mrs Collins no longer looked dusty brown. In fact she looked really quite respectable. Nani, seeing me coming, had already put down the phone and wandered off.

'Ravi,' I hissed into the receiver. 'Come now. If you don't, then don't blame me.'

I could still hear Ravi laughing in my ear as I put down the phone. In the kitchen Nani and Mrs Collins were talking.

'You mustn't call me madam, Mrs Collins, it sounds so formal.'

'What shall I call you then? Mrs Datta?'

'You could call me by my name, Kamala. It means lotus.'

'Now what would I call you if we was in India?'

'In India? You'd probably call me Kamalaji. *Ji* means respected and we always add that on.'

'Kamalaji. I'll call you that then. And you must call me Edna.'

'Ednaji.'

Wasn't it all just so sweet and cosy. I resolved that if nobody else was worrying then neither would I. Once again we all settled into our routines. Mrs Collins took over two shelves in the hall cupboard, started putting her shoes next to ours on the shoe rack. She befriended both Cheryl and Annie, who would lap up her stories of upstairs and downstairs, sculleries, cauldrons of clothes and shining silver.

'In one place, Jewish bankers they were, they had so much silver that it took the whole Friday to polish it all. We could only work as long as there was daylight y'see, because after that everything had to be shut down for the sabbath and we went off duty.'

Mrs Collins started to accompany Nani to jumble sales; they picked up an old sewing-machine and she then got busy transforming old clothes into smart outfits for herself. She also started to buy *The Lady* to 'look for a position as housekeeper companion'. Nani encouraged her, and by the time Ravi came up to visit, she really was both presentable and companionable. Ravi was quite taken by her, she called him 'Master Ravi', enquired about his studies, told him how she'd heard lots about him from Nani.

Mrs Collins even started to keep the fast with my grandmother, and one day I overheard her telling Cheryl that Nani didn't like it that my friends shortened my name, Divya, to Dee and Div.

'They don't mean anything, you see. But Divya has a meaning, it means divine. And they believe, you see, that words and names have energy. And she chose that name for her you see.'

And then there was that time when Simon came. Simon was a friend of Ravi's. He arrived early and Mrs Collins let him in. I heard them talking in the sitting-room; Mrs Collins appeared to be telling him the story of Durga, who she was, why she rode a tiger and the meaning of all the weapons in her arms.

'Hello, Divya, you didn't know I knew all that, did you, dearie?' She smiled at me as I came in.

'Hello, Div,' smiled Simon. 'Do you know all these wonderful stories?'

'Kamalaji, the mistress that is, is a wonderful storyteller. But I must tell you truthfully that I was a bit frightened of all these when I first saw them until I found out that they're all stories and ideas really.'

Maybe I felt a bit jealous. I hadn't listened to Nani's stories for years and my mother and father were always too busy. And now she'd been telling them all to Mrs Collins. That night it was I who couldn't sleep and got up to creep around the house. Mrs Collins remained fast asleep.

It was the following Friday and I came home early and caught Mrs Collins rummaging through Nani's bag in the hall. She hadn't heard me open the front door as the kettle had just started to whistle. But when I came into the kitchen she looked startled.

'Your gran's not feeling too good.' Her tone seemed unsure. 'She had a dizzy spell, so I'm making her a hot drink.'

That night after a long time I once more heard the floorboards creak and the doors squeak. Mrs Collins was again prowling around.

The next day, Nani came into my room early to ask if she could borrow some money as she had mislaid her purse.

'I had a fall when I went out yesterday,' she said. 'On my way to the bank.'

The image of Mrs Collins and the bag flashed through my mind. 'How much did you have in it?'

'A hundred and fifty pounds. I'd just got it from the bank. I had a fall. I must have dropped it somewhere.' Nani was trying to remember.

Of course, I knew better. 'Did you say you fell on your way to the bank?'

'Someone once told me,' continued Nani, 'that if you turn a glass upside down and ask St Anthony to help, then whatever you've lost will be found. We can try it now, shall we?'

And if it's not lost, but stolen, will St Anthony catch the thief, or maybe even the thief repent, I said to myself as I went to the kitchen to get a glass.

Mrs Collins was sitting in her sunny spot reading *The Lady*, and marking things up as she went along. Butter would definitely not melt in her mouth, I said to myself. She looked up at me. 'Everything all right?' she asked. So innocent! It was unbelievable. I started to wonder how many other things she had stolen during all the weeks she had had free rein of the house. I wrestled with the idea of confronting her there and then but my throat felt blocked. I walked out with the empty glass. Maybe St Anthony would sort it all out.

Later, I called Annie and told her about Nani having lost her purse. I told her how upset Nani was, which wasn't true. I knew Mrs Collins could overhear.

'Was there money in the purse your gran lost?' Mrs Collins asked when I came back into the kitchen.

'Of course there was. She'd just been to the bank, hadn't she!'

Mrs Collins closed her magazine and looked uncomfortable. And so she should, I thought. Maybe I also thought I was giving St Anthony a helping hand.

The next morning Nani came into my room looking fragile and bewildered. 'Ednaji is not there. She has taken all her things and gone. Did she say anything to you?'

I was taken aback but pretended otherwise. 'Nani, can't you see that she's just stolen your money and left.'

'But she didn't need to do that, Divya. She could have just asked me, she knew that.'

'Well, she was not what she seemed,' I said with great certainty. 'I warned you at the very beginning.'

'Did you say something to her, Divya?' Nani's voice was very gentle.

'No. I just told Annie. She heard me and realised her game was up and left. It's so obvious, can't you see?'

Nani just nodded absently.

It was early Monday morning that the bank called. I was getting late for school, but I picked up the phone. They had found Nani's purse. She'd dropped it there. There was money in it and would she like to come and identify it.

I didn't go to school that day, or the next. I went instead to Victoria station and wandered around through the lockers, the benches, the ladies, the platforms, the cafes. Then I wrote out an advertisement for *The Lady*.

'Mrs Collins, Ednaji. Please come back. Forgive me. Divya.'

I was crying, so I didn't hear Nani as she slipped into my room, but was soothed by the lilt of her voice. It was her special storytelling voice.

'Life is full of lessons. And there is always more to learn.' I swallowed my tears and held my breath. 'Long time ago now, when the partition riots were going on and we were trying to make our way out of Lahore, to the new Indian border, I got separated from my family and couldn't find them anywhere. I was very frightened. I was only twenty and it was such a terrible, terrible time. Everything seemed to be on fire, and the air was thick with smoke and hate.

'A Muslim family who had themselves just escaped from India and lost their own daughter on the way, took pity and adopted me. They called me Rashida. They protected me, and in spite of all their sorrow, and at great risk to themselves, they eventually got me to safety. I vowed never to forget, never. As it was Ekadashi I decided to keep the fast in memory.'

The Ekadashi fast is reputed to develop inner strength and wisdom. I've kept it for seven years now and the lessons of that time continue to unfold.

We never did hear from Ednaji again, and I still read the personal column in *The Lady*. But since that summer I have never been the same. I grew up then, and sometimes, I wonder if Mrs Collins appeared just for that to happen.

THE WOMAN AND THE CHAIR

Shamshad Khan

She was walking on the back of a gold, red velvet chair. She lifted her bare foot and placed it on the cold brass mound in front of her. Half-danced to the top. Breathless, she paused. Knelt down and leant to look over the edge. Dizzy heights, strange lands, new worlds, endless possibilities.

Another day. For now she slid down the other side of her hill. Landing on the worn velvet floor at its base, she untangled her hair from around her legs. Deftly plaited its length with Indian fingers and then wrapped it around her waist. She was a strange sight, dressed in silk tunic and *shalvaar*, her wrists encased in bangles, her tiny feet laced with *mehndi*. She laughed at the thought of herself, Lehla M. walking on the top of an antique English chair.

Lehla had no recollection of how she had got here and little memory of where she had come from. But her yearning to find out why she was here she knew would be answered if she searched. She stood straight, her feet set apart, her toes pressed into the chair's velvet covering. She looked up at the room's brightening sky. It was as though she was trying to make contact with her world, hoping for some communication.

None came. Lehla gave up her attempts at spiritual communion, it seemed she would have to take direct action.

She set off to explore, seconds after seconds passed, hill after hill. Then, just as she was beginning to know the rhythm and pattern of things; a magic ring. No hill. She stepped over the edge on to a bright field of crimson velvet. Enticed, she lay down, stretching out against the softness of her land. Time stopped. She slept a long, deep, dreamless sleep, awoken by the sound of a distant flute and whining sitar. Unfolding her body, she rose and danced endlessly. Smooth, delicate, powerful movements. Finally exhausted, she sat down to dine. She opened her sequinned bag, drank water from a deep green glass bottle and ate coconut sweets until she was nearly full. Brushing crumbs from her clothes, she stood, picked up her bag, counted to three and stepped out of the circle; magic slipping from her as she walked away.

Her last hill passed, Lehla came to the end of the chair. She bent down, holding on to the golden beam. Beneath her, in the corner, laced between the gaps in the back of the chair, a web-woven hung. She settled one leg among the feathery threads and, easing herself down, she turned and climbed on to the net. There just below she was sure she saw the first word. She climbed down to reach it, leant and tore it away. 'STARS' she read. That could mean so many things; the position of the stars at the time of her birth or maybe meetings with famous people. Either way, the first clue didn't seem too bad. The stars shone a gentle light, playing shadow games on her hands. She folded them and put them in her bag. Pulled a thread from the web, and swung down. She landed on the arm of the chair, always cushioned by velvet. The words in mind, she walked the length of the arm, resting from time to time.

Her head taken up with thought was interrupted, jolted as her foot hit something hard. She bent to pick it up. 'DANGER'. Lehla stopped in her tracks. Suddenly there was darkness all around, her life threatened, but by what she did not know. Stars and danger, what was she to make of this? Lehla decided her fate was set in the stars, to avoid imminent danger she would have to tread carefully, and maybe even then she wouldn't be able to avoid it. Her heart beating fast, Lehla took careful steps forward. The sun was at its highest and she had much further to go; many more words to find. The seat of the chair was her next stop. The carved wood should be difficult to climb down. She knelt over the arm, turned around and felt her way with her feet. Her legs weary, her hands sore, her silk tunic torn, she climbed and slid, until, finally, she landed.

She rested a while, her head swirling. She looked out to see the acres of land that spread out on all sides. The soft fields gave way to rough canvas terrain and then, just by her feet, a great abyss. She peered cautiously to look in. Great metal coils. Underground serpents lying in wait; guarding some great treasure among the straw they nested in. A musty warmth, overpowering, swept up from the depths. Danger on all sides; which way should she turn? She would have to take the risk and plunge. She breathed long and slow before diving. Her hands catching hold of the metal, her legs wrapped around; sliding down the snake. She looked up, dust and sundrops spiralled in the light above. Her eyes adjusting to the darkness below, Lehla began to make out the shadows. She felt her way around the silhouettes, her head a little dazed by the heat. The air was thick with words; heavy tortuous words. She reached out and plucked them from the air. 'EXHAUSTED', 'FRIGHTENED' and 'DEFEAT'. It had all come to an end. There was no further to go. Her life, as she had always feared, would end in tragedy. 'Frightened and defeated', 'frightened and defeated', Lehla repeated the words to herself and then lay down in the straw. She had given up hope.

As she nestled down in defeat, her head rested on something soft and warm. She turned to see what it was: 'LOVE'. She had nearly forgotten. Her heart lifted and in a moment she had forgotten all danger and exhaustion and leapt to her feet. Old Indian movies flashed before her eyes. Lovers in fields of flowers sang to her. Then more words: 'PASSION', 'HOPE' and

'RETURN'. The Indian movie dream lived on. She imagined herself the star of the screen. She had always secretly believed she would have her name in lights. Lehla M. stars in *Arp Kee Kismeth*. There would be passion, endless, endless passion, and hope, as the long-lost brother who had become a villain returns home a prosperous lawyer. Flowers and stars, that was why she was here.

Then a little doubt crept in. If she was to be the star of an Indian movie, what was she doing sitting here in the middle of an English chair?

'Life has its funny ways,' she tried to console herself. She had a few more years, no doubt she would get there somehow. But the doubt had already taken root and Lehla could soon feel it growing inside her. She collected the different words together and read them one more time before putting them into her bag. She set off again, singing old Hindi love songs in an attempt to keep her spirits high. Then again in the half-light she saw more words. 'DELIBERATE', 'DEATH' and 'FORGOTTEN'. Words that hung in the air in a heavy mist. Like a shawl they fell to rest on her shoulders. Death gripped her with ice fingers, Lehla's heart sank. She had been silly, she was no movie queen, there was no final love scene. The words had been plain to read. 'Defeat, tied and danger'. And the love and passion just things of the past. The stars were only there to light up her failings, they were not a destiny of fame. Lehla looked at the three words she had just found, deliberate, death and forgotten. Yes, she had forgotten where she had come from and where she was to go. Her life an endless struggle to comprehend. Deliberate, was this deliberate as in to consider options, or deliberate as in a considered, conscious action? Lehla sat in the dark as her mind spiralled down into the depths. Why did she even bother trying to work it out? This was a riddle she wasn't meant to understand. She would give up. Right here and now, she would stop trying to make sense of things and just live. She stood up and looked for a way out. Her senses awoken spurred her anew. She pushed her way through head-high straw, great grass needles lying across her path.

The light above was beginning to weaken, and she knew she had little time left. She began to make her ascent, her head lightening, her lithe body scaling the snake. Reaching its head she looked out and saw in the distance what looked like a cliff side. Drawn towards it, she realised it was the pages of a book piled high. Lehla opened the cover, the crumpled yellow paper crackled as she climbed on to it. The moon shed its watery light on the page and as it filled she began to read:

> Your life in the ————
> is set.
> Frightened you may be
> ———————— by the . . . .

This wasn't making any sense either. Then Lehla noticed her bag sparkling in the moonlight and remembered the words. She pulled them out of her bag and began to roll them into place one by one. So, she was to be answered after all. All her misunderstandings and misinterpretations would be explained. Would she be the movie queen or was she to die unknown, unremembered; she was soon to learn. The blueprint of her life lay stretched out in front of her. Lehla placed the last word in its space and read again:

> Your life in the stars
> is set.
>
> Frightened you may be,
> exhausted by the
> trials of life.

But don't lose hope.
There are ways to overpower
defeat.

Deliberate not too often
but open your heart
to knowledge, love and passion.

From death you will return
to learn
what you fear
you have forgotten.

Things were beginning to make sense. Lehla tried hard to remember the words. Coming to the last verse, she sang the words gently to herself in the hope that they wouldn't be forgotten.

In search of your meaning
you will ask again
                    and will be answered
                        one more
            with
        the
            turning
                of
                    a page.

As Lehla read the last word she lost all recollection of what she had learnt. The full moon overflowing poured into the room, lifted her from where she lay. Words wrapped around her and caught in her long, long hair, spinning threads of wisdom a butterfly cocoon.

THE VISIT

Sue Thakor

It may seem odd to those of you who did not know her but at the time the very simplest of acts became disjointed in her mind. Or so she was told. Her life, something that looked so much like an open book, became complicated. Or so it seemed. It began with such a simple act. The shops. Shopping. An ordinary enough pastime but something that led her into an unfamiliar world. Decisions made without her knowledge. For the best. A phrase that she would hear again and again. She distrusted it. The taste of it. For the best. The sound of it. For her it was the beginning. The beginning of her distrust. The sound of a door slamming shut. Shut against her. Shutting her in.

Spring was early that year. Flower stalls began to sell the sunshine buds. Just looking at the bright array was enough to put a spring in anyone's step. A crisp Spring day. A day similar to many other days in her life. Similar but different. They went to the shops. A journey that was familiar as the parade of shops itself. Usually she only had time for a brief nod or fleeting smile as she hurried on her way past friends and neighbours. Armed with shopping bags and with her head full of worries she would make her way along the invisible path. An invisible string would pull her along the path, that well-worn path that recognised each footstep and guided her to her destination. To places that she recognised and that recognised her. But this time it was different. She had time to browse. She found it difficult not to worry about the mundane things – like the peas defrosting, or what birthday present to buy his sister. She remembered thinking about the peas. Should they try another brand? It was so boring buying the same things every week. Did they buy his sister a photograph frame last year? Or was it someone else? It's strange what passes through your mind on these occasions.

But this visit was hers. All hers. They were going to buy clothes. Just for her. Clothes for the evening and maybe something to wear on the beach. Something light and airy with added layers if it became cooler later. And why not? She deserved a weekend away. It had been a long time since she had done anything for herself, without the added burden of thinking what the family might think or need or want. Working around their lives. Their schedules. Their traumas. But what about her? Didn't she have a life too?

Her life was an appendage. Something that was there but no one noticed. Until the visit. Then they watched her. Then they watched to see what she would do or say or even how she acted. They watched to see if she put a foot out of place. Watching to trip her up. But they never did. They never could! Why? I can hear you ask. Because she knew them. She knew them all. Each and every iota of their personalities. She had worked around them for so long that she knew every niche of their characters. But they did not know her. They never knew who she was. They did not know the person who liked going to the ballet, taking long walks in the country, dancing or doing the crossword. They only saw what they wanted to see. A fragment of a being who knew what was needed at different times. A dislocation that fitted a pattern of other people's making. Let her out and she would dream – a dream of life and happiness.

They drove down. To the coast. They often went to the coast when the children were younger. Not now. Not for a long time.

It was their favourite guest house. In fact it was the only one they stayed in. They had tea at others, of course, but never stayed. Never stayed overnight. Things change. People change. People had made changes at the guest house. All new and shiny. Very different from the old beams and copper kettles. If you were a fly on the wall, you would see her sitting in a chair by the window, bewilderment echoed in her eyes. She was looking for something. You could see that. There was no sign. No sign of recognition. No sign of anything familiar. Can you see her eyes travelling across the room, searching every crevice for recognition? Again and again. Searching. She looked closer still and saw another door close. You could see she wasn't sure. She wasn't sure if she liked it. Not sure if she was ready for all of this. White walls with framed flowers. All shiny. Too shiny.

People came and went. Some would stay. Some would go. Some would wander around nomadically. Each searching. Each knowing where they were going but not knowing why. She sat and watched. Was she a reflection? Their reflection. Images of different people reflected in each others' eyes. Waiting to be recognised. Waiting. Waiting, for the right time. Not the in-between time. Not the timeless time that finds its own way through the ticking of the clock. But her time. Her own time. Her beginning.

But they weren't ready. You see, it was their time. Now was their time. They were ready. They answered their questions. They said it would be all right. But did they know what 'all right' was? If it was the same as before, she didn't want it. They asked her how she felt. What did that mean anyway? Feelings! How was she supposed to feel? If they gave her a hint of what they wanted, then everything would be all right. She would have her own tools. She would have something to chisel away at. Something to hold on to. But all they did was talk. Talk. Talk. Talk. Meaningless chatter that echoed around her head. Stop.

Can you hear her? Listen, and you will hear her. Stop and let her think. If only they would let her think then maybe she could understand. Look again and you can see her sigh. The room became silent. She took a deep breath and expelled the air slowly. Another sigh. That's right. Relax. That was all she needed. Rest. Silence. Peace. Rest from their endless questions. Peace from those distant voices. Silence to think and remember. It was all too much effort to be their comforter, companion, lover. All things to all people. All too much for her to think about. Rest, that's what she needed.

But that was not to be. Day and night became one. Her day thoughts did not differ from her night thoughts. Why? Why did this happen. To her. Or them! Maybe! Maybe she would have to wait. But that was all right. It was all right to wait. It was all right to remember. It was all right to remember the journey. After all, there was time to remember.

Time passed, as it does for all of us. Too long ago to remember. They said. Details. They said. But it was details that had kept her life's blood pulsing through her veins. Details in her life. Details of the past. Her loss. His loss too, but he never spoke of it, so how could he feel the same pain. The same memories. To remember. That was all. To say goodbye. That was all. It was so little to ask for, in the scheme of things. To say goodbye and then to live her life – in peace.

Memories slowly edged their way through the clouds. Years blown away. So many years. So much time. She began to watch them. They would visit her. Often. They didn't like it. Their inner discomfort covered them like a hard shell, surrounding and protecting them. From what or whom she never knew. But their discomfort did not stop her. They brought with them their restlessness. She would stare, drinking in each detail, trying to remember. Waiting. Wanting some response. Some emotion. Any emotion would do. Any emotion except for what she could see. Embarrassment. Their naked embarrassment. What could she do? Ignore it? Look away. Respond? How could she! There were no answers left. Every look, every tilt of the head gave her a hint of what was. Hidden in the past. Happy memories. Sad memories. Memories that were part of her life. She looked closer. Inspecting. Suspecting. Maybe there was something else she had forgotten. As each cloud cleared, she saw fragments creep into her vision. Memories that had built her life to what it was and will be. Today, tomorrow and yesterday.

There they were, sitting in front of her. Why not smile and say hello. That's easy enough to do, isn't it? Waiting. They do look as if they are waiting. So why not smile. What was the harm! But there was no answer. No answering smile. No familiar smile. In fact, there was no reaction at all. Only silence. What a time for silence! What could she do? What could she say? The sea. Always a popular subject – like the weather. Is it grey/blue/green/windy/calm. Limiting.

Finally she turned away. She saw the distance in their eyes and she turned away. Their pain could still hurt her. She looked towards the only other exit. Looking out, through the dust speckled glass, she looked past them. Onwards. Hot tears would burn inside her but they could not see. They could only see the other one. Their invention.

The leaves became golden brown, warmly welcoming with each gush of wind. She saw the changing seasons from her window. It was often a more accurate reminder than the ticking of that clock. She liked the view. It had not changed – not really. People came in and out of it, giving relief from the static figures around her. Children splashing. Balls flying through the air. Footprints of people as they walked or ran along the beach. Hints of time passing while she remembered a time that had long been buried, dug out to be dusted and then returned to its rightful place. Now the cobwebs had gone, she could return – to her rightful place. But where was that place? Would it be the same as before? No, never again. Too much had changed to go back. Too much had changed in her. She was different. Stronger. Yes, she was different. That was the key. She was strong enough to face the past and the future. Together. After all they had always been together, just unable to communicate. It would be different now. They had even laughed at a corny joke. She smiled to herself, remembering. Remembering other beaches, other times.

Boredom. She wanted to leave. What could she do to leave? Act. She had done that all her life. A performance. Now that would be easy enough. That was it. She decided to start right away. No time like the present. When they were next due to visit her, she would talk to them. The suit brigade. That's what she called them – secretly. Sometimes the white suit brigade. Yes, that was it. She would talk to the suit brigade, but not about the weather. No – definitely not the weather. Not this time. Not even a joke. This time. Not too much in the beginning. She would build it up. Slowly. She could even wear some of her new clothes. Where had she put them? Look. They still had the labels on them! That was easy enough to remedy. Where had she put her scissors?

'Oh. Excuse me. Much better. Thank you.'

She decided to sit outside for a while. She would tell them when they came. A comfortable chair in the sun. The sun was glorious. Maybe it would help with her cause. Everyone looks better after a bit of sun. That's her – better. For better or worse – that's her.

ATONEMENT

Siu Won Ng

Late summer charges through time, scorching hot bodies and dulling alert minds. Too hot to be in a hurry, Cara lingers, following the paths of the uneven pavement squares.

Cara walks, building up courage. She hesitates, searching her mind: *Are you crazy?* She is thinking: *But this is a test and I shall pass.* Black mackintosh draped around her body, she melts but she cannot let go of the security the long coat offers her.

The pavement is dirty and crowded. *Why don't those people get away from me or I shall drown in my claustrophobia? They hum and they mumble, I listen but I can't hear what they're saying. They block my view on this hot tiring day. I wish God would part the sea of people.*

This is when she saw her, sitting on the dirty wide steps gazing into space. Cara watched her. She stood by the side of the road, causing a people jam, and watched her. Cara couldn't help it, she looked exactly like Yit-Mun . . . when she was alive, but ten years older. As Cara stood and stared at her, it was just as though she stood in her own layer of time looking through into another layer that led to the future – it could have been ten years into the future. A fragile red web had begun to spin over her face, spinning from her nose to her cheeks and she thought, *I must help before it is too late and she dies again, if it is her. After all, she could have come back in another guise, testing me to see whether I would help or whether I would allow my destiny to lead me to hell where*

I'd fall deeper than any torturing depths can contain me.

As Cara stood to watch, she caught her moments of despair as the woman gazed into space. Yet something was going to happen – she could sense it, and Cara could see it on her face, planning, plotting with great determination. Then a child ran past, breaking her concentration, and her eyes lingered longingly after him – hungry eyes devouring an already fading memory.

Cara said, 'Sister,' and the woman looked at her with scared-looking eyes, round, like two suns shining in the summer sky.

She sat and stared and stared and would not talk to me. Cara's outer skin was making her inner skin prickle with the heat, *and the sun was beating me, beating me down into human pulp.* 'I want to help – that's all.' *And she looked at me through those broken telescopic eyes even more strangely as if to say: is there something wrong with you or what? Why are you, a stranger, staring at me and offering to help me?*

Cara felt like shaking her, to rattle some sort of life into her bones. As Cara moved towards her, the boy, who was about four or five years old, tried to run between them playfully but tripped over Cara's feet.

'Are you all right? There, let me help you to dust yourself – that's better. Where's Mummy, or don't you want Mummy to know that you fell?'

The more I talked to the child, the more her eyes danced. They caught and reflected the dazzling colours of the afternoon sun. She stooped to pick the child up adding, 'Let me help you,' but the child's mother appeared on the scene at that moment. She hesitated but asked:

'Do you have one of your own?'

Cara faltered, not wanting the past to swamp her on this hot heavy day, but it seemed to be the only link she had with this woman. 'Yes, but he died at birth . . . It seems such a long time ago now.'

The woman wanted to share something with Cara. She pulled

something out of one of her many pockets and indicated, 'My son.' She was holding a creased black-and-white photo of a young boy smiling uncertainly to the camera as though waiting for instructions on what to do next. 'My son, smiling at me,' she added and Cara could sense how precious he was to her. She cradled the photograph as though it were a shell, a delicate fragment of a larger part of a lost and unknown past, and Cara could sense her struggling, wanting to tell her more. The sun beat mercilessly down on both of them. Was she drowning in her past like Cara was in hers? Cara wanted her to tell but she seemed to have forgotten how to talk and it was so hot and she seemed more unreal the more she looked at her.

'It's too hot to stand under the sun!' *Was that a loud echo from deep within me?* 'Look, are you all right? Let me help . . .' *and I was caught before I fell through the final layer of the mist, caught by safe strong arms and pushed towards the step that had been her seat.*

'You don't look well. Let me take you for some tea,' the woman demanded. 'I'm Jade, by the way.'

I blinked her into focus and nodded. 'Cara,' she whispered.

They walked down the steps into the Crypt – you know, the one under St Martin-in-the-Fields, full of black tables and dark chairs – a dark, dark place, with classical music pumping through Cara's ears. It was too crowded though, too many people closing in on them, who didn't give them enough space to walk, enough space to breathe. *I walked us back to the top of the steps through the sea of people who were looking and looking, up and out to the top.*

'I'm sorry, but I can't stand to be near too many people. Look, I know another café that's open in one of the side streets and we can talk there, if you want,' Cara ventured. Jade nodded in consent. She attempted to throw a thin smile at Cara and followed her slow processional walk to the almost deserted side-street café. Bliss, a place almost devoid of people, seems too good to be true.

So they sat and watched the steam rise from exhausted urns,

listened to cutlery cutting into plates and the rhythmic munching from eaters nearby while they waited for tea.

The door jangled hard and three young men, all about sixteen, jostled and crammed into a small front booth. A few voices that sounded familiar kept stabbing and stabbing into Cara's ears slicing up the past in front of her. They jabbered like magpies. Their voices appeared like spirits from her previous life, following her, allowing her no peace. *Haunting me when I least expected them to. I knew I had to stop listening to the tone of the voices or they would take over the present. I could feel anger burning my soul, rising higher and higher through my body, a fearful bright substance full of venom and revenge.*

They jabbered like magpies *and I know what they do.* They steal good memories away and replace them with nightmares.

I want to be free from having to carry dead memories inside me, carry such scorching pain and fierce voices that torment me on a daily basis, fear that wavers inside, panic that smothers me and an image playing over and over in my head, chasing me, beating me, oppressing me down down so many layers of time until I lose track of where I am, who I am, what I will become, and the panic becomes stronger and stronger, until it engulfs me, conscience and all.

Isn't it merciful that when you least expect it help always comes? Isn't it a miracle that calmness descends, weaving its fine strong thongs over panic, binding it over and over again until it is squeezed out of shape into an unrecognisable form?

So Yit-Mun appeared, as blackness covered the earth, and she is smiling a forgiveness that burns all other things out of sight.

'I'm back, but you must redeem yourself,' she said.

Do you remember, how I rocked you in my arms when you said you were afraid and you wanted to be cradled in God's arms? How I got you your first measure of angel dust and sprinkled the stars inside you? Then you had felt so warm and bright inside you. You were smiling and smiling and said that you were being rocked inside an angel's wings and you tried to turn round to look at your angel's face but stared into mine instead. You didn't see me, though, and thought you had travelled to heaven in a blink of an eye and were ready to stay. But you were afraid of the world outside of your body because you had no control over it. So when the warmth left you, you felt all cut up and cold inside and you needed to feel the warmth and brightness inside you to build up the courage to find your path in this life. That need was so great that you gave up your life for it so you could stay warm inside for always.

'I did not come back to deny my past in my own undoing but I do remember that you had sprinkled stars inside me when I needed to shut out the cold and hardness of the world. I also remember being afraid of being trapped in a meaningless life that sucked me down deeper into its bowels, ready to spew me up when I was least ready. So I needed the stars to shine inside me all the time so I could live off their bright light. But then I so desperately needed to remain in perpetual brightness that I swallowed too many stars, and each one was fighting to shine the brightest so that all of them won and I got blown out of the orbit for ever.'

And your breathing got slower and slower and you didn't want to wait for help to arrive or you would be pulled back to a hard hard world full of spite and envy. Well it got so that you were breathing so slowly that you stopped altogether because you forgot how to breathe. But you sighed out of happiness did you know that? I left.

I had to leave you, not because I was heartless but because I was self-ish enough not to see beyond the need for my own freedom and I didn't want them to find us together or they would jail me for daring to rob your life from you, and they would never understand because they will never see the beautiful side of life, will they?

But you knew I was helping you, didn't you, Yit-Mun? I did bring warmth into your life, didn't I? Even for a little while until you came back from your place of warmth and then wanted more until the warmth turned into a fire which consumed you.

Cara's name hurtled through the darkness and parted the black curtain that had separated her from the earth, albeit temporarily.

'Cara!' Jade whispered again, more urgently. The hot tea was gently steaming Cara's face and Jade's whisper threw a jagged breeze across her face, bringing her back to the present. 'Are you all right? You were miles away. I was telling you about my son. Remember? He's at an age when he needs me . . . I know we've only just met but I need your help. You said you wanted to help.'

I encouraged her by nodding, slowly so I would not break her concentration nor her fragile determination.

'My son – he's with his father and I haven't seen him for . . . is it six months now? I keep losing track of time. He told Social Services that his son was at risk and that I wasn't responsible enough to look after him because of my drinking problem. So he was granted a residence order and I've been denied the right to see my son. He's our only son and I don't want him being corrupted by his father – do you understand? At least I was able to protect him while I was with him, but now I can't hide his father's lack of warmth, gentleness, his staying from home for days, his violent temper . . .

'I have something that I need you to give him. Will you do this for me? I have this jade bracelet which my mother used to wear. It has been through so many years of hardship. I know it will protect him from harm as it protected my mother and me. Please, give this to him.'

A small price to pay. I must do it as I knew what I had to do back then. You knew what you wanted too, didn't you, Yit-Mun? You said you didn't want to feel cold and all cut up inside any more, so I got you your first measure of angel dust and sprinkled the stars into you. They melted and warmed you from inside to out. It made you feel so warm and safe didn't it? Then you wanted more . . .

SUHAAG RAAT

Parminder Sekhon

They made a dandelion necklace for me in the front garden. One picked and the other threaded. I could hear them giggling and whispering as they crept up behind me. Sangeeta placed Amrita's yellow scented hands over my eyes and whispered: 'This is our wedding present to you. We hope you will always be this happy.' With that, they let the flowered gems fall into my lap and I kissed them both, big and happy.

Amrita was my baby and Sangeeta loved me. For most of the afternoon we sat on the grass, encased in blossoms that hung like *sehera*. Fistfuls of pink petals fell all around. Crumbling and spilling, flirting with every breath of air. Spring is such a divine season. Everything feels so good for all right now and you just know there's so much more of it to come.

Sangeeta hardly stopped for a second. She was playing on the swing with Amrita. She was smiling my way, smiling every-where. I sat still on the grass. I sat and watched the light change from minimum to optimum, counted the seconds it took my unlit skin to burn. I watched Sangeeta's hair change from black to red to brown. She was really beautiful.

I liked her skin; it was the same as mine but darker, smoother, full of *sai kashish*. I liked the way her hair hung below her waist, thick and black and often tangled. I liked her make-up-free face; it was different from mine except the *surma* in her eyes.

Sometimes it would make me cry just to look at her. She looked like Smita Patel. We would have many daughters together, we would sit and *vat ladoos* until all our fingers were swollen and broken, until there was no one else left to feed.

It was a special day. She was wearing a white *makesh kiti* sari and I a plain saffron one. We had been in the morning to the Gudwara to *matha tek*. Neither of us were really religious. Only when I married did I truly believe in God, believe He was a man and that He was born ten times over and that he cared little or none for any feminist lesbian separatists. But all the same I wanted to be there.

I wanted to see and be near other Indian people so they in turn could see and witness us. I wanted the peace and the sacredness of something special like it could never have been before.

When we sat crosslegged on the sheets, Sangeeta took my hand, she held it tight all the way through the *paat*, breaking our clasp only to receive the *parshad*. My eyes took in the splendour and my ears swam with the sound. For a converted car-park, it was quite a sight. Fairy lights and Christmas decorations in every corner. I could tell they had spent a lot of money on it.

But for the time it took my hands to empty, I felt different. Felt changed. My focus had disintegrated, my thoughts slipped, leaving my mind wide open to all that I had worked so hard to close it to. Thoughts gatecrashed, and racked my brain.

Lots of people were coming up now after eating their langar and any one of them could have been Ma or Papaji. I knew none of them but recognised them all. Took me back. Made me feel like I could see in infra-red. Not just the most vivid things like the *pherias*, the *chura* soaked in milk that scrape your hands to blood and *shallaly* or the *vasin*, the *dahi* they scrub and wash your body with, the *laddoo*, the *mehndi*, the *theil*, the *paise*, the *ghungra*, the *cleria*, but it was everything the videoman and the music. *Nach ne pabhiye nach vir da vyah nach* (Dance, sister-in-law, dance, it's our brother's wedding). I felt sick. I remember now that I was remembering Alyce hard. How I wanted her so badly, said I would do anything, said I wasn't proud, said it was good not to have any pride, I would be big, so big . . . She said she couldn't be with me any more because we both knew I'd have to have an arranged marriage some day and anyhow I'd always known she wasn't a lesbian. I'd heard those lines so many times.

Over the years I'd learnt how to stop the tears from falling in public. Grinding my teeth and sweeping my eyelashes in a rush, I would send them back.

I looked at Sangeeta and told her with my eyes that I was ready to go.

In the garden it was high afternoon. I was sitting on the grass, my elbows resting on my knees so my hands lay across my eyes. I sat this way for a long time. I felt Sangeeta come and sit down tight behind me and slip her arms around my waist. Legs astride, she tucked them neat against me so we were almost one shape; only the colours of our saris divided us.

I felt her head resting on my shoulder, her fingers tracing patterns on my back, felt her begin to kiss. First dragging her mouth lightly across the base of my neck then kissing higher and deeper on the inside, her fingers pushed up through the roots of my hair, dragging up the heel of her hand. Soft and slow are our kisses these days, just because we have all the time to do it that way.

No more hard and fast fuck-kisses torn from scrappy hours left over from heterosexual lives, with bodies skewered so deep it takes up all your time just to make it all right. Now the only hard and fast kisses we share are the ones we do over and over just because we don't want to stop, don't want to wait because we already have done for too long.

When I opened my eyes I saw the red in her hair, it was streamed through an immaculate parting. Holding her head, I scraped back her hair so I could see more clearly.

'Who put *sindhur* in your hair?'

'I did. Why? Do you want me to put some in yours?'

She was smiling, teasing. I nodded yes, mouth closed, half laughing. Eyes down, she made me feel shy. Then she spoke softly. Stroking my face she said simply:

'Talk to me, Mehtab, please.'

She shouldn't have said that, just the knowing and feeling of her presence gave such relief to the weight inside me. My eyes began silently to flood and wet, tears fell and I had no desire to try and stop them.

I tried to smile because it really was too much, all these tears. I remembered Raj once said to me to stop crying because it made me look damn ugly. I knew most of my make-up had come off so I reckoned I must look twice as ugly now. She ran her hands through my tears, holding me near.

I smiled properly and turned round to look at her. Really I was OK.

'What were you thinking?' she said.

I was going to protest, say it was nothing, it almost felt like it was nothing now, certainly nothing to make a fuss about, just sad things, stupid things that don't even matter any more and then I told her everything. Told her of how I'd been watching her sitting on the swing and looking at the *pallu* of her sari which was blowing so beautifully in the air behind her and how that made me look at mine and feel the softness and the plainness of chiffon against my skin, how it reminded me of the day I got married, how I'd cried so much I couldn't see anybody's face when it was time to get in to the car, I kept using my *chunni* to wipe my face over and over but the *gota* was made of tinsel-like material and I didn't know until the next morning but my face was covered in scratches and it hurt so much when I cried because it stung like anything and that reminded me of how I'd ever said yes in the first place and that just reminded me of how unhappy I'd been and just how different it was to how I was feeling now and that it really can be OK and for a long time after all.

'Oh, but you know how I love you, you know it, Mehtab.'

'I know, but it's such a miracle, it's so hard to believe we ever met.'

'It's kismet.' She said it seriously, as if she meant it, and then she began to smile, slyly. I had to laugh, it was funny. Hindi movie *Kismet*.

'*Theek hai, apene sitary bujay.*' (That's right, our sky stars are tied together.) Yes. That was it.

'Besides, it doesn't have to be a fly-by-night chance or a fluke, like women aren't making it every day, because they are.'

'I know. It feels good to know you. I know with what eyes I used to look when I saw women together smiling and touching, and now, now it's happening to me.'

She gathered up the pleats of her sari and gave me a finger lip kiss and walked down to the bottom of the garden to look for Amrita. I knew she would find her there through the fence of the next-door garden, spiking worms or something. I went to the bedroom and stared into the mirror hard.

We drove for two hours and arrived at the hotel before dark. Two weeks in a white seaside town is what we had chosen. God only knows why.

I said, 'I don't want to prove a point Sangeeta, please.'

She said, 'But I want to be by the sea. Amrita will love it and so will you, I promise.'

Wants to be by the sea, we could go to Verarval if she wants to be by the sea, we could go to the Seychelles if she wants to be by the sea like other people.

We arrived in Torquay with our crumpled saris and our non-Indian English accents, speaking Punjabi a mile a minute. It felt good, signing the reception book with *mehndied* hands, it felt good to even be in Torquay.

Our room was large. I set the bags on the bed and began to inspect the doors and the ceramics like I was going to lay a deposit down on it or something. I threw open the windows and checked the view. The sea shone for miles and miles.

I turned around and smiled at Sangeeta who was sitting on the bed. 'It's OK, I like it.'

We unravelled our saris, let them fall where they fell, let them merge like melted-down ice-creams mango and vanilla, as our tongues merged in multilingual ecstasy, seamlessly, languages from two states and one country were ours. Our bodies not yet naked, still covered in silks and cottons, fingers travelling, dragging up skirts of silk, moving across the lengths of calves and thighs to find a softness so wet, so salty sweet, I suck till she drops down in front of me, shaking. I hold her still, her hair loose and heavy falls around my shoulders, her eyes tightening and then opening up wide, pressing, pushing hard against each other, into each other, couldn't get any deeper if we tried. Sweat rises up between us like dew and bones lock for ever. Keep it that way, keep it that way for a long time. I untie the strings of her blouse, it falls from her, she guides my hand over ribs sculptured perfect to underneath her right breast, fingers trailing over the faded remains of a tattoo. It would have been a leaping fish, blue and green.

Let love spill out and over the balcony, on to the promenade and into the pockets of those who cannot dream, into the sea.

BIOGRAPHICAL NOTES

Rukhsana Ahmad taught English literature at the University of Karachi before moving to Britain in 1973. She has freelanced as a writer, journalist, translator and playwright since 1985. Besides short fiction she has published *We Sinful Women*, Contemporary Feminist Urdu Poetry (The Women's Press, 1991) and a translation of Altaf Fatima's novel, *The One Who Did Not Ask* (Heinemann, 1993). Her play *Song for a Sanctuary* toured London and the regions in spring and autumn 1991, was published by Aurora Metro in 1993 and broadcast by BBC Radio 4. She has recently finished her first novel *The Hope Chest*.

Smita Bhide was born in Bombay in 1961, and grew up in India and in Britain. She has worked in women's organisations and in documentary television as a researcher. Her first novel is *The King of Fear*, and she also writes for film and for theatre. She lives in West London with her six-year-old son.

Maya Chowdhry is a writer, film-maker and live artist. She was winner of the BBC Radio Young Playwright's Festival with *Monsoon* (Aurora Metro Publications); the Cardiff International Poetry Competition; and the Littlewood Arc Short Story Competition. She is author of *The Heart and Heaven* (BBC Radio); her poetry is collected in *Putting in the Pickle Where the Jam Should Be* and in *The Popular Front of Contemporary Poetry, Crazy Jig*, and other anthologies.

Leena Dhingra was born in India, grew up in Paris and was educated in France, England, India and Belgium. Her work includes the novel *Amritvela* (Women's Press, 1988) and contributions to anthologies, *Watchers & Seekers* (Women's Press, 1987), *Right of Way* (Women's Press, 1988), *So Very English* (Serpent's Tail, 1991) and *Borderlines* (Serpent's Tail, 1993). She lives in London and has recently resumed an acting career.

Joyoti Grech: To start with, I was born in Dhaka, Bangladesh when it was still part of Pakistan. My mother and father brought me up believing I was fabulous, and I still hold this close to my heart despite attempts to convince me of the contrary. I also have a fabulous sister and two fabulous brothers, one fabulous nephew with a sibling on the way, and several fabulous cousin-sisters as well. My mother comes from the Chakma tribe of the indigenous Jumma people in the Chittagong Hill Tracts, Bangladesh. My father is from Malta. Our own family history taught me early on the rich fluidity of culture and the absurdity of imposed national boundaries. Most of all, I want to say, Thank You Ma.

Rahila Gupta spent most of her formative years in Bombay and came to London at the age of 19 to do an M. Phil in English Drama. She has worked as a journalist and freelance writer for many years and is currently producing and editing publications for a housing charity on a part-time basis. She has contributed short stories, poems and polemical essays to a number of anthologies, the most recent being *The Virago Book of Love and Loss* (Virago, 1992) edited by Georgina Hammick. Also due to be published in 1994 by Harper Collins is an autobiography of Kiranjit Ahluwalia which has been translated and written by Rahila Gupta.

Tanika Gupta has been a member of the Asian Women Writers' Collective since 1989 and has been actively writing for the past eight years. In 1991 she was a finalist in the BBC Young Playwright's Festival and had her first radio play *Asha* broadcast on

Radio 4. Since that time she has had four episodes produced for the Radio 5 twenty part series, *Kiss Me Quick*, a single play for children called *Badal & His Bike* for Radio 5 and a thirty minute play *Pankhiraj* produced for Radio 4. In 1993 she was a finalist in the BBC Black Screenplay awards and is working on a treatment for television called *Nasreen's Flight*. She is also working on developing a stage play *Bande Mataram* through Talawa Theatre's black women writers' project and is developing a short film called *Bideshi* with an independent film production company.

Tanika divides her time between working as a community worker for Islington Council, bringing up her two small daughters – Nandini and Niharika – and writing deep into the night!

Seema Jena graduated from Madras University and came to Britain on the Commonwealth Scholarship in 1988. Currently she is a research student at the University of Loughborough. Founder editor of the first South Asian literature journal *Daskhat*. She won the national competition for Black British writers sponsored by Jonathan Cape with her first story 'In Another World', which is being developed into a novel. Published work includes: a critical text titled, *Voice and Vision of Anita Desai* (Ashish Publishers, New Delhi, 1989).

Shamshad Khan was born in 1964 in Leeds, Yorkshire. She now lives and works in Manchester, where she studied Animal Behaviour. Her present job involves campaigning, research and advice on employment rights issues. Shamshad also performs her poetry and runs creative writing workshops. She is currently working on her first novel and shortly hopes to publish a collection of her poetry.

Janet McDermott is an Asian woman who lives in Sheffield, where she grew up. She works part-time as a community worker with other Asian women. She is Anglo-Indian, a member of a community of mixed race heritage in India dating back to the eighteenth century. Her first novel, *Yasmin*, was published in 1992 by Mantra.

Afshan Navid Malik: I came to the UK at the age of 11, grew up in Yorkshire, lived in London and am now living and working in Wales. I work as a lecturer of Biochemistry in Cardiff University and am actively involved in medical research. I write as a hobby in my spare time both in English and Urdu and my work includes poetry, songs, comedy, short stories and a half finished novel.

Preethi Manuel is a new writer, currently completing her MA in Screenwriting at London College of Printing. She was an Outreach Worker for the AWWC between 1989–90 and has previously been a lecturer and Media Resources Officer. She also cares for her daughter who has cerebral palsy.

Ameena Meer is an Indian of the diaspora, usually living between New York City, Mexico City and Brixton, with her daughter Sasha Iman Douglas. Her first novel, *Bombay Talkie*, is published by Serpent's Tail (April 1994). Her writing appears in *Bomb, Frieze, Harper's Bazaar, Interview, The Portable Lower Eastside: New Asia, South* and *Spin*, among other publications. Currently, she is composing descriptions on the back of athletic underwear boxes and working on a fictional history of her extended family.

Vayu Naidu is a storyteller who retells Hindu myths and epics, Muslim legends and folk and oral tales from the Indian subcontinent. Her *Biswas* stories for children are published by Collins Educational (1990–1992). A short story 'The Hedge' was published in a Black Literature issue of *Critical Quarterly* (ed. Rukhsana Ahmad). She has published her poetry widely and is the founder member of *Brumhalata* Intercultural Storytelling Theatre.

Vayu Naidu was born in Delhi, educated in Hyderabad, Ranchi and Bombay, hails from the South of India, and now lives in Birmingham.

Ravinder Randhawa is the author of *A Wicked Old Woman* (Women's Press, 1987), a teenage novel *Harijan* (Mantra, 1992) and has published short stories in several anthologies. She lives in London.

Sibani Raychaudhuri was born and brought up in Calcutta. She has written short stories for children in Bengali and translated Bengali poetry into English (some of these translations have appeared in the *Times Literary Supplement* and the *London Magazine*). She has written for *Spare Rib* and *Artrage*, and her short stories and poetry appeared in *Right of Way* (Women's Press, 1988). She lives in London and works freelance in education and has written articles on educational issues.

Perminder Sekhon has been a member of the AWWC since 1990. She lives in London and works full-time in an Asian Women's refuge. She is also an actor and photographer.

Anya Sitaram was born in Bombay in 1963. Her family moved to Britain when she was five. She works as a reporter for Independent Television News. She is married to a journalist and lives in London. 'Naukar' was based on real events during a year the author spent in India after leaving school.

Siu Won Ng was born outside her Motherland. She writes about her experiences across two cultures and currently divides her time between housing advice work, reading a Master's in law and CWRG. In 1989 she joined AWWC to develop her writing and has contributed to *Artrage, Feminist Arts News* and various anthologies.

Sue Thakor was born in 1962 in Leamington Spa and moved to Gloucester when she was five. She studied Literature, History of Art and Women's Studies at the University of East London and now lives and works in London. She has written several short stories and poems and is currently working on her first novel.

GLOSSARY

·····◆·····

abba: father
abbajan: father
abbu: father
Allah: God
Allah mian: dear god
aloo-paratas: potato filled paratas
alpana: auspicious paintings, done by women on steps of houses to
    welcome good times on occasions of festivity and celebration
'Amar Sonar Bangla': 'My Golden Bengal', the national anthem of
    Bangladesh, written by Rabindranath Tagore (1871–1941), the
    great Bengali poet
amma: mother
ammi: mummy
Angrezi: English
apsara: nymph
'arp kee kismeth': your destiny/fortune
awara: footloose
baba: father
badtameez: ill-mannered
baji: older sister
basin: gram flour
behen: sister
beshurum: shameless
beti/bete: daughter/child
bhai/bhaijaan: brother
bibi: miss
bidis: Indian cigarettes
biryani: rice and meat cooked together
chachi: aunt (paternal)
chacha: uncle (paternal)

chappal: sandal
chichi: shit
chilman: bamboo blind
chitti: letter
chokidar: caretaker
chup: keep quiet
chura: wedding bangles
cleria: silver and gold bridal decorations that hang from the wrist
dadaji: grandfather (paternal). *Ji* is a term of respect.
dadiji: grandmother (paternal)
dhai: yoghurt
dhania: coriander
dhobi: laundryman
didi: sister
doodh-wallah: milkman
duppatta: long scarf worn with a punjabi suit
ehunni: scarf
garam masala: spice mixture used for cooking curry
ghungru: ankle bells
goonda/gunda: thug, layabout
gota: ornate scarf edging
hain: okay, yes
haram: forbidden
haramzadi: female bastard
ishq: love
jamadarni: toilet cleaning woman
janat: paradise
kafirs: non-believers (contemptuous)
khadi: woven cotton
khala: aunt
kismet: destiny/fortune
kissans: farmers
kulfi: ice cream
kurta pyjama: two piece outfit
laddu/ladoo: Indian sweets
maharani: queen
mai: servant
mamoon: mum's brother
maskesh kiti: sequinned

masterji: teacher
matha tek: bow
maulwi: muslim priest
mehendi: henna, used to decorate hands and feet
mittai: sweetmeat
mullah: priest (often used as a term of contempt)
mussalman: muslim
naukar: servant
neechi zaat: low caste
nikaah: formal wedding ceremony
paise: money
pakoras: spicy teatime snack
pallu: top end of the sari worn over the shoulder
pan: betel leaf
parshad: blessed food
perias: Sikh wedding ceremony
sahib: mister
sai kashish: beauty
salan: curry sauce
salwaar/shaluaan kameez: two piece outfit originally worn by women
    from Punjab
sehera: bridegroom's head-dress made of flowers
shaitan: satan/devil
shaitan ki bachi: satan's daughter
shallay: blisters
sharab: alcohol
sharam: modesty
sindhur: red powder used in the parting or on the forehead to denote
    marriage
surma: khol
Sylheti: a dialect of Bengali, spoken in the Sylhet district of
    Bangladesh
theil: oil
toba: asking God for forgiveness
tongas: horse drawn carriages
vat: shape and mould
Veraval: seaside town in Gujerat
zamindar: land owner